THE SPECTACULAR SIMON BURCHWOOD

a novel by

SCOTT SEMEGRAN

MUTT PRESS

Austin

Mutt Press
Austin, Texas
http://www.muttpress.com
info@muttpress.com

ISBN 978-0615758114

Photo of Scott Semegran by Lori Hoadley
Cover by Alchemy Book Covers and Design
Illustrations by Scott Semegran
Edited by Brandon R. Wood

Books by Scott Semegran:
Sammie & Budgie
Boys
The Spectacular Simon Burchwood
The Meteoric Rise of Simon Burchwood
Modicum
Mr. Grieves

Find Scott Semegran Online:
https://www.scottsemegran.com
https://www.goodreads.com/scottsemegran
https://www.twitter.com/scottsemegran
https://www.facebook.com/scottsemegran.writer/
https://www.instagram.com/scott_semegran
https://www.amazon.com/author/scottsemegran
https://www.smashwords.com/profile/view/scottsemegran

What Reviewers Are Saying About The Meteoric Rise of Simon Burchwood:

"This book will have you rolling in laughter at a man who cannot or will not realize who and what he is. Nonstop laugh beginning to end." -- 5 Stars / *Free Book Reviews*

"A very good novel that was humorous throughout." -- 4 1/2 Stars / *Red Adept Reviews*

"Simon Burchwood Is A Genius, It's True!" -- 4 Stars / *Bitsy Bling Books*

"Cracked me up! Overall a very good and funny read." -- 4 Stars / *Ashton the Book Blogger*

"Verdict: An ambitious, enjoyable read with a superb ending that changed my interpretation of the entire text." -- *IndieReader*

"A clever and surprising twist... cutting observations of the writerly demeanor." -- *Kirkus Reviews*

Accolades for *The Meteoric Rise of Simon Burchwood*:

Inductee into the Indie eBook Hall of Fame for General Fiction

5 Best Summer Indie Beach reads (July 2011) - Huffington Post

For Nathan, James, Albert, and James. Thanks for helping me get through one of the toughest years of my life.

Table of Contents

An Introduction, Failure, Truth

Things don't always turn out the way you plan, at least that's what they say. It's true. Things have a way of becoming a goddamn mess. I know, I know, that's so cliché. You can thank the French for that word. They think they're so goddamn smart, the French, the way they can analyze the banal and coin a phrase. When things don't go your way, they will say "c'est la vie" too. You know what I say? Eat shit. Yep, that's what I have to say. Eat shit.

Why does life have to be so goddamn hard? That's more difficult to sum up than saying something like "that's life." That's not good enough for me. I need something more concrete. I need something more scientific, something that's closer to the truth, not hyperbole. Life can be a bitch. It's true. Why is that? Let's find out. Don't you want to know why? Of course you do. I do.

Since we last spoke, a lot of shit has gone down. So much so, I thought it best that I catch you up on what has happened to me in the last few years since the publication of my novel, *The Rise and Fall of a Titan*. In short, it was a disaster, a goddamn disaster. I never made it to New York like I had planned. Instead, I ended up in the emergency room with a concussion, the result from the effects of a pill that was supposed to relax me, not lay me out. That bartender in the airport lounge tricked me, for sure. What a cocksucker. I guess he was mad at me for stiffing him. His service left a lot to be desired though.

And that singer on the plane, Grant, he was a crazy motherfucker. Crazy I tell you. He was yelling all over the goddamn place, bouncing up and down in his chair. I guess once that pill hit my gut, it was lights out for me. I don't remember a goddamn thing. Not one thing. It's true.

Except (and I'm quite embarrassed to admit this) I had this crazy dream that my best friend Jason committed suicide on account of his shitty marriage and all. It all seemed so real, the dream. I was so immersed in that dream world that when I woke up in the hospital, I was screaming my goddamn head off like an idiot. My poor wife, bless her heart, thought I was going crazy. But what do you expect when you witness a crazy thing like that? It can be just too much to handle. It's true. As it turns out, Jason is just fine. He's still living in his rundown house in his rundown neighborhood in bum-fuck Montgomery, Alabama with his whore wife. And that's where he will stay and continue on. It's a goddamn shame.

My novel fell flat, selling a whopping 43 copies in its first month. Then hit its stride in the following month, selling another 72 copies. And then, well, that was that. What can I say? Like I said, it was a goddamn disaster. In less than three months, my novel came and went like a meteor in the sky then evaporated. It was all just so disappointing.

When review copies were sent out, a handful of excruciatingly bad reviews tainted its arrival and crushed any chance of it having some success. The social web of the internet then wrapped its rancor and disdain around my novel and choked the life out of it. The promise of a new career as a writer came and went like that, like a finger snap. Snap! Done! Over! It was a goddamn shame. It's true.

What was I to do? I did what every man has done at least once on his journey toward greatness: I crawled back to my former employer and begged for my job back. Sad but true. I put in a call to that rat bastard Mr. Folsom and prepared myself for two things that I knew would happen. 1) I would, without question, be unable to keep my attention away from his twitchy, lazy eye and 2) be subjected to an excruciatingly large amount of condescending bullshit that would leave me feeling small and worthless. Suffice it to say, I was absolutely right. Mr. Folsom sprinkled his annoying cackle throughout our brief meeting, gazing at me with his one good eye while his loose, twitchy, lazy eye spun around all over the goddamn place. I mustered all the strength I had to not pounce on his desk, grab a sharpened pencil, and jam it halfway through his diseased eye socket. Sorry to disappoint you but I did not stab his lazy eye with a sharpened pencil like I wanted to. I took his bullshit like a man because I knew I needed a paycheck. Sometimes, you just have to take someone's bullshit like a man, even if you don't want to. You can take that advice to the bank and cash it. It's true.

For a few months, things were good. But it didn't last. As most tech companies do, a round of layoffs followed the news of a bad financial quarter for the company. And my position was included in the immediate RIF (reduction-in-force, dummy). Just like that. Snap! Done! Over! Delivering the bad news to my wife Jessica was just as demeaning as begging Mr. Folsom and his goddamn lazy eye for that job in the first place. She wasn't too thrilled about it at all, not one bit. But can you blame her? She depended on me to be a provider and I wasn't doing a very good job of it at that moment. In fact, in hindsight, I was doing a pretty good job of fucking up most everything in my life at that point. She really let me have it too with the yelling and the screaming and the crying and all. Women are really good at laying their emotions on pretty thick and Jessica was the best, a real pro. If anybody had the skill to make a man feel like a turd, it was Jessica. She should put that skill on her resume, right at the top. I'm sure a future employer of hers would appreciate that ability. It's true.

As you can imagine, my layoff and subsequent stint in unemployment did wonders to my marriage, leading the way to the inevitable and irreparable damage that comes from wallowing in your own misery and self-loathing. Why did Jessica not understand that I had greatness within me? Why did she look at me like I was dog shit when I told her that I knew, deep down in my heart, that I was truly meant to be a writer and a novelist and not a tech support schlub? It's easy to beat a man when he's down. And boy was I down. When she told me, after a few months of unsuccessful job hunting, that she wanted a divorce, I was devastated. It was a swift kick to the nutsack and a heavy realization: I was a failure.

That's life, they say.

Eat shit.

Failure.

The last conversation we had before she packed her bags and the kids' things and left was pretty intense. She went on to list ALL the things I had done in our marriage that disappointed her. She concluded that I was a spectacular failure, a spectacular asshole, a spectacular letdown, a spectacularly bad lover, a spectacular idiot, and a spectacular waste of time.

"So, I see a theme here," I said as I watched her zip her suitcase shut and lead the kids out the door.

"And what is that Simon?" she asked, hurrying to leave.

"You think I'm spectacular."

Turn lemons into lemonade, some people say. I'm not sure who coined that phrase. I'll have to Google that later. Probably not the French, I'm sure.

The Spectacular Simon Burchwood. I like the sound of that. It has a nice ring to it, like I'm a superhero or some shit like that.

The Spectacular Simon Burchwood.

The Spectacular Simon Burchwood.

The Spectacular Simon Burchwood.

The Spectacular Simon Burchwood.

The Spectacular Simon Burchwood.

The Spectacular Simon Burchwood.

So, that brings me back to my question: Why does life have to be so goddamn hard? That's a tough one, really, even for a superhero. We all have hopes and dreams and desires and those things can be easily crushed into oblivion by matters that seem so out of our control. I didn't agree with Jessica's assessment of me, I didn't agree with TechForce's choice to have a RIF, and I didn't agree with the criticism heaped on my novel. But what was I going to do about it? I was on a mission for enlightenment and I found the truth. Would you like to know what it is? I bet you would. I'm sure of it. It's true.

1.

I got my job working for the State of Texas by accident. Well, maybe not by accident. Luck, that might be a better word. Pure luck. After getting laid off from TechForce, I received unemployment benefits for a period of time. What a sweet deal that was! Every week I had to call this phone number and promise that I had been looking for work then I would get approved to receive $212. That's it. Easy street. The next day, $212 was direct deposited into my checking account. It was like getting a check from your grandmother for Christmas, you know, because you had admiration for your grandmother and appreciation for the money but you never actually saw her much. The government is kind of like your grandmother: old, admirable, and distant. It's true.

I had devised a plan, just in case anyone from the unemployment office decided to show up at my apartment, to make myself look destitute in an effort to keep the unemployment checks coming as long as possible. It seemed like a good idea anyway. I bought Ramen noodles by the case and stacked them in front of the counter at the end of my kitchen. I didn't particularly care for Ramen noodles but everyone assumes that if you have Ramen then you must be broke. It's true. But no one from the unemployment office ever showed up at my place. Lazy goddamn government workers. They never do a goddamn thing right.

I eventually found an ad in the newspaper for a tech support position that seemed to have a good pay rate so I decided to call the number and check it out. I was reluctant to get another job in tech support but when you need a paycheck it's hard to be picky. The girl who answered the phone had a sweet voice, like a little bird, cooing her greeting and the scripted formalities. She sounded so sweet I almost felt like vomiting.

"Good afternoon! Thanks for calling blah blah blah bluh blah blah blah where it's a great day to start a new career. My name is Carey. How can I help you on this blah bluh blah blah blah?" she delicately rattled off, syncopated words beating like the flap of a hummingbird's wings.

"Uh," I said. Her fucking sweetness was suffocating. I had a hard time finding the words. Can you believe it? It's true.

"How can I help you today, sir?"

"Oh, I'm calling about the ad in the newspaper for a tech support position."

"Certainly, can you hold please while I look up information on that position?"

"Sure."

"Thanks so much."

The phone made a few clicks and zaps then some music came on. I'm pretty sure it was Herb Alpert's "A Taste of Honey." Most people would associate this song, which is now relegated to Muzak for elevators and shopping malls, to cheesy swingers from the 1960s. But when I was a kid, my parents had a copy of Herb Alpert's album "Whipped Cream and Other Delights" in their record collection. I would take a peek at it when I could, and marvel at the cute brunette who awkwardly sat under a mound of white goop that was supposed to be whipped cream. I imagine it was a shocking image at the time it was released. It was a shocking image to an eight year old boy in the 1970s. But time has a way of whitewashing past titillations into caricature. It's true. That album cover now looks no sexier than a box of cereal. Anyway, the phone clicked and zapped again, Carey's sugary voice cutting off "A Taste of Honey."

"Hello, Mister..."

"Burchwood. My name is Simon Burchwood."

"Hello, Mr. Burchwood. I have the information for you. It's a tech support position located downtown. Past experience preferred but not required. They will train you. There are two steps to the application process. Number one: email your resume to jobs@techneat.com so we can enter your information into our database. Number two: go to the onsite meet-and-greet tomorrow at 1:00pm, take your resume, and signup for an interview. I'll let them know to expect you, after your resume is received here, of course. Any questions, Mr. Burchwood?"

It all seemed too easy. What a goddamn formal production for nothing. It's true.

"Let me think. Can you tell me the name of the company that is hiring?"

"The Texas Commission of Employment and Benefits."

"Really?"

"Yes, Mr. Burchwood. Is that OK with you?"

"Yes, of course."

"Then, on behalf of TechNeat, and on behalf of your potential future employer, thanks for allowing us the opportunity to attempt to place you in gainful employment."

At first, I wasn't too excited about the opportunity to work for the State of Texas. And the Texas Commission of Employment and Benefits? That sounded like a real crock of shit, I tell you. I mean, like I said, government workers are a lazy bunch of numbskulls. But after a second or two, the idea that I could be a lazy numbskull while getting paid started to sound pretty good. Actually, the idea of being a lazy, goddamn numbskull while getting paid while I worked on my next novel sounded pretty fucking fantastic. It's true. I began to feel pretty grateful for the opportunity all of a sudden. I felt the need to thank Carey and her sweet, sappy goddamn voice.

"Thanks, Carey. I appreciate the opportunity."

"You're welcome, Mr. Burchwood. Have a nice day and good luck."

"Thanks. Thanks again. Uh, Carey?"

"Yes, Mr. Burchwood?"

"Is the Texas Commission of Employment and Benefits a nice place to work?"

The phone went silent. I think the question threw her off. She probably wasn't expecting something that wasn't scripted for her. I could hear some papers shuffling around, like she was looking for something. It took her a few seconds to get back on the line. She must have been nervous, nervous and worried.

"I don't have that information, Mr. Burchwood. It's not in our best interest to judge the working environments of companies that hire us to find employees for them. It is our job to place qualified candidates."

"So, you know nothing about the working conditions there?"

"No, I'm sorry Mr. Burchwood."

"Nothing at all?"

"Good luck, Mr. Burchwood. I have another call."

"But..."

She hung up the phone. How rude! I couldn't fucking believe it. Here I was trying to be nice and all and she hung up on me. I stared at the phone in disbelief. I decided, right then and there, that I wasn't going to let this slip. In fact, I thought this was a good opportunity to really speak my mind. I decided that when I sent my resume attached in an email to jobs@techneat.com that I would inform whomever responded to this email that Carey was a rude, unprofessional, bore. I was really going to let her have it. It's true. I fired up my trusty laptop and began to furiously type my disgruntled email. I wrote:

To: jobs@techneat.com

From: simonburchwood1972@aol.com

Subject: Your Rude Receptionist and My Resume

Message: To whom it may concern, I called today about a tech support position and I just wanted to let you know that your receptionist, Carey, was rude. Just thought you should know. Also, I've attached my resume, as Carey requested I do. And thanks for the opportunity. Sincerely, Simon Burchwood.

At exactly 1:00pm the next day, I arrived at 101 East 15th Street, dressed in suitable attire for an interview and with my resume in hand. I was ready as can be, having slept quite well and I was full from a nutritious breakfast. I was going to get this job, no matter what. It's true. I was determined to make it happen.

Once inside the drab government building, I was greeted by a security guard of African descent. She seemed reluctant to do any kind of work and was quite annoyed that she had to deal with me. I thought it funny that she would be annoyed at all, especially since she wasn't really doing anything, just sitting there typing away on her cell phone, probably texting dirty suggestions to her boyfriend or baby daddy or whoever. Then I thought to myself that this place would do quite nicely, especially if I could sit around doing nothing, just like this lady. It made me smile a little. It's true.

"Are you here for the meet-and-greet and job interviews?"

"Yes," I said.

"Then sign in here. Driver's License?" she asked, extending her hand. Her fingernails were an inch long with jewels glued to them. I imagined it would be pretty goddamn hard to shoot a pistol with fingernails like that. In fact, it would be pretty hard to do pretty much anything with fingernails like that. How would she pick her nose without scooping out the inside of her cranium? I'm sure pushing buttons of any sort was a catastrophe with nails like that. Or typing? Can you imagine typing with those goddamn fingernails? It was just unbelievable. It's true.

I gave her my driver's license. She glanced at it and scribbled her initials next to my name on the clipboard. "Go down to the basement. Room B-112."

"Thanks."

"That way," she said.

I went downstairs.

2.

Room B-112 was a small room holding 12 cubicles and it was full of people. 11 technicians occupied 11 small cubes and a dozen or so applicants were applying for the lone seat. I imagined it would be a nerd-fight-to-the-finish. Now when I say nerd, I don't mean it in any kind of derogatory way. Nowadays, it's more like a classification than a term of derision. When I was a kid growing up in Montgomery, Alabama, nerd was a pretty nasty word. It meant that you were smart but (and this is a big BUT) it also meant you were awkward, probably filthy, unattractive to anyone of the female persuasion, and socially inept. It was almost as bad as the word nigger, a word I heard quite often in Montgomery, considering Montgomery is full of goddamn rednecks. The funny thing about rednecks is that they think they are smart but they are as dumb as a pile of used tampons. I'm not sure where they got their superiority complex from but it's rather misguided. It's true. Anyway, just as rappers and such appropriated the word nigger and turned it into a term of endearment, nerd has simply become a word of classification for someone who is smart and into the tech scene. It's weird how words can change their meaning over time, isn't it? It's true.

Now, Room B-112 was pretty sparse and the walls were painted that government version of gooey tan that you see in practically every government building, and there wasn't one goddamn window in there to let in some sunlight. But it had a busy air to it and I felt I could work there for the time being while I wrote my next novel. Off to one side was a door to another room and the dozen or so nerds were in some kind of line, moving towards it. I figured that's where I must be going. I kept to myself while I waited.

It didn't take too long before it was my turn to go in there for my interview. I sat in front of two men. One was a bald, older-looking fellow wearing a white, button-down shirt with a red tie, pocket-protector securely fastened in his shirt pocket. The other was a rather large, but kind-looking African-American man. They both had forced smiles, the kind of smiles brought on by long days of interviews with know-it-all nerds. I was ready for any questions they had.

"My name is Mike," the bald guy said, extending his hand to me for a shake. He had a limp handshake.

"And my name is Rod," said the African-American fellow. His handshake was like a fucking vise. He practically crushed my hand into dust with his massive goddamn hand. It's true.

"I'm going to let Rod lead this interview since he's the lead support technician. If hired, you will be following his instructions. He is a very capable and knowledgeable technician. Take it away, Rod."

Rod squared me up with his eyes, studying me, like he was a chess master or something. I could tell he was carefully choosing his line of questioning. But something told me he really knew his stuff. Sometimes, you can tell if someone knows their stuff by the way they carry themselves. It's true. Rod carried himself like a brick house.

"Have you supported the Windows environment before?" he asked.

"Yes," I responded.

"What do you do if a customer says their document won't print?"

"Check to see if the printer driver is installed and check their print queue for any messages."

"What do you say to a customer who says they used their CD-ROM tray as a coffee cup holder and the cup spilled coffee everywhere when the tray automatically went back into the computer?"

"I'd tell them they were fired."

Rod burst into a hardy chuckle, a laugh so deep and thunderous that it startled me. He gave me a quick glance. I was ready for more questions but he gave Mike a wink and that was it.

"Well, it seems Rod likes you. Tell me about yourself. Married? Have children? Any hobbies?"

"I'm recently divorced. I have two kids named Jessica and Sammie. They are my pride and joy. And for a hobby... well, I wouldn't call it a hobby so much as a passion. But I like to write in my free time."

"Really? What do you write?"

"Novels."

"Novels? How fantastic. I love to read, especially westerns. Louis L'Amour, Anthony Burgess, even Cormac McCarthy, although he doesn't write westerns much anymore. You know, I've always wanted to be a writer..."

Oh shit, here it went. Once I mention to someone that I'm a writer, it never fails that they always say how much they want to be a goddamn writer and write the great American novel and shit like that. It's guaranteed like the sun rising in the east and setting in the fucking west. It's true. It's like a curse, listening to these goddamn idiots explain to me how their dreams of literary success is always thwarted by other things going on in their lives, what, with their bratty kids and their bitchy wives and their goddamn jobs and life in general getting in the way. Life has a way of messing things up for everyone. Like I said, life can be a goddamn mess. It's true. But I didn't want to let his bullshit get into my head. If you let someone's bullshit get into your head, then writer's block can set in. And the last thing a writer needs is to let writer's block set in. Writer's block is the devil. So I focused on a spot on the wall while he blabbed his goddamn head off. It took a while too, the blabbing. But he eventually moved on.

"...but, you know, I have my career here. I'll write when I retire," Mike said. He was finished talking, thank God.

"Yes, when you retire. Good time to write."

"When can you start?" Rod asked.

"Aren't you going to ask me more questions?"

"Do you want me to ask you more questions?"

"Well..."

"I usually get a good or bad sense about people pretty quick. I don't need to ask you anymore questions, unless you want me to. So, when can you start?"

"Tomorrow."

"Good, be here tomorrow at 7:50am, sharp."

"OK."

I stood up and extended my hand for a shake. I got another limp shake from Mike. I braced myself for Rod's vise grip and he didn't fail to deliver. His grip was just as firm as the first time, like a goddamn vise. I grit my teeth and took it like a man. I smiled and said thank you.

Walking out, the other nerds gave me a concerned stare. They knew, deep down in their nerdy hearts, that they had the knowledge and skill set to get this nerdy job. But little did they know that the job was mine and I didn't have the heart to tell them, the poor bastards. They were smart enough to figure it out for themselves. It's true.

3.

When I was a kid, I loved comic books. I loved comic books more than anything, more than bikes, more than girls, more than just about everything. It's true. I especially loved Marvel Comics, Spider-man, X-Men, The Avengers, The Fantastic Four, but particularly Spider-Man. The Amazing Spider-Man. The Spectacular Spider-Man. I collected issues of Spider-Man. Everything Spider-Man. Not only did I relate to Peter Parker, Spider-Man's awkward alter-ego, I was enamored with the writing of Stan Lee and the artwork of Steve Ditko. There was real poetry in the narrative of the life of Peter Parker. He was a nerd, a reject, and a very three-dimensional teenager. And that, right there, made him unique in the comic book universe.

Now, there were some very established characters in comic books. You had the tried and true characters from the DC Universe: your Supermen, your Batmen, your Flashes. But these characters had been around for decades before the Marvel Universe. And they were grown men, older fellows far removed from my pimply youth. But Peter Parker, he was a kid just like me. He was covered in pimples and was awkward and love struck with his girl and hormonal and unsure of himself. Even with his newfound powers, he doubted he could do anything worth anything. After kicking a super villain's ass, he still thought he was a piece of shit. I liked that. I could relate to that. I felt just like Peter Parker, except I didn't have shit for powers. Sometimes I struggled with Peter's doubt and self-deprecation. I would say to myself, as I pored over issue after issue, "Come on, man. You're fucking Spider-Man! You can climb walls for Christ's sake. You have motherfucking Spidey sense. What's your problem?!" But I knew his problem. He was a teenager. And so was I.

Because of Spider-Man, I knew when I was a kid that I wanted to be a writer. I thought Stan Lee, the creator of the Marvel Universe, was a genius. And Steve Ditko's artwork was perfect. Their talents were a match made in heaven. And I decided, right then and there after studying their work, that that was what I wanted to do too when I grew up. I wanted to be a comic book writer. But I couldn't draw for shit. So what was I to do? I'll tell you what I did. I enlisted the only friend I had that was a willing accomplice: Jason. Now, Jason couldn't draw for shit either. In fact, he made stick figures look retarded without trying to make them look retarded. He had a God-given gift for drawing stick figure retards, which meant any kind of heroism or dramatic flair was completely out of the question. It's true. But I was driven. I felt, deep down in my misguided heart, that I could nudge Jason's talent for drawing retarded stick figures into something, anything, that resembled Steve Ditko's beautiful artwork. Boy, was I wrong. I tried. I really did.

But Jason's artistic talents resembled more that of a kindergartner's autistic scribbles than a Marvel masterpiece. Our teamwork was short-lived and an abysmal failure. I soldiered on alone.

Jason became more than a collaborator. He became my cheerleader. He encouraged me to follow my dream and I did. Without Jason's support, I wouldn't be where I'm at today. It's true. I love that goddamn bastard. He's the one who introduced me to Kurt Vonnegut. Once I read Vonnegut's work, I knew I didn't need to team-up with an artist and create comic books. I could simply be a writer. Vonnegut's characters spoke to me in the same way that Lee's did. They were all tragically flawed in an outlandish way. His work was profound, funny, and poetically absurd. Hi ho.

When I arrived to my first day on the job at the Texas Commission of Employment and Benefits, I brought along a few personal items. 1) A framed photo of my kids, Jessica and Sammie 2) a copy of Breakfast of Champions by Kurt Vonnegut 3) a copy of Amazing Spider-Man, Vol. 1 by Stan Lee and Steve Ditko 4) a copy of Mad Libs, in case I needed to work out some writer's block (you never know when you'll need a copy of Mad Libs to work out some writer's block. It's the goddamn Devil, you know?) 5) and finally, a shmapple. What's a shmapple, you may be asking? Well, it's an ordinary apple. But Sammie has this cute way of changing words by adding a "shm" to the front of the word. So he might say something like this to me, "Daddy, a shmapple a day keeps the shmoctor away." And then he would giggle his little head off. I love that kid.

Rod came by my desk, crushing my goddamn hand with his handshake again, and gave me a quick run-through of the phone system and the call-logging application. It was pretty straightforward. Being a tech support guy was a pretty goddamn straightforward thing. Idiots call and you tell them what to do. Done. Log it in the system. The user's an idiot. Fixed it. Next.

"I have faith that you know what you are doing so you really won't need any formal training, will you?" he asked, cocking his head in a wink-wink fashion, if you know what I mean?

"Sure."

"Good. I'll assign another tech to help you if you have any questions. He's a bright kid... uh, a little strange at times but he knows his stuff."

"OK."

"Let me know if you need anything."

"Does my computer have a word processor on it?" I asked.

"Yes, it has a full Office suite installed. And everything else you will need to perform your work. Just push the green button on the phone when you're ready. That will put you in the call queue."

I quickly gathered my things together and put myself in the queue. And then, nothing. The phone didn't ring off the hook, like I expected.

At my old job at TechForce, the phone rang off the goddamn hook. It was fucking ridiculous. I barely had time to breathe let alone go to the bathroom to take a leak or blow my nose or write my fiction. Well, I made time to write (a writer always makes time to write. Duh!). But going to the bathroom? That was another story. I hate to admit this but I once had to take a piss so bad while stuck in the call queue that I peed in my trash can under my desk. It's true. I couldn't get up from my goddamn desk because my managers wouldn't let me out of the queue. It was that busy. It was goddamn ridiculous if you ask me. But apparently at the Texas Commission of Employment and Benefits, the phone didn't ring off the goddamn hook. Apparently, it barely rang at all. So, after 15 to 20 minutes of staring at my phone, I decided it was time to write. I fired up the word processor, slipped my portable flash drive into my computer, and opened the file containing my new novel.

Now, the key to writing a good novel is very simple. So simple, in fact, that I'm almost afraid to tell you. Great writers, like great magicians, don't give away their tricks and secrets. But I like you, I really do. So I'm going to drop some knowledge on your unsuspecting head. I know you'll appreciate the goddamn gesture. I'm sure of it. The key to being a good writer is "preparation." That's it. Preparation. What do I mean by *preparation*? It's simple. The best analogy I can give is that being a writer is a lot like being a really good cook. To prepare a good meal, you have to gather and measure your ingredients. You need to prep the oven, utensils, and cookware. You have to set your prep and cook times, so on and so forth, etc. If you follow the directions and take the appropriate steps, then you'll have a goddamn delicious meal or dessert or whatever when you're done. It's easy as pie. It's true. Although, I have to admit, making a pie really isn't that easy and neither is writing a good novel.

I spent the last six months preparing this novel and I was ready to belt it out. What is it about, you ask? I had this brilliant idea to write a memoir that was completely fabricated. Now, if you watch even a smidgeon of TV, you probably know of a shithead named James Frey, a writer who duped Oprah Winfrey in front of her TV audience into thinking his memoir was a goddamn masterpiece. But he later admitted that it was only partially a masterpiece and also partially a goddamn lie. What a doofus! Telling lies on TV will get you in hot water. It's true. But I remember thinking, "Why partially fabricate a memoir? Why not completely fabricate a memoir?!" It's fucking genius!

I didn't get halfway through a sentence before I was bothered by a jingly noise behind me. I turned around to discover a nerd in my cube, all snaggle-toothed and hunch-backed and awkward. He was the epitome of the nerd stereotype: greasy hair, cheap ill-fitting clothes, pens in the shirt pocket, and so on and so forth. He was a goddamn nerdy mess. It's true. As he stood there in my cube, gawking at me, his hand was tossing whatever was in his pants pocket (coins, lint, game tokens, paper clips, Dungeon and Dragons dice, car keys) along with his testicles. It was the most vigorous display of pocket pool I had seen in my entire life. And he was shameless about it, a goddamn nightmare.

"My name is Ryan. What's your name?" he asked, smacking his nerd lips over his nerd gums with gingivitis so potent the air around us curdled.

"Simon. My name is Simon. I'm the new guy," I said, shielding my nostrils from his bad breath or at least trying to.

"You worked tech support before?"

"Yes, at a company called TechForce."

"Oh, TechForce!" His nerd eyes lit up like a goddamn Christmas tree. "I heard that place was cool."

"Not really."

"Oh," he wheezed. He looked genuinely disappointed, like the data he had about TechForce in his nerd brain was corrupt or something. His brain quickly shuffled around the bad data, putting it into archive mode, and switched back to awkward nerd mode. "You got any certifications?"

"Sure. I have a Microsoft Server certification. Some Unix training."

"I'm an MCTS. I got my certs a few months ago," he said. For you uninitiated, an MCTS is a Microsoft Certified Technology Specialist. It's also nerd-speak for 'I got skills.' What a bunch of bullshit. "I plan on running my own network at another company very soon. I won't be around this dump much longer."

"That's cool."

He continued to play pocket pool with his loose change and his nuts and his keys while he occupied what little space was left in my cube. It was pretty goddamn uncomfortable. The dank, stinky fog from his mouth was turning my cube into a toxic gas chamber. But his phone rang from his cube to save the day. He craned his neck, peering in that direction.

"Oh shit, my phone," he said, running to answer it, tripping and stumbling over his untied tennis shoes.

My phone suddenly rang too. It surprised me. I placed the headset over my ears and read the tiny caller ID screen on my phone. It read, "V. Johnson - 5106." V. Johnson? Could this be a man or a woman? Now, I don't want to sound sexist because really, there is nothing worse than a goddamn sexist. But, and this is a big BUT, woman are more difficult to support with technical calls than men. It's true. In fact, most women really seem uninterested in technology period, unless it's a cell phone. But computers, TVs, printers, scanners, streaming players, all things technical, women could give a rat's ass about. So trying to assist a woman with problems related to these technical things was a goddamn catastrophe. It's like trying to communicate with a Chinese man who only knows two English words: McDonald's and basketball. Huh? Anyway, I had to answer the goddamn phone. I picked up the receiver.

"Thanks for calling The Texas Commission of Employment and Benefits technical support line. My name is Simon. How can I help you?"

"Hello?" I heard some clicking and a muffled thud or two, then the sweet voice came through again. "Hello? Is this technical support? Sorry, I dropped my phone."

"Yes, it is. My name is Simon. Can I help you?"

"Hi, Simon. That's a nice name. I've always liked that name: Simon."

"Oh... thanks."

"If I had another boy, then I'd name him Simon. Not after you, of course. But because I've always liked that name."

"Ummm."

"Right, technical support. I called for help, I know, not to talk."

"What can I help you with this morning?"

"My computer, it..."

"Yes?"

"It's acting weird this morning." See? What did I tell you? How in the world can you troubleshoot a technical problem like that? Acting *weird*? Give me a goddamn break. I could already tell that I was in for a long morning in the vortex of technical support hell. It's true. "It's doing this thingy where the screen freezes up and the input fields flash and the mouse goes crazy and I can't do my work."

"I see. When was the last time you rebooted your computer?"

"Oh, I don't remember. Am I supposed to do that?"

"Do you remember seeing any warning screens saying that updates have been applied to your computer and for you to reboot?"

"Uh, I..." she paused, the embarrassment revealing itself. "I... I really don't know."

"OK, I can't help you unless you help me."

"Can you just come to my desk and fix it?"

Uh oh. She wanted me to leave my cube and go help her? Since it was my first day, I had no idea how to get around the building and where certain departments were and the protocol for this and the procedure for that. It seemed to me that she was asking a bit much of me. But then I thought, "What the hell? I'm supposed to help people, right?" I went against my better judgment. It's true.

"OK. Where are you located?"

"Third floor. Room 335," she said, sounding relieved.

"I'll be there shortly. What is your name?"

"Valerie. Valerie Johnson."

"See you soon, Valerie."

She hung up the phone. I sat my headset on my desk and turned my phone off. I stood up and leaned over my cube wall, telling Rod about the situation. He was on the phone with a customer but got the gist of what I was saying. He gave me the "thumbs up." So off I went to dive into the vortex of technical support hell.

4.

Walking through a government building is kind of like walking in a time warp, a dreary, depressing, moldy time warp. It's true. The interesting thing about most government buildings (and the building for The Texas Commission of Employment and Benefits was no different) is that when they initially come into the consciousness of the officials with the power and authority to assign government funds to establish and build them, there is so much promise and hope placed upon them. Things like this are said: "This new building will help serve the great people of Texas" or "this building will be the symbol of hope for the citizens served by The Texas Commission of Employment and Benefits." A bunch of goddamn pomp and circumstance is thrown around like confetti in the wind. It's all very exciting at first. So millions of dollars are thrown at contractors and the buildings are built. It's made out to be a glorious fucking magnificent thing. And then, once the buildings are completed and staffed with enthusiastic government workers, the reality of the world sets in and the maintenance of these magnificent buildings goes to the way side. All the promise and hope dissipates and what is left behind is a drab building staffed with drab employees. It's true. My building, it seemed, was stuck in the horrific color palette of the 1950s: grey walls, grey floors, grayish green tile in the bathrooms, grey carpet in the offices, grey everywhere. It was an interior decorator's goddamn nightmare. It's true. If there was one interesting thing about my building, if you want to call it interesting, is that apparently tunnels went underground from my building to intersect with tunnels from several other buildings around the city, including The Capitol building. I thought that was pretty goddamn interesting and decided I would have to traverse them one of these days, just not this day.

I climbed the barren stairwell to the third floor. The hallways were empty and lined with several doors with numbers on them. I was looking for room 335 and found that the numbers on the doors didn't have any discernable pattern: 301, 312, 317-A, 324, 329-C. What the fuck? Who was in charge of assigning room numbers back in the 1950s? Probably Lyndon Johnson, I bet. What a crazy character, that Lyndon Johnson. I bet he assigned these asinine numbers to these rooms thinking it would be a pretty goddamn funny thing to confuse us poor lowly government worker bastards. At least, the thought of Lyndon Johnson doing that was pretty goddamn funny, if not far-fetched. Supposedly, that cocksucker was a real prankster. I once read that he liked to pee with the bathroom door opened to annoy his staff and that he would splatter the toilet water all over the goddamn place like a filthy pig. He thought it was funny. That Lyndon Johnson. What a character. We celebrate his birthday as a state holiday in Texas, you know? I don't have to work on Lyndon Johnson's birthday. It's true. Anyway, I eventually found room 335 and went inside.

Room 335 was filled with cubicles that had dividing walls roughly five feet tall, dozens and dozens of cubicles set in neat rows. I could tell there were a lot of desks in there but since the walls were so tall, I couldn't tell if they were occupied or not. With all the click-clacking from fingers tapping on plastic keyboards, it seemed as if the room was filled with busy, dreary, government worker bastards. But you never really could tell. It was an optical illusion; no doubt, put in place to show that tax dollars were hard at work (don't you see?). But I'm pretty sure the workers weren't doing anything more than browsing the internet for bikini-clad models, silly videos of cats playing piano, and deals on shoes or tube socks. It's true.

I didn't know exactly where Valerie Johnson sat and I didn't want to ask anyone so I walked up and down the aisles, peeking in and around them for name plates. I discovered quite a few workers doing various things though none of them actually looked like they were doing a goddamn thing of any importance. I saw a guy picking his nose, another guy resting his head on his desk, a lady filing her nails, another lady putting on makeup, and a dude watching videos on his computer. It was a fucking miracle that this goddamn place even conducted business. It's true. I eventually found a cubicle with a name plate that read, "Valerie Johnson." I poked my head inside and found a young woman staring at her computer screen, as if staring at it a few minutes longer would fix whatever problem she was experiencing. I was pretty sure that wouldn't accomplish a thing. It's true.

"Valerie?" I asked, muffling my voice so I wouldn't disturb the other lazy assholes in the cubes nearby.

"Hi," she said, quickly shuffling some papers around on her desk, then making room with a swipe of her arm, pushing aside whatever junk was there. She pulled a second chair out from her desk and patted the seat softly with her hand. "Please, have a seat."

I sat down and gazed at some framed photos she had on a shelf above her desk. There were pictures of a couple of sweet looking kids, a dog, a cat, and various combinations of the kids, dog, and cat in cutesy poses. The cat appeared to be at the bottom of the family totem pole of importance; one photo showed him being mauled by the dog while the kids laughed, his cat face frozen in photographic horror. Poor little bastard. Cats usually get thrown at the bottom of the family totem pole, mainly because sometimes they can act like such pompous assholes. It's true. Cats can be real shitheads. I had this cat once that had issues with his litter box. That little fucker would squat in that box and hang his feline ass off the side and shit or piss right there on the floor, even if you were watching him. He would just look at you with disdain while he did it. So I thought I would be smart and line up three cat boxes instead of one for him to fit his fat ass in but he still would mount himself in the last cat box and hang his fuzzy butt off the side. I wanted to choke his skinny cat neck but I didn't. You know why? That little bastard had personality for miles. Sometimes, personality trumps urination / defecation issues. It's true. Valerie's cat looked like he had a long road ahead of him living with that sadistic dog.

"Is your computer still having the same problem," I asked. Stupid question, I know, but sometimes you just have to break the ice with strangers by asking stupid questions. Don't ask me why because I don't know. It's just one of those things.

"Yes. It's been giving me problems for the last few days."

"I see. Can I sit there?"

"Oh, sure." She stood up, quick yet awkward, and accidentally tripped herself. She stumbled sideways and I instinctively put my hands out to catch her. I caught her at the wrist by her shirt sleeve and commenced (accidentally I tell you, *accidentally*) to ripping her shirt sleeve right off her goddamn blouse. I stepped back, with my one hand raised to my mouth, and stared at the loose sleeve in my other hand with utter disbelief. It was one of those freaky moments, moments that are so out of your realm of everyday normal moments, that when they happen, it's like getting struck by lightning. I couldn't believe it was happening but there I was, standing like a goddamn idiot with a strange woman's ripped shirt sleeve dangling in my hand. At that moment, right then and there, I couldn't think of another time where I had embarrassed myself so thoroughly. I felt like dog shit.

"Oh... my... I'm so sorry," I said, holding the sleeve like it was a baby bird with its wing crushed. To my surprise, all she did was giggle. She giggled like it was the cutest thing in the whole goddamn world. "I'm really sorry."

"It's OK," she said, giggling some more. She was really starting to laugh it up too, even though her face was as red as a baboon's butt. She had tears welling up in her eyes, giggling so hard. She then grabbed her other sleeve, and with one hard yank, pulled it right off her goddamn blouse. She was now completely sleeveless. She handed me the other sleeve then sat down like nothing happened. "Now you have a matching set."

There are moments in your life when you encounter free spirits and those moments are pretty goddamn hard to miss. It's true. Most of the time, you glide along in your normal routine and encounter normal people, people so devoid of adventure, insight, and uniqueness that they just pass right through you, like ghosts. But free spirits, they are like hurricanes. They are pretty fucking hard to miss when you encounter them. They have the potential to do some real damage to your own calm existence but they are a beauty to behold. Lucky bastards. It must be nice to be a free spirit. They get to do what they want and not have the fear or worry about what other people think and frolic in an existential meadow and rip off their own sleeve like it was the most fucking normal thing to do in the goddamn world. It's true. I decided right then and there to just move on, move forward, and act like nothing had happened. I poked around on her computer then ran a simple diagnostic test. It was the right thing to do.

"This test shouldn't take too long. I can come back in a little while, if you want," I said.

"No, there's no reason for you to aimlessly wander around the building."

"Oh, OK."

"Tell me about yourself. How long have you worked here?"

"This is my first day."

"Really?! Your first day? And you got to rip a woman's sleeve off her blouse on your first day?"

"I guess so." Boy, I didn't think that she would rub it in but that's what free spirits can do sometimes. They don't give a shit about anyone else's feelings but their own, which is part of being a free spirit. Did I mention that? I guess not. Free spirits can be pretty goddamn selfish bastards sometimes. It's true. "I said I was sorry."

"I know you did. Are you married?"

"I was. I'm divorced."

"Oh, I'm so sorry. I know how hard that is. I'm divorced too. How long were you married?"

"Ten years."

"I was married 15 years. I married quite young. I never should have gotten married so young but then I wouldn't have my wonderful children. Do you have kids?"

"Yes, I have two kids, Jessica and Sammie."

"Ah, what great names. I bet you're a proud father, aren't you?"

"Yes, I am." I glanced at the diagnostic test and it was about halfway done, not soon enough though. She was really starting to get nosy and all, asking some pretty goddamn personal questions. She was really getting on my fucking nerves, what, with the questions and the guilt and the free spiriting and the goddamn nosiness. It was getting to be just too much to handle. It's true. But I soldiered forward. That's what a good support tech would do, right? That's what I thought.

"Well, you seem like you would be a great father. I don't meet too many of those, you know? Great fathers, that is. When you get to our age and you get divorced, the dating pool really starts to shrink."

"Ummm."

"Do you date?" She was really starting to get on my last nerve. The diagnostic test was just about done. Almost. Goddamn it.

"Not really. Well, sometimes. I don't have a lot of time to date. You know? Because of the kids."

"That's true. It does make it hard. Why does life have to be so hard?" BINGO! There it was. She said it. Why does life have to be so goddamn hard? I could see it in her eyes. She was an introspective person, just like me. Maybe she wasn't a selfish bastard after all. Maybe there was more to her than I originally thought. Sometimes, people can be pretty complex beings and the good ones, the really good ones, are hard to find. It's true. I think this was her way of letting me know that she had empathy for me, being that she was divorced and had two kids and regretted getting married and all and thought about it all the time. It was just too much to take. It's true.

"Yes, why does it have to be so hard sometimes?"

"Ah, Simon. Don't take this the wrong way..." She leaned over towards me and placed her hand on my knee. Something was up and it was making me pretty goddamn uncomfortable, so uncomfortable that I really didn't want to know the answer to my question anymore. I didn't want to know anything at that moment. I just wanted to run away. Fuck what a good support tech would do. Fuck free spirits. She gently squeezed my knee and as I felt the jolt of adrenaline surge through my body, the diagnostic test on the computer signaled that it was complete. The computer beeped one of those BIOS / system beeps, the kind straight out of the 1980s, and I knew it would reboot itself and be just fine. I decided right then and there that it was time to go. It was time to get out of that free-spirited, floozy, divorced, nosy coworker's cubicle. I quickly stood up and she withdrew her hand, startled.

"Your computer will be fine after it reboots."

"Simon?"

"Have a good day."

I left her cubicle and bolted straight for the door. I heard her call my name one more time but I didn't turn around. I didn't acknowledge that I heard anything. I just left her and the other lazy government bastards to do what they were doing before I came in. Nothing.

5.

Divorce is the scourge of our society. Absolute pile of shit. It's true. Nothing destroys families more than divorce. Marriage is tough enough. Mortgages. Children. Compromises. Jobs. School for the kids. Death of family members. Car loans. Groceries. Clothing. It all adds up to one big challenge. Then, when things get really tough, sometimes you decide it's time to give up. Divorce. Then you pour salt on that big gaping wound. More hurt. What do you do? You allow the government to decide what is best for your family. What a pile of shit. It's a goddamn travesty. When you decide to take the route of divorce in Texas, all the state cares about is your property, assets, and debts. No matter what led to the divorce, the state piles up all your assets and debts and says, "Divide up your assets and debts. Sayonara." You have kids? Great. "Here's your custody schedule. Hasta luego." Need a lawyer? Give them all of your money. Why do you need a fucking lawyer? Everything that is written up for a divorce is in a language that no one understands but the lawyers. My divorce decree makes absolutely no sense. It's a bunch of gibberish that cost a pile of money to draw up. "Thanks for your time. Good luck. You, my friend, are a failure." It's true.

For 10 years, I spent every single night with my children. Now, I have them in an altering array of weekdays and every other weekend. "It's what is best for the children." Bullshit. My children are suffering. "Too bad. You are a failure." Child support. Twenty five percent of my paycheck is siphoned off for the benefit of the children. I pay it to the state to be divvied out minus a fee, of course. "Thanks for playing. Try again." Fuck you, assholes. Fuck you.

I try to make the best of it. My family is now destroyed but I make the best of it. I have a new place, a new life, and new challenges. When my children cry at night, telling me they miss all of us being together, I tell them I'm trying my best. I am trying my best. When they are gone, I cry too. When they are with me, I try to be strong. It's the only thing I can do now.

On Tuesday evenings, the night before Jessica and Sammie come to stay with me, I go to the grocery store to get the things I need for them. Stuff to make their school lunches, snacks, ingredients for dinner, bathroom toiletries, kid stuff, everything that I will need to be a good daddy. I love my children and I want the best for them. Plus, we like to bake cookies together. Baking cookies makes everything better. It's true. Baking cookies with your children is like watching the sun rise. It's magical. It brings a smile to your face. It's what families do.

I pulled into the grocery store parking lot and found a space toward the front. Inside, I found a cart with the least amount of bird shit on it and pulled out my grocery list. The weekend before, I was by myself. I subsisted on ham and cheese sandwiches and ice water and my refrigerator was completely empty. So I had a pretty lengthy list of things to buy. Jessica made sure to tell me that she wanted macaroni and cheese and Sammie wanted peanut butter to make sandwiches. Done and done.

I pushed the cart up and down the aisles, loading it up with the things I needed, crossing items off my list as I went. Macaroni and cheese? Check. Peanut butter? Check. Cans of soup for work? Check. At the end of the aisle, I noticed a little boy, not much older than Sammie, rummaging through some cans of ravioli, looking for something. I watched him as he rummaged. He didn't see me because he was in a zone, looking for beefaroni or lasagna or cheese raviolis or some shit like that. Watching him made me miss my kids. I wondered what they were doing right now. Were they happy? Were they hanging out with their mother and the bastard who wedged his way between our marriage? I looked around for his mother. She was nowhere around. So I decided, right then and there, that I would check on the kid, see if he was all right. I slowly pushed my cart forward, trying not to disturb him. He was really rummaging through those cans, like a squirrel who knew he buried a nut somewhere and couldn't for his life remember where it was. I parked my cart right next to him and pretended I was selecting an assortment of Ramen noodles. I still had cases of Ramen at my apartment but I acted like I needed some more. Ramen is disgusting, by the way. It's true.

"Are you lost?" I asked him. He flinched a bit then continued rummaging. "Did you lose your mother?"

He pretended to ignore me even though I knew he heard me. His little squirrel hands were really going at it. He was looking for something special, I could tell. What could it be? He kept me in the corner of his eye.

"My mommy told me not to talk to strangers. I don't know you mister."

"Your mother is right. You shouldn't talk to strangers."

"OK." He continued on, rummaging.

"Do you like beefaroni?"

"No. Beefaroni is disgusting. It makes me want to barf." He put his index finger up to his mouth, puffing his cheeks up as if to hold back an imminent projectile barf. His face turned red from holding his breath.

I laughed, hard. What a character! Most kids are real characters. It's true. Kids speak without any filters. They always say exactly what is on their little minds. I admire that. Adults don't do that. Adults talk a lot of bullshit, nothing but bullshit. It's true.

"Then what are you looking for? Ravioli?"

"Ravioli is disgusting too. I like fish sticks. Fish sticks are the bee's knees. Fish sticks are yummy. My mommy makes me fish sticks and ketchup. I like to eat fish sticks for breakfast." See? Unfiltered. Kids are so great.

"Oh. Then why are you rummaging through the Chef-boy-r-dee?"

"I lost my Woodle."

"What's a Woodle?" I asked. What the hell was a Woodle, anyway? How interesting.

"Not what. Who. My Woodle is my friend. And I lost him."

"You lost him in the Chef-boy-r-dee?"

"Yes, I lost him. The last time I came shopping with mommy, I hid him here because my mommy didn't want me to bring him. And now he's gone. I put him right in here and he's gone. Someone stole my Woodle." Little tears appeared in the corners of his little squirrel eyes. He looked like he was about to start bawling and there is nothing worse than a little kid bawling over something that is important to him. It's true. It's a goddamn shame, really.

"Do you want me to help you?"

"OK!" he chirped, a smile stretching across his little face. "You look behind the ravioli. I'll look behind the spaghetti with meatballs. My name is Cameron."

"Hi Cameron. My name is Simon."

"Do you have kids, Mr. Simon?"

"Yes, I have two kids. Their names are Jessica and Sammie."

"Where are they?"

"They are with their mother."

"Oh. I wish they were here. They could help me look for my Woodle too."

"Yes, they would help you look for your Woodle. I'm sure of it."

"Are they nice?" he asked. What a cute little squirrel! I bet he was the same age as Sammie. He looked about the same age. I wondered if he went to my kids' school. I wondered if Sammie knew who he was. I wondered if they played together. I wondered a lot of things. I sure missed my kids. I missed my kids something awful. It's true.

"Yes, Cameron. My kids are very nice, sweet kids."

"You are nice, mister. You're not like a stranger at all."

I looked behind the cans of ravioli and spaghetti and meatballs and beefaroni even though it was obvious that the Woodle was nowhere to be found. Some goddamn grocery store employee probably found it during the early morning stocking hour and discarded it with the rest of the trash. The bastard. People can be real assholes sometimes, finding things that aren't theirs and throwing them away without a care in the world. It's true. I'm guilty too, finding things and throwing them away without a care or a thought to who may be missing what I found. I felt terrible thinking about that.

"I don't think your Woodle is here anymore, Cameron. I'm sorry."

"Don't say that, mister. He's here, I know it."

As we continued our search, I felt a presence behind me, an eerie presence. I turned my head and saw another cart behind mine. It was filled with all kinds of crap, Ding Dongs, Twinkies, Cheetos, an assortment of junk that would make your insides turn to mush. I heard a familiar goddamn voice. It was the voice of a real bastard too.

"Simon Burchwood? Is that you?"

I stood up and discovered the asshole of all assholes. The king of the cocksuckers. The epitome of douchebaggery. Mr. Folsom, my former boss. My nemesis.

"Mr. Folsom?" I wiped my hands on my pants, straightening myself up. Cameron noticed too. He gazed at Mr. Folsom's lazy eye, its bulging presence spinning around out of control. It must have freaked Cameron out because that little squirrel bolted like he saw the boogieman. He ran as fast as he could, leaving behind his Woodle. It wasn't there anyway, poor kid. It's true.

"What are you doing?"

"I was helping him find his Woodle."

"His what?"

"His... nevermind. I'm grocery shopping."

"That wasn't your boy, was it? What was his name? Johnnie? Frankie?"

"His name is Sammie."

"Right, right. That's it. Sammie."

"No, that wasn't Sammie." His goddamn eye was spinning something crazy, like it was ready to pop out of its goddamn eye socket and roll around on the floor. What a cocksucker.

"You find another job?"

"Yes, I did. Tech support for the State of Texas."

"Great. Just wanted to let you know that your layoff was nothing personal. It was just business. You know that, right?"

"Sure." What a bastard! What a fucking smug bastard! I wanted to cram a can of soup in his mouth and shove it out his diseased eye socket. I wanted to kill him, right then and there. I was red hot. I was livid. I wanted to cry. I was a ball of confusion and anger and resentment. I was a mess. It's true.

"Great. Good luck to you. Take care." He extended his hand for a shake but I didn't shake it. I clinched my fist, as if I was going to throw it. I wanted to knock his goddamn block off. He saw my fist and grimaced. "OK then." He pushed his cart away. I watched him round the corner until he was out of sight.

I felt the rage boil up inside me. I wanted to hurt him something bad. I wanted to make him pay. Revenge is an evil thing. It really is. But sometimes, just sometimes, it seems like the right thing to do. Sometimes, when you are all out of sorts and confused and angry, it seems like the only thing that makes any sense. And the only thing to do was let things be the way they were going to be. It was time for action. It was time for revenge.

I grabbed my cart and pushed it the opposite way up the aisle. I turned the corner and saw Mr. Folsom down the next aisle looking for more crap to throw in his cart, more bullshit to stuff in his rotten gut while sitting behind his comfortable desk at his comfortable job. I continued on to the next aisle, one filled with chemicals and household items and cleaners and detergents and sponges and shit like that. I found a bottle of bleach and thought I could do something with it. But what? Pour it on him? Throw him to the ground and drain it down his throat? I grabbed the bottle of bleach, clinching it in my angry hand, scheming something in my mind. I rounded the corner and waited at the end of his aisle. I saw him examining a package of Little Debbie cakes, deciding to take it or not. I unscrewed the top of the bottle of bleach and knew what I was going to do. The scheme went off in my mind like a firecracker, quick and bright and brilliant. I cocked my hand back like a professional bowler, lifting the bottle behind me. I took three careful steps and slid my foot forward, sliding the bottle like an eight pound bowling ball. The bottle slid across the floor, swiveling out of control, bleach spurting out the top. He saw it coming but not quick enough to do anything about it. Score, direct hit! The bottle slammed into the wheels of his cart and tumped over, spilling bleach all over the floor. The slippery liquid pulled his feet out from under him. He danced a spastic dance, losing his balance, spinning around, his feet flailing for firm ground. He saw me, for a split second, with his lazy eye. It focused right at me. And before he could say anything, yell for help, he grabbed for a shelf to catch himself but his weight was too much. The shelf gave way, falling down, spilling the cheap snacks on top of him. He crumpled to the floor and the rest of the shelving gave way, dropping heavy cases of food on top of him. It was like an avalanche, violent and quick and loud. And then time stopped.

"Uh oh," I thought. Revenge. It sounded so good for a second. It didn't seem like such a good idea anymore. I grabbed my cart and went in the opposite direction, pushing frantically.

Check-out aisle 12 was empty so I unloaded the few groceries I had. I knew it was time for me to go and leave the Woodle behind and Cameron the cute squirrel and Mr. Folsom and his goddamn lazy eye and the rest of my groceries for me and Sammie and Jessica. The clerk looked a little frazzled, not knowing that I was the culprit. The commotion from the falling groceries sent a buzz through the store and the employees didn't know what to do or how to react. I acted like I didn't know what was going on either. Suckers.

"Sounds like something fell over," I said, nonchalantly, discreetly.

"Yeah, it didn't sound good," she said.

"Nope, it didn't."

"Need stamps or ice today?"

"No."

"How about a candy bar from the sale basket?"

"Sure, a candy bar would be great."

I paid for my groceries and the candy bar and left. I wondered if Cameron had found his Woodle. I wondered if he eventually found his mother. I wondered if Sammie and Jessica were all right. I wondered what I was going to make for dinner. I wondered if Mr. Folsom was hurt but I didn't wonder about that very long. Revenge. It's not what it is cracked up to be. It's true.

6.

Things were a lot different when I was in elementary school. It seems, nowadays, that the world is filled with goddamn pedophiles and creeps and rapists and kidnappers and lunatic bums who claim that Jesus told them to steal your children and make them their sex slaves. It's all enough to make a parent want to slam their head against the wall and lock their kids up in their homes, sheltered from the perverted world. It's true. When I was a kid and it was time for me to go to school, I really don't think my mother and father worried that I would get scooped up and kidnapped. My mom would load up my Spider-Man lunch box and make sure my things were in my backpack and she would wave goodbye to me as I rode off on my Huffy BMX bicycle to school. The elementary school was a mile or two away and, 99% of the time, I made a beeline straight to the school, occasionally stopping to mess with a pile of fire ants or perform a jump off a curb, just for kicks. Kids do that kind of shit for no reason, you know? But I never encountered any strange creeps or anything like that. In fact, I don't remember ever even hearing about strange creeps in my neighborhood. Today, you can't turn on any news channel or news show without hearing about these slimy bastards all over the United States going after your children. John Walsh and Nancy Grace and all of the concerned talking heads on the boob tube warn us about the scumbags every day, 24 hours a day, seven days a week. And that, my friend, is why I drive my kids to and from school (when I have them, that is). Today was no different. It was my day to have the kids and I waited for them behind the school in my car, same spot as the time before.

The elementary school devised a pretty goddamn complicated pick-up system for the children and all of the parents were supposed to follow it but no one did, mainly because most of the parents were selfish bastards. It's true. When people are in their cars with their personal distractions like car stereos and MP3 players and cell phones and DVD screens and their makeup and their cheeseburgers and their creepy rat terriers or whatever else they have distracting them, they are oblivious to everyone else in the goddamn world. It's enough to make you want to ram your car into theirs in a fit of nasty yet justified road rage. But, in an effort to remain calm (and not go to jail, thank you), I decided early on in my kids academic career to avoid the car line and the school's silly pick-up rules and the other distracted assholes and their mongoloid children and park on the street across from the school. It was a safe place for me to wait and watch for my kiddos.

I enjoyed doing a couple of things while I waited for my cutie pies. One of the things I enjoyed to do was to observe the body language of the teachers and guess their marital status. You can easily tell if a woman is married or not by the way she carries herself. It's true. Some of the teachers wore outfits that were so hideous and so unbecoming of the female shape that they seemed to create a force-field so impenetrable that even the sexiest of the sexy bastards couldn't woo them. These frump-a-linas were obviously married to some poor schlubs who were deprived of sex and instead showered with bitterness and condescension so relentless as to render them neutered. Poor bastards. In contrast, other teachers wore outfits so sexy and unbecoming of an elementary teacher that the site of the little boys buzzing around them like horny honey bees brought huge, shameless smiles to their faces. With the boys buzzing around, they would bend over and expose their breasts to the poor little bastards, sending their confused hormones to a heightened state. Obviously, these women were divorced and shameless, full of regret and the urgency that comes from aging and the inevitable loss of beauty that makes snagging a husband more difficult. They were one misstep away from pedophilia. It's true.

The men in the teaching profession, on the other hand, were there for two reasons: 1) they were on reprieve from their previous careers as devious accountants, micro-managing assholes, or conniving salesman and 2) they were trying to woo the bitter frump-a-linas and the shameless cougars. It's true. Why else would they be teaching small children? There is no prestige in being a male, elementary school teacher. None. Why else would they be there besides trying to get laid? It's true.

The other thing I enjoyed doing while waiting for my children to get out of school was completing Mad Libs. As I've mentioned before (in detail, I might add), Mad Libs are an excellent tool to relieve mentally constipated writers from the cruel grasp of writer's block. It's true. A perfect example of a Mad Libs puzzle goes like this:

"Mary _____ her yellow _____ while she _____ her _____."

Now, as you can see, there are a dozen ways to complete this puzzle. A proficient writer like myself might complete the puzzle like this:

"Mary <u>drives</u> her yellow <u>automobile</u> while she <u>calls</u> her <u>sister</u>."
Perfecto!

On the other hand, an ignorant jackass like my best friend Jason would have a ball with this exercise. He has no desire to exercise his mind. He just likes to make light of everything, like everything in life is a goddamn joke. It's true. He tries to make jokes at everyone's expense all the time and laughs his ass off like a goddamn hyena, hemming and hawing and cackling all over the goddamn place. He probably would complete the puzzle like this:

"Mary <u>porks</u> her yellow <u>dildo</u> while she <u>barfs</u> her <u>lunch</u>."

And he would start giggling like a goddamn jackass, I'm sure. He has no idea how hard it is to keep the creative mind sharp. It's true. Sadly, most people don't.

This little exercise got me wondering what good ol' Jason was up to, though. As much as I rag on him, he really is a good guy and all. It's true. He can be all kinds of sweet and supportive and just what a friend should be. It's sad that he is married to a goddamn whore. It's just too sad. She doesn't deserve a nice guy like good ol' Jason, that bitch. I decided right then and there that I would send him a text message and see what he was up to, maybe see if he wanted to take a break from his crappy marriage and pay his best friend a visit in beautiful Austin, Texas. I sure could have used the company. It's a sad state of affairs when you're divorced and living alone. It's true. I pulled out my trusty cell phone (an old junky flip phone but a trusty one nonetheless) and sent the following text message:

Hey buddy! I was working on Mad Libs and thought of you. Hope you're doing OK. Would you consider coming to visit? That would be nice. Simon

Done and done. I placed my trusty cell phone back in the glove box and realized (very suddenly, I might add) that I had been sitting in my car for quite some time and my kids were nowhere to be found. In fact, most of the kids were gone, with only a few stragglers and a few frump-a-linas left behind to watch them, waiting for someone to come and pick up the last of the little nose-pickers. The poor bastards. But where were MY KIDS? I jumped out of the car and ran toward the school. One of the frump-a-linas saw me coming and she looked concerned. Surely she didn't want to deal with a concerned parent like myself and surely she was pondering what to say to me. The little nose-pickers sat there on the cement doing what little nose-pickers do, smashing boogers on each others' t-shirts. I stood next to the teacher, wheezing and huffing and puffing from running. I was a goddamn mess. It's true.

"Excuse me. Where are my kids? They are supposed to be here waiting for me."

"I'm sorry, sir. What are your kids' names?" she asked. What a goddamn, nincompoop. This lady was responsible for watching these children after school? That was a shame.

"Their names are Jessica and Sammie."

"And their last name?" she asked, rather sheepishly. This was turning into a goddamn nightmare. It's true.

"Burchwood. Their last name is Burchwood."

"Let me see if someone else picked them up." Someone else? Now who could that be? No one was supposed to pick them up today but me. She pulled out a clipboard from behind her back, scanning through the pages, looking down the roster of names, names of the nose-pickers no doubt. The majority of the names had a checkmark next to them, I guess to indicate that they had been picked up. It didn't take long for her to find my kids' names. Since Burchwood started with a "B," they were on the second page. "Someone already picked them up."

"Who picked them up?" I asked. I was really starting to get pissed off with this frump-a-lina. She was getting on my last goddamn nerve.

"I don't have that information, sir. Just that someone picked them up. See?" She pointed to my kids' names. A green checkmark perched next to each name. It was all just too confusing. It's true.

"Did you see who picked them up?"

"No."

"Then who wrote down these checkmarks?"

"I don't know, sir. It could have been any of the teachers that were out here helping with the car line. I'm really not sure. I just know that they were picked up and their names were checked off. See?" She pointed to the names with her chubby index finger, tapping the clipboard. Her finger looked like a hot dog that had been boiled for way too long. It's true. "The checkmarks mean they were picked up and marked off by a teacher."

"I can see that. So what am I supposed to do?"

"What do you want to do, Mr. Burchwood?"

"I want to pick up my kids."

"They have already been picked up, sir." I was about to blow my goddamn top. I was getting all sorts of pissed off and angry and upset. I was seething on the inside. This frump-a-lina had absolutely no idea how angry I was getting. I wanted to grab that clipboard from her chubby hands and cram it down her throat. I was THAT mad. "I'm sorry."

"Yeah, me too," I said. There wasn't much else I could do at that point, really. What was I to do? Ask her to perform a miracle and have my kids pop out of her ass? That wasn't going to happen. So I decided right then and there to go home and figure out what I was going to do. "Thanks."

I turned around and began to walk back to my car when she called out to me, "Is there a relative who could have picked them up?"

I turned her way and said, "Sure."

"Then if I was you, I would call them first and see. Maybe a relative picked them up."

"OK. Thanks."

I turned around and walked away. When I got back in my car, I noticed I had received a text message while I was chatting with the frump-a-lina. It was from Jessica, my ex-wife. It said (and I quote the dismal message verbatim):

Simon, I picked up the kids from school. We are moving to Dallas. I have a new job, a new house, and a new life there. Goodbye.

All I could think was:

Shit.

Or as my son Sammie would say:

Shmit.

7.

The best advice anyone has ever given me was this gem from my grandfather: Always, always brush your teeth. Insight from a 90 year old man (who still has all of his teeth, for crying out loud) is priceless. It's true. Unfortunately, old people get the short end of the stick from society most of the time. It seems young people get too caught up in the fact that old people can be forgetful or cranky or smelly or sentimental or resentful or all of these things rolled up into one cantankerous son of a bitch or one spiteful old witch. The one thing most young people gloss over is the fact that they themselves are selfish to the point of narcissistic catastrophe. It's really a goddamn shame. It's true. Young people can be a bunch of selfish assholes, the whole lot of them. Now, it is true that I've encountered some old folks who smelled like a McDonald's Filet-O-Fish sandwich that had been left in a sock drawer for an indeterminate amount of time, which is quite horrifying in the olfactory sense. But that is beside the point. So here it is: to live to be 90 years old is a real feat and any insight into how someone gets to be that old is important. Period. Because to be honest, I'm surprised that some of the idiots I encounter on a daily basis live to see tomorrow. It's true. Young people can be a bunch of goddamn idiots.

Back to what is important here. I was sitting with my grandfather and some of his good buddies one time when I was a teenager. They were all quite old, as old as my grandfather or close enough I'd imagine, but were all very lively and talkative and happy. They were all beer drinkers and very enthusiastic about making each other laugh so jokes were being volleyed about between sips of beer. They weren't much into being reflective unless someone asked and for some reason, I felt like asking for advice this time. Once I did that, the floodgates opened. "Finally!" I imagined them thinking collectively. "A youngster interested in what we have to say!" I wanted some general good advice, what was I to do as I moved forward in age toward adulthood. And here, in no particular order, is what some of them had to say:

- Don't get attached to your job
- Never hit a woman
- Ejaculate at least once a day, either through intercourse or masturbation
- Drink at least one alcoholic beverage a day, preferably beer
- Keep in touch with your parents
- Volunteer your time to people in need
- Drink plenty of water and eat lots of fruit and vegetables.
- Always ask for bacon on your cheeseburger
- Follow your dreams

- Never be boring
- Be true to yourself
- Eat ice cream when you're sad
- Never judge a book by its cover
- Etcetera

When it was my grandfather's turn, he said, "Always, always brush your teeth." Of all the advice given that day, this one piece of advice seemed to get the largest amount of consensus from the group. An agreeable mumble was groaned as they all nodded their heads. It was an amazing goddamn thing to witness. It's true. Their collective age must have been over 1,000 years and this was the best advice: Always, always brush your teeth. So, being young and foolish and curious and a goddamn idiot, I asked my grandfather why that was good advice. He said, "Son, of all of your bodily functions, eating is the top of the heap. They have remedies for the other functions but this one, it's the most important. If you can't walk, then they'll put you in a wheel chair. If you can't crap right, then they'll put a diaper on you. But if you can't eat, if you can't enjoy your sustenance, then there ain't no remedy for that. Life ain't worth living if you can't chew your own food." So there it was: wisdom from the elders. Who was I to question this wisdom? They obviously had lived a long time and I was just a little shit. It's true. It must be very important advice.

The reason I bring this up is because my coworker (who will now be formally nicknamed Snaggle) had the absolute worst teeth I had ever seen on a human being in my entire goddamn life. The slang term snagglepuss was invented specifically for Ryan, my young genius coworker, whose teeth looked like they had all been pulled out with pliers at some point in his early life and jammed back into his gums by a maniacal chimpanzee on mescaline. It's true. Snaggle had one busted-up grill. However, his dental condition didn't keep him from socializing. In fact, he was at my cubicle at every opportunity to flap his gums and play a vigorous game of pocket pool, yapping about computers and software and programming and batch files and girls. He loved talking about girls but, I imagined, he probably had never touched a girl in his entire life. With the way his breath smelled, I was absolutely sure of it.

I felt pretty down about what had happened to my kids and was trying to decide what to do about it. The last thing I wanted to do was go to work. Work has a way of making a shitty day even shittier. It's true. The phone queue was relatively quiet when I heard the sound of coins and game tokens and paper clips and Dungeon and Dragons dice and car keys jingling behind me. That jingle, it was the warning sound. Snaggle was in my presence. He and his abused testicles were right behind me.

"What's up?" he asked, his hand in his pocket furiously tossing his nuts like a squirrel working on an acorn.

"Nothing. Working."

"I was bored last night so I built a Linux server in my living room. Took me an hour."

"Really? Sounds interesting."

"You ever been to Costa Rica? They say you can get a hooker there that looks like a super model to give you a blow job for only $2."

"Uh, I've never heard of that."

"Did you know that Abraham Lincoln was really a grand dragon in the KKK?"

"What?"

"Are you going to request any Microsoft training this year?"

"No, probably not."

"There are dozens more planets in our solar system but the government and NASA are keeping them secret. Chimps were sent to Planet UZ-37 in 1966 but they still haven't arrived."

"Ryan?" I asked, annoyed.

"Yes?"

"Are you bored?"

"Kinda."

"I'm trying to figure something out and I would appreciate some privacy, if you don't mind."

"Privacy? At work?" He started to laugh and cackle and guffaw all over the goddamn place, his lips smacking against his mangled teeth, little globs of spittle flying in the air. As weird as this may sound, he reminded me of Jason the way he laughed like that. It was one, weird, nerdy déjà vu. It's true.

"Yes, privacy would be nice."

"That's really funny, Simon. I would think that..." Just then his phone rang and he ran for his cubicle, the coins and dice and paper clips pouring from his pocket as he tried to get the call before it went to the next tech in the queue. Nothing looked worse on your job performance report than calls passing you in the queue because you didn't answer them. They would dock your pay if you missed calls, so if the phone rang and we weren't at our desks then we would run like wild men to catch the call. It was a goddamn sight to see sometimes. It's true.

With Snaggle gone, I could get back to the task at hand which was to figure out where my ex-wife Jessica was taking the kids. She mentioned moving to Dallas in her text message but that was it. She didn't give any other information. Typical. I tried to call her but got no answer. I sent her emails but got no replies. I sent her text messages but got no responses. It was all so disheartening. I told you divorce was a goddamn mess, the scourge of society. It's true. We had an agreement that neither of us would move and take the kids out of a certain geographical area but, as you can see, agreements don't mean shit to anybody. People do whatever they goddamn well please. It's true. Selfish bastards.

Here's the thing: 9 times out of 10, when you make an agreement with someone, they have absolutely no intention of keeping that agreement. It's true. It's a rare thing to find an individual who will look you in the eye, shake your hand, and keep their fucking word, even for menial little things. A friend might ask, "Can I borrow your drill?" And of course, you say yes. "I'll bring it back to you tomorrow." Sure, no problem, buddy. But guess what? Say goodbye to that goddamn drill because it will vanish in a dark hole of bullshit agreements. And it doesn't stop there. It goes all the way up the ladder of society, all the way up to the top. How many times have you heard leaders of various countries say they have come to an agreement with a foe or a disgruntled neighboring country or a terrorist group or whatever? Guaranteed, the minute that shit is signed, any intention of upholding that agreement vanishes into thin air, just like that. Bye bye. Those bastards look at you and think to themselves, "I can't believe they think I'm going to sign this thing and keep my promise. Suckers!"

Divorce is no different. In fact, divorce is the grand sucker of all sucker agreements. Here it is: ex-spouses pay lawyers thousands and thousands of dollars to help them come to an "agreement," an agreement that involves their property, their finances, their time, their retirement, their children, etc. This agreement devised by lawyers...

Jingle, jingly jingle, jingle.

Jingle, jingly jingle, jingle.

Jingle, jingly jingle, jingle.

I heard the jingly noise coming from behind me. It was the warning sound. Remember? I peered over my shoulder. Snaggle was in my cube again. He stood over me, his snaggle-teeth bursting through his terse smile, remnants of his breakfast on his shirt pocket. He was a goddamn pig dressed up in nerd's clothing. It's true.

"Did you know that a woman's clitoris is 100 times more sensitive than a man's penis?" he asked. I don't need to tell you what he was doing in his goddamn pocket, do I? Of course not. The jingly jingle, jingle was sufficient enough. His testicles must have looked like 6-month-old tennis balls by now.

"I did not know that." He was in my cubicle for less than 30 seconds and he was already getting on my last goddamn nerve.

"Did you know that some land crabs in Cuba can run faster than a horse?"

"Ryan?"

"Uh huh?" he said, his hands plunging deep into his pant pockets, probing for places on his testicles that had not been touched before. It was fucking unbelievable.

"Seriously, are you that bored?"

"No. Why do you ask?"

"Because..." I tried to think of the most polite way to ask him why he was fondling himself in public in a very unashamed fashion. But that was very difficult to do. Unfortunately, you need to be polite to your coworkers in this day and age unless you fancy getting shot in an unprovoked display of workplace violence. Believe me, all of your coworkers are capable of killing you at any moment. They are probably thinking about killing you right now. It's true. "Oh, nevermind."

"Do you know why chickens can't fly?" he asked.

"No." I laid my head on my desk. It was all just too much to take. Really. All I could hear in my head, over and over, was 'Why does life have to be so goddamn hard?' Life could be a real kick in the pants, you know? It's true.

"Simon, are you OK?" Snaggle sounded genuinely concerned, which was nice to hear. Sometimes, it's pretty easy to underestimate people, especially coworkers with fucked up teeth and the habit of pulling their pud in the company of others. Maybe I was being too hard on Snaggle. Maybe.

"I sure could use some time to relax. Or a massage. That sounds nice, a relaxing massage."

"A massage?" he asked, his voice perking up. "Boy, do I have the perfect thing for you." He skipped over to his cube, fumbled around on his desk, shuffling papers and shit, and skipped back to my cube. He had a smile stretched across his snaggle-puss that would make the Cheshire Cat look modest. It's true. "Here you go."

He handed me a business card. It said, "For a Relaxing Massage, email Jenny."

"You should make an appointment," he said, cackling his goddamn head off. "She'll definitely give you a *relaxing* massage."

"Really?"

"Uh huh."

"Thanks. I'll do that."

Snaggle's phone rang and he bounced back to his cube. Maybe I was being too hard on him. I remembered back to that time when I was hanging out with my grandfather and his good old buddies and another piece of advice from one of the old men that I forgot to mention earlier was never judge people too quickly. I remembered the old man telling me that the cliché of not judging a book by its cover was very true and he recounted many instances to me about how he had failed to see the good in people because he was too busy judging everybody in the goddamn world. He said to me, "The only person that you should judge is yourself." Well, I judge myself all the goddamn time. That's part of my personal repertoire of self-deprecation and self-loathing. But sometimes I don't realize how hard I can be on others. It was really a goddamn shame. It's true. I decided right then and there that I would give Snaggle a break, at least for one day. He deserved it.

Now, if only he would stop playing pocket pool in front of everybody in the goddamn world. I have a feeling my grandfather and his old buddies would agree with me about that. I'm sure of it.

8.

I emailed Jenny and she promptly replied with directions to her massage studio and specific instructions on where to park and what to do. To be honest, it almost seemed like too much work for a goddamn massage. I mean, she asked that I not park in front of her house but to the side of the house and to not come early so as to not disturb the other goddamn clients and the relaxed state they were in and to be careful approaching her house because she had a dog that didn't like strange people lurking around and so on and so forth. It was a lot of goddamn work just for a massage. But, and this was a big BUT, I needed to relax and what better way to relax than by getting a massage. A good massage is like a gift from God. It's true. I could feel the tension being released from the knots in my shoulders already. Isn't that amazing?

The only thing of concern to me was that her studio was on the east side of town, which if you didn't know, was the fucking ghetto. East Austin is the biggest shithole in the entire world. It's true. Well, maybe not the biggest shithole in the entire world (that's a bold statement) but a shithole nonetheless. I'm sure there were bigger shitholes in India or Africa or some other crappy countries like that. But in terms of this Texas city, East Austin was the black eye of this otherwise beautiful town. It was shitty enough for me to give it a second thought. If you have second thoughts about driving into a certain part of town, then there must be valid concerns, and I wasn't in the mood to be concerned. I wanted to relax.

Anyway, right then and there I decided to put the second thoughts aside and to just go for it. So I did. I promptly left work and headed for Jenny's studio on the East Side of Austin. As I drove east on 7th Street, I noticed several businesses that had crazy names like "My T Sharp Barbershop" and "Bertha's Pretty Hair Salon and Nail Bo-Teek" and "Your Mama's Liquor Store" and "Holy Smoke BBQ" and "Juan in a Million Taco Shack" and so on. It was pun after terrible pun of bad business names. How is anyone going to take you seriously if you have a business name that sounds like a second grader came up with it? Maybe that's why East Austin was such a shithole. Not only were the businesses badly named but the streets were filled with all kinds of bums and people standing around looking like they weren't doing much of anything, which means they were up to no good for sure. They were probably waiting around for their welfare checks to arrive in the mail so they could cash them at a check-cashing place and spend their hard earned cash on malt liquor and crack and hamburgers. Crack! Of all the names in the world, crack had to be the silliest name for a drug that anyone could come up with. It's true. It was all just too ridiculous.

After passing block after block of welfare bums, I finally found Chicon Street and made a left. When I straightened out my car I discovered a small crowd of African-American fellows congregating in the middle of the street. They paid no attention to me and my vehicle and stood there yapping and laughing and patting each other on their backs and butts like they scored a touchdown and were celebrating, what, I don't know. I sat there a minute, my car idling in the middle of the goddamn street, hoping they would notice me but they didn't. They just continued on with what they were doing which was probably no good. I debated if I should honk my horn but decided that was the last thing a scrawny, slightly balding white guy like myself should do in a neighborhood like this. I would likely get killed, shot with an illegal firearm, and dumped in an alley like a bag of garbage. The thought of that gave me goosebumps, so I waited. And waited. And waited. Finally, one of the home boys noticed me and waved. I wasn't sure what to do so I waved back. Then he approached my car, walking with a stiff limp. He came right up to my window and knocked on the glass. I was scared shitless. It's true. He looked like he could tear me apart with his bare hands. He knocked again so I lowered the window a few inches.

"What's up, Steve Martin?" he asked.

"What?"

"You heard me, Tom Hanks. Wazzup?" I sat there baffled, not knowing what to say. I could feel the urine in my bladder pushing down, inching its way toward catastrophe. I almost peed my pants right then and there. It's true. "You lookin' for somethin'?"

"Uh, I'm just trying to get to my destination."

"Which is wha'? Funky Town!" He started laughing and cackling all over the goddamn place like a jackass. He really thought his joke was something else. It's true. He soon got over himself and turned serious. "You lookin' fo' some smoke?"

"No. Just trying to get where I'm going."

"You said that already, motha fucka." His demeanor turned from serious to dead serious. I thought he was going to bust my window and pull me out of the car and rape me right there in the street. It was just too much to take. "If you not lookin' fo' smoke, wha cha doing in my hood?"

"I'm looking for 435 11th Street. Just trying to get where I'm going."

"Oh shit, homie! Why did'n you say so?! That's just right up the street." He yelled something to his friends, waving his hand in the air, and they dispersed from the street in a quick fashion. They all bowed down, lined up along the side of the road, extending their arms out like a maitre d's at a fine restaurant, directing me to drive on through. I slowly pulled my car forward. I felt like I was being boobie trapped. It's true. "Good day to you, sir."

"Thank you." What a nice fellow! Seriously, sometimes you can judge a book by its cover and get it all wrong. My grandfather's buddies were so right.

"And if you want some smoke, I be right here. You get that, Bryan Adams? The name's Marvin." As I pulled away, I could see them congregating back in the street as if I was never there. It must be nice standing in the goddamn street all day with your buddies, selling dope to strange people, and patting your friends on the back like you were actually accomplishing something. What they were accomplishing, I had no idea. "See you soon, Bryan Adams! Just ask for Marvin!" he yelled.

After a few blocks, I found 435 11th Street and remembered to park at the side of the house, not in the front. I pulled behind a late model Honda Accord, beat all to hell and dirty as fuck. It looked like that car had been to hell and back and was in desperate need of a car wash and a good waxing. I was a few minutes early for my appointment so I decided to park my car and wait a few minutes. I didn't want to disturb the serenity of whoever the hell may be in there right now, mainly because I won't want to be disturbed when I'm in there.

The second I turned my car off, literally, I saw a guy leaving the house. He was a supreme fat ass and must have weighed somewhere in the vicinity of 400 pounds. He was massive! He lurched off the front porch and slowly made his way to his clunker. I could see that his fly was open and part of his shirt poked out the front of his pants. He was a really humongous goddamn mess. It's true. I imagined a scene in the studio where the petite masseuse (I'm sure she's petite, you got that?) attempted to massage the massive slob, climbing on a stool to reach his nether parts, rubbing globs of fatty tissue with her small but firm hands. It was just too much. I was snickering and giggling like a little nose-picker in elementary school.

Soon the giant slob took off in his hell-hole clunker, probably off to buy some crack from Marvin down the street and his lazy goddamn buddies. I decided to make my way to the front door. The house was completely surrounded by a chain-link fence, encircling the property like a prison barrier, and "Beware of Dog" signs were affixed every 10 feet or so along the fence. It was a cute goddamn little house, probably built in the 1950s, recently painted white with dark brown trim. But if anything was an indication of just how shitty this part of town was, it was this chain-link fence. Jenny meant business, obviously, by letting her neighbors know that they weren't welcome on her property. I imagined she probably had a vicious dog too, one of the terrier varieties with a lock-jaw bite and a taste for human flesh. I unhinged the gate at the front of the property, looking around for the vicious guard dog, and slowly made my way to the front door. I wasn't sure if the dog was lurking about, maybe hiding behind a bush or something, so I kept myself attentive. The last thing I needed was a vicious goddamn dog clamping his jaws onto my nuts. It's true.

I rang the door bell and heard a dog barking from inside, a bark that seemed to be from a dog that was less than vicious, more appropriate for something that would nuzzle in your lap. I heard footsteps inside, steps that were making their way across a wood floor. The door opened slowly, a pair of beautiful blue eyes peeping out up top, a small dog's head popping out at the bottom of the entrance, its tongue lashing about. The dog looked like that creature that perched next to Jabba the Hut in the movie The Empire Strikes Back, a Muppet-looking extraterrestrial that was scrawny, mostly bald, and had a tuft of hair at the top of its head that poked straight up like a goddamn ostrich plume. The dog tried to jam its head out the door so it could like my shoes. It was a sight to see! That little bastard almost had a heart attack. It's true.

"Can I help you?" a delicate voice asked.

"I'm Simon. I'm here for a massage."

"Yes, come on in." She opened the door and motioned for me to come inside. "Don't mind the mess, please. I'm Jenny," she said, extending her hand for a shake. She was... gorgeous, absolutely, fucking unbelievably gorgeous. It was going to be difficult controlling the raging erection I knew would come the minute she placed those delicate but firm hands on my skin. I was already embarrassed. It's true.

"I'm Simon."

"Follow me, Simon."

Her house really wasn't that messy and was decorated in a tasteful, hippy style that was more Pier One than Goodwill. And she was barely taller than five foot three with a silk robe draped over her thin frame. She glided across the wood floor like an ice skater, her Muppet-looking extraterrestrial dog at her heels, its squinty brown eyes watching me closely as she led me to her studio.

"How is your day so far?" she asked.

"Good."

"Great. Take off your clothes and lay on the table. There's a sheet there to cover you, if you want."

"What?"

"Just be careful. My previous client broke the table but I think I fixed it. I'll be right back."

She and her Muppet-looking extraterrestrial dog vanished in a side room and left me there alone. The room was pretty sparse, a massage table, a dresser, a mirror, a radio, a chair, and that was about it. I will say this though. That room smelled fantastic. I'm not sure what the smell consisted of but it was so soothing and calming that I knew I would be put into a state of relaxation in a matter of seconds. It's true.

I began to take my clothes off when I noticed some movement through the window blinds. I peeked through the blinds and there was my car, parked on the street, and Marvin the drug dealer was inspecting it, sauntering around it like a used car salesman. What the hell was he doing out there? I was about to blow my goddamn top! I had to fight the urge to bang on the window and tell him to fuck off. I decided right then and there to just ignore Marvin, take a deep breath, and relax. I was there to relax and I didn't need a two-bit, unemployed drug dealer ruining my day. It's true. I took a deep breath, removed my shirt, and placed it on the chair. I saw myself in the mirror, slightly pudgy, slightly balding, and I thought, "Damn, I'm a goddamn mess." Growing old sucks. It's true.

I climbed up on the massage table and laid my pudgy, growing-older-by-the-minute body down. The table was a little rickety, courtesy of the goddamn fat ass who was in there right before me. He must have given this helpless table a real goddamn challenge, plopping his gigantic body on top of the reinforced aluminum frame of the table. Thank God for modern engineering! The table had a fighting chance because of the team of well-trained engineers who designed it. It's true. I could hear Jenny fumbling around in the room next door, the Muppet-looking extraterrestrial dog yipping and yapping all over the goddamn place about something, probably about me. Dogs. What a goddamn waste of time. If I could go back in time and find the first prehistoric idiot who domesticated dogs, then I would give him a real swift kick to the nuts. Seriously, I would kick... she burst into the studio.

"I'm going to lay this sheet over your legs," she said, unfolding a sheet to lay over me. "Sorry it took so long. My dog doesn't like to be left alone."

See? Fucking dogs. They are a goddamn waste of time.

"No problem." I lifted my head to face her and I could see that she had changed clothes. But before I could get a good look, I felt her hand on my head, turning it.

"Place your face here, on the head rest. Relax. Keep your head down."

"OK," I replied, my voice muffled. My face was smashed into the goddamn headrest. It wasn't the most comfortable position in the world. In fact, it was not the relaxed position I imagined I would be in. It's true.

"I'm going to light some aroma-therapy candles. Do you want me to put on some music?"

"No, not really."

"Great. No music." She seemed really professional about the whole thing, placing sheets over my body and lighting candles and asking me what I wanted about this and that. Most people don't give a shit about what you want. They just do whatever the hell they please. But Jenny, she was a real goddamn professional. I could tell. It's true. "Are you comfortable?"

"I'm getting there."

"I know it can feel awkward at first but just relax."

"OK."

She began rubbing my shoulders. It was magnificent!

"Do you mind if I talk to you?"

"Of course not."

"Some people don't like being talked to but I find it makes the time go by nicely."

"Oh."

"What do you do for a living?"

"I'm a writer," I said. Well, that was only partly true. There really was no point telling people that I had a tech support job because, honestly, that's not who I was. I'm a writer. Period. Telling people you were a computer support technician was really fucking depressing and sad and pathetic, even if in my case, it was partly true. Once you declare your job to be who you are, then that is really who you are. It's true.

"Really? I've always wanted to write." Oh shit, here we go again. Goddamn it! It never fails when I tell people that I'm a writer that they start blabbing about wanting to be a writer and so on and so forth and blah, blah, blah. It gets SO old. But what was I to do? I had my face plastered in a headrest on a goddamn massage table. I was just going to have to listen and to take it like a man. So I shut up and took it like a man. It's true. "I love to read. I read so much. I'm constantly reading."

"Oh yeah? What do you like to read?" I asked, her hands easing their way down my spine to my lower back. Heaven, I tell you, heaven. It's true. A massage will almost make you forget about people blabbing about their miserable hopes and dreams. Almost.

"I like to read feminist writers. I go to the library and ask for them and the librarians bring me books by Margaret Atwood, Kate Chopin, Sylvia Plath. I devour them!" She worked my sore muscles like a master sculptor, mashing and tweaking them until the tension evaporated. It was an amazing feeling to behold. It's true. "I find I only enjoy reading books written by women."

"Really?" Now, that was a goddamn ridiculous statement to make. That's like saying you like to eat ribeyes but don't like to eat New York Strips. That's like saying you like ice cream but don't like milkshakes. They're the same goddamn thing! It's true. Not that I blame her though. Many of the great authors were misogynistic bastards who wrote novels about macho men who liked to abuse their vulnerable women. Not that my books were that way. I mean, I like to write about relationships and all but gender politics was just too boring to me. And feminists? They're no different than the misogynistic bastards, just at the other end of the spectrum, the estrogen end. It's true. "It makes no difference to me if a book is written by a man or a woman. A good book is a good book."

"If you say so. What brings you here?"

"What do you mean?" I really didn't know what she meant. That was a pretty goddamn vague question, if you ask me.

"Why did you schedule a massage? Most people have a good reason, you know?"

"Oh, well... I've had a rough year, I guess. Divorce."

"I'm sorry," she said and she sounded very sincere about it too. Her voice turned sweet and her touch became firm. I could tell that she was choked up about something. Were her parents divorced? Did she get a divorce? It was all just too much too take. It's true. "I really am. Divorce must be difficult."

"Yes, it is, especially when kids are involved."

"You have kids?" she asked, surprised. That really seemed like a shocker to her. How strange.

"Yes, I have two kids, Jessica and Sammie."

"How cute," she said. Women always get sweet and sappy when you talk about your kids. It's in their nature to get that way, I guess. Every woman is a potential mother, even if they don't want to be. It's true.

She worked her way down to my legs and right then and there my ding dong squirmed. It wiggled and wiggled and flexed itself, prodding me under the weight of my body, letting me know that he knew what was going on. Ding dongs are funny that way. They jump into action at the most inappropriate times, even if you don't want them to. It was a goddamn curse.

"I love my kids dearly."

"So did you and your ex-wife have an amicable divorce?" she asked, rubbing my feet and working the muscles between my toes. Her touch sent my ding dong into full-on attention. My blood was flowing down there like a tsunami.

"Well, yes and no. It seemed pretty normal until the other day."

"What happened?"

"She sent me a message saying that she was moving to Dallas and taking the kids."

"No fucking way!" she said. She walked around the table to where my head was resting and I could feel her through the strands of my hair, what little hair I had. I could smell her perfume which was intoxicating and sensuous and all kinds of sexy. She must have put it on in the other room because I'm sure I would have notice it when I first came into her house. It was a goddamn aphrodisiac. It's true. "What are you going to do?"

"Uh, what do you mean?"

"I mean, what are YOU going to do? You said you adored your kids. I imagine you couldn't live without them."

"Yes."

"So are you going to get them?"

"You mean, go to Dallas?"

"Yes, I mean go to Dallas and get them. It's really the right thing to do. Not many men love their kids like you say you love them. They deserve to be with you as much as they deserve to be with their mother." Bingo! She was absolutely right. It was genius. Why didn't I think of that? Why not assert myself and go to Dallas, tell Jessica that the kids needed to be with me, and bring them back to Austin? I mean,

Dallas is an OK city and all but it's not a place to raise your kids. And who did Jessica think she was for taking them away from me? It was all becoming very clear to me now, what to do, what I should be doing. I needed to go to Dallas. It's true.

"I guess you're right," I said.

"I know I'm right. Now, turn over." Uh oh! Turn over? Was she fucking crazy? If I turned over, I'd poke her in the eye with my raging erection, which by the way, was as hard as could be. How embarrassing! Now, boners are great and all but they aren't that great when they are not wanted. There's nothing more intimidating and embarrassing than an inappropriate boner. It's true. I was in a quandary. I didn't want to move. "Come on, turn over."

I reluctantly turned over with my eyes closed and fortunately, my ding dong found a way to lean toward my body. Hopefully, and this was pure hope, she wouldn't touch me in a way that would make him move. The potential for a humiliating disaster was one touch away. It's true.

"I didn't think about going to Dallas. You think I should?"

"I know you should." She started at my feet and massaged my lower legs, slowly moving upward, pushing and squeezing my leg muscles, working the tension from my calves, moving toward my crotch. "Open your eyes."

I opened my eyes to discover that all she was wearing was a pair of black, lacey panties. She was naked otherwise, her small, perky breasts exposed, her skin covered with tiny goosebumps. She reached for a bottle of oil, poured some in her hands, and rubbed it on my chest. I was absolutely dumbfounded. I felt paralyzed, like in a bizarre lucid dream, where things were dancing and spinning around me, and all I could do was observe. Once the scent of that oil reached my nose, my ding dong decided it was time to make his presence known. He stood at full attention, raising the sheet like a makeshift tent. She giggled a little, pulling the sheet from my legs, exposing the rest of my body.

"Ummm." That's all I could muster to say. Absolutely ridiculous.

"I know just the thing to make you relax." She slid her oily hands around my ding dong and electricity shot through my nerves, hitting my brain like a bolt of lightning. It had been so long since I felt the hands of a woman on my body. But something just wasn't right. I felt paranoia slip in, wondering if Marvin and his bum friends were outside the window, prodding my car for an unlocked door or window. I wondered if the police were nearby, waiting to bust in and apprehend the two of us. I thought about my kids and wondered what they were doing and if they were thinking of me. It was all just too much to take. It was driving me crazy. "You can touch my breasts, if you'd like."

Right then and there I jumped up, hopped off the table, grabbed my clothes, and tried to dress myself as I ran out of the room. She yelled something to me, something like where are you going and you owe me this and you shouldn't leave like that. The Muppet-looking extraterrestrial dog was yipping and yapping all over the goddamn place in the next room. I could hear it scratching at the door of the room it was in, trying to get out to maul my ankles or some shit like that but I didn't care. I continued to get dressed so I could get out of there. I wasn't looking for a hooker. I just wanted to relax. It's true.

"Hey! You can't leave. You owe me $120!"

I reached into my pant pocket and pulled out all the cash I had, maybe $15 or so. I tossed it on the floor and was out the door, half-dressed, ultimately humiliated, ready to go. I hopped in my car and cranked the ignition. I slammed on the gas, tearing down the street, right at Marvin and all of his goddamn buddies. They saw me and ran for either side of the street. They were lucky because I was on a tear. I turned right on 7th Street and didn't look back. I drove away as fast as I could. I could hear Marvin, yelling at the top of his lungs.

"Come back, John Mayer. Come fo' yo' smoke. It's the shit! Bill Murray?! Where ya goin'?"

I watched Marvin in the rear-view mirror until he was a tiny brown speck. Then he was gone.

9.

Let me get one thing straight because I don't like to be misunderstood. There is absolutely nothing in this world that is worse than being misunderstood, misinterpreted, or judged. Here it is. Are you ready? I am not a prude. It's true. But I have to admit that there is nothing more startling than having a strange woman touch your ding dong. I mean, no one goes into a situation like getting a massage by a professional thinking they are going to have their private parts manhandled. I mean, it really sounds nice and all. It really does. But fantasy and reality are two different things altogether. All men fantasize about a goddamn thing like that, especially if you're a fucking pervert. I am not a pervert. It's true.

I realized pretty quick that Snaggle must have been playing a trick on me, that sneaky bastard. Who does that kind of shit unless it's a prank? Really? And from a goddamn coworker? So either that goofy bastard was a real grade-A pervert or he was absolutely clueless. I thought about it for a while, really analyzed the hell out of it, figured things from left and right and from top to bottom. I didn't really know him all that well. Who really knows anybody when you think about it? But after overthinking it, maybe a bit too much, I decided that Snaggle must be fucking clueless. He was too goofy and awkward and naïve and snaggly to be a sneaky bastard. I was sure of it.

I have to admit that the even though Jenny was a goddamn whore, she was absolutely right. I had to give her credit when credit was due, even for a hooker. I was going to have to go to Dallas and get my kids. There was no other way around it. I mean, when you're a concerned father like myself, and you love your goddamn kids with all of your heart, there is nothing more important than doing the right thing for your kids. It's true. Kids deserve that more than anything. Look at the goddamn world we live in now, filled with divorce and broken homes and absentee parents and runaway children and pregnant teens and deadbeat dads. It was all a goddamn mess. My only problem was figuring out exactly when I could get the time off from work to go all the way to Dallas. I mean, I just started my job and all. I probably didn't have the time to take off being that I had absolutely no seniority and shit like that. But when something has to be done, you always find a way. It's true.

When I got to work the next day, I had two things on my to-do list. 1) Figure out if I could get a couple of days off so I could drive my ass to Dallas and 2) start my next novel. All I had so far was months of preparation and a partially written sentence. Not good, not good. How can I claim to be a writer with THAT? It was a goddamn pathetic situation. You can't claim literary greatness to the world and not have anything to show for it. It's true. Well, that's not entirely true. I mean, I had a novel under my belt, *The Rise and Fall of a Titan*. What a turd! It was an absolute disaster, sorry to say. I was going to have to write a masterpiece to make up for that pile of dog shit.

I walked into the office and had a strange feeling. Everybody was *looking* at me, really staring it up. Did they know? Were they judging me? Were they thinking, "What a goddamn pervert?" I didn't know for sure but something wasn't right. I saw Snaggle peeking from behind his cubicle, curious and shit. He watched me walk to my cube. That sneaky bastard. He knew what had happened to me. I just knew it. And I wasn't at my desk for more than 30 seconds when that goofy bastard appeared behind me. I turned around and glared at him, his hand plunging in his pocket giving his testicles a run for their money. He was a filthy bastard. The filthiest.

"So?" he asked, juggling the change in his pocket, gazing at me with his bloodshot eyes, his teeth jutting between his chapped lips.

"So what?"

"Did you get a *massage*?"

"Yes, I got a massage."

"Was it *good*?" He was really talking it up, all goofy and awkward and snaggly. What a goof! "Did you *enjoy* it?"

"Maybe." I think he was trying to get me to admit that I was as perverted as he was. I wasn't falling for that shit. It's true.

"Well," he said, pausing for a second, gee-whizzing it like a country bumpkin. "I was just curious. I've never been to see her. I've always wanted to but I've never made an appointment."

"What?" I was shocked, really. I could tell he was telling the truth. He was standing there like a little kid, like my kid Sammie. I could tell he had no idea that Jenny was a goddamn whore, standing there kicking his foot back and forth. It's true. "You've never been to see Jenny for a *massage*?"

"Nope."

"Never?"

"Nope. Never. I saw a stack of her business cards at the 7-11 when I was buying a Slurpee. Sounded nice, a massage. But I've never gone."

"Oh." I realized right then and there that goofy bastard wasn't sneaky. He was absolutely fucking clueless, a real goddamn naïve doofus. It's true. I had him figured all wrong. Everyone makes mistakes and I just made a really big one.

"Did you know that urine is drinkable in small amounts?"

"No," I said, chuckling. "No, I didn't know that."

"Did you know a trout's brain weighs .02 ounces?"

"Uh."

"Did you know..." I raised my hand, stopping the insanity. I had to start working on my novel and I wasn't going to do it with this goofy bastard asking me if I knew a bunch of goddamn nonsense. "Sorry."

THE SPECTACULAR SIMON BURCHWOOD

"I'll talk to you during my break."

"OK." He skipped back to his cube, popping his headset on. What a goddamn dork! Or as good ol' Sammie would say, 'What a shmork!'

I was really starting to miss good ol' Sammie and my cutie pie Jessica. I wondered if they missed me, thought of me. I hadn't seen them in a while and that was weighing on me something fierce. The idea of them living in Dallas with their mother killed me, absolutely killed me. I guess it made sense that their mother would want to move there being that her parents lived there too but that didn't make it right. I imagined her parents hated me now. Jessica had a way of exaggerating things and I imagined she made up some bullshit story about me and that I was a bad father and a bad husband and an absolute failure, spectacularly bad, and all. As much as I wanted to start writing my novel, I had just too much on my mind to do that. Life has a way of killing any creative energy you have with a bunch of bullshit. It's true.

So, rather than work on my novel, I decided to send my supervisor Rod an email. If I was going to drive to Dallas to get my kids, then I had to do it sooner than later. Waiting any longer was going to be a big mistake. It's true. I put my thinking cap on and started writing an email. It went like this.

To: Rod
From: Simon
Subject: Death in the Family
Rod - Recently, my grandmother of 89 years passed away. She was like a mother to me. She helped to raise me and even paid for my college tuition. Can you believe that? As far as grandmothers go, she was the best, a real special person. In addition to being the best, she was also a saint. Really! Whenever the Christmas holidays came around, she used to buy homeless people hamburgers and shoes. Anyway, I think it's important that I attend her funeral. I know I haven't worked here very long and I probably don't have the vacation time to use but I would really appreciate it if I could have the time off to go. I'll work extra hours when I get back. I promise! Thank you. Simon
Sometimes, and I mean sometimes, when you need to get your way, you have to lie. I'm sorry to say that but it's true. I mean, a little white lie never hurt anybody. But if you're going to lie to someone, it has to be pretty goddamn believable. And if you really need to make something happen, what better way to do it than to pull the "my grandma died" card. It was fool proof! No one ever questioned something like that. It's true. You'd have to be a pretty jaded and unsympathetic bastard to question someone when they told you their grandma just died. Would you question it? I didn't think so. But here's the thing. Once you pull that "my grandma died" card, you'd better be wary of ever pulling it again because people only have so many grandmas. It's not like you say "my grandma died" whenever you needed to take time off from work.

People remember shit like that, unless you get a different job, which in theory, puts the "my grandma died" card back in your deck of excuses. But I'm getting ahead of myself. Rod had no idea that my grandma was healthy and alive and enjoying retirement with my grandfather. That was really none of his business. It's true.

In a matter of seconds, Rod replied that it was OK for me to take off and that he was really sorry and all and that he felt bad for me because his grandma had passed away recently and that I wouldn't get paid while I was gone but that it was fine with him that I go and this and that and blah blah blah. It worked! What did I tell you? The "my grandma died" card worked like a charm. I popped my head up in my cube and saw Rod across the room, giving me the thumbs up. I returned the thumbs up with the satisfaction of knowing that I would be seeing my kids soon. I felt like celebrating! And what better way to celebrate while you're at work than taking a break? I needed a break. I was working too hard. It's true. I took myself out of the calling queue for a well-deserved break.

I found a sweet spot outside in the great lawn separating my building from the Capitol building on a bench under a huge oak tree. It was a beautiful goddamn day, evident from all the other goddamn government workers strolling around the lawn or sitting under the trees or napping in the grass or doing anything but working, just like me. It was beautiful to see. I think people underestimate government workers. Many assume that the people working for the government are a slovenly group, not fulfilling their potential. But that is making the assumption that money is the only thing that matters in a career. I believe that government workers are a smart bunch, mainly because they value their time over money. It's true.

I closed my eyes, feeling the cool breeze hitting my face, thinking about how soon I would see my children, when I heard a noise behind me. It was a very familiar sound, the sound of coins and keys and stuff. You know that sound? Of course you do.

"Did you know that squirrels are very adept swimmers?" Snaggle said.

I placed my weary head in my hands, shaking a negative but, goddamn it, he continued on.

"Did you know an ostrich's eye is bigger than its brain?"

"How did you find me?" I asked, annoyed.

"Don't know. I just did."

"Do you need something? Is Rod looking for me?"

"No but he did tell me your grandma died and I wanted to say that I'm sorry. My grandma died last year." Oh shit, here we go again. Why is it that people feel the need to tell you about their goddamn relatives kicking the bucket whenever they find out one of your relatives kicked the bucket? How annoying! I mean, he didn't really know that my grandmother was still alive and I didn't really care that his grandma bought the farm and was hanging out with Jesus right now. It was just too much to take. It's true. "I miss her like you probably miss your grandma."

"Mmm hmm."

"It's OK to cry, if you want."

"I don't want to cry."

"Well, you can if you want to, if you change your mind." Snaggle sat his goofy ass next to me and that was the last thing I wanted him to do. Really. He smelled of peanut butter and donuts and Coca Cola, a real nightmare. I wanted to vomit. "I find crying to be very therapeutic. I think all men should express their emotions more."

"Really?"

"Yes," he said, turning his head to the sky, letting the sunlight warm his face. "Men are more complex than just testosterone and muscles and chivalry. To be a complete human being, one must have access to all of their mental and physical abilities as well as their full range of emotions."

Holy shit! Did I misjudge this goofy bastard? This aw-shucks, silly, nerdy bastard just dropped some knowledge on me when I wasn't expecting it. He really did. Crazy! I always go back to what my grandfather and his buddies told me in situations like this. It's true.

"Thanks. I appreciate that. I really do." Now I felt bad. Here I was letting on that my grandmother was dead and she was alive and kicking just like it was yesterday. I was feeling something awful. It's true.

"When are you leaving for Dallas?" he asked.

"Oh, probably Thursday. That way I have a long weekend to get up there and back for work Monday."

"You know, if you need some company on your trip, I'm not doing anything this weekend. I'm never doing anything except playing video games or building computers. I have nothing better to do."

"You want to go to my grandmother's funeral with me in Dallas?"

"Sure." Unfucking believable. Really. I barely knew Snaggle at all and here he was trying to invite himself on a trip to do something that wasn't going to happen. What a nut job.

"Well, I don't know. It seems kind of strange."

"I have lots of money saved up."

"So?"

"We could make a road trip out of it. Maybe do some stuff on the way. Turn a sad trip into a fun trip." As crazy as that sounded, he was really starting to wear me down and make some sense. I mean, he was starting to appear to be a lot sharper than he led on with all of his goofy trivia and incessant games of pocket pool and his snaggle teeth and his bad breath and all. And without Jason around, being that he lived in fucking Montgomery with his whore wife, and I didn't have any other friends around, it was nice having someone offer to hang out and be my copilot. I didn't know how to break it to him that my grandmother really hadn't kicked the bucket. But for that one moment, it really didn't seem to matter. It's true.

"Let me think about it," I said.

"Did you know that babies develop their finger nails in the uterus?" I started to laugh my fucking head off. I was laughing like a goddamn jackal, spitting and spatting all over myself.

"For once, I did know that."

"You let me know if I can tag along. I'll bring lots of soda."

"What the heck. Sure."

"Sweet!" He jumped up from the bench and danced a retarded jig, flailing his arms and legs about like a rooster who had his head chopped off. He looked like a mental patient hopped up on caffeine. It's true.

"I have something I have to do tomorrow so I can leave on Thursday."

"No problem. I have to get back to the call queue."

"OK," I said, watching him skip back to our building. What a goofy bastard! But it really started to seem like a good idea, what, with it being a long trip to Dallas and all. Maybe having Snaggle along would help me. I could dictate some of my stories to him on the way. Maybe bounce some ideas for my novel off of him. We could complete some Mad Libs. It all seemed like such a fantastic idea. It's true.

10.

People say that if you analyze your dreams then they mean something. Crazy, huh? But that's what they say. And I always seem to have crazy, weird dreams. It's true. So, the thing is, you can't analyze them in a literal sense because dreams can often be pretty fucked up. You have to analyze them in a metaphorical sense, dummy. Got it? So, with that in mind, then you have to hear about this fucked up dream I had last night because I want to make sense of it all. It was really *far out*! It was like I was on acid, although I've never taken acid before. But I imagine if I ever did take acid (and that's a big IF because acid is a goddamn disgusting thing to do), then this dream is how I would see the world. Maybe it was the combination of beer and Oreo cookies I had in the hours proceeding going to sleep that brought on the crazy dream. Who knows?! But get this, you're not going to believe it when I tell you. I'm sure of it.

The dream started out innocent enough. It was a tranquil scene, me with the kids at a water park next to a huge lake. It was all very scenic and colorful and fun and serene and perfect, like a goddamn bullshit commercial for a Caribbean resort like you see on TV. It was just too good to be true. I felt very present in my dream though and being that I was self-aware, I paid extra attention to my kids and their demeanor. They seemed very happy, which is good. Nothing is better than seeing your kids happy even if it's in a goddamn bullshit dream. It's true.

It went on for a long while like this with me observing my kids, watching them have fun. Time has a way of slowing down in my dreams. Then out of nowhere, a guy approached me and asked me if I'd be interested in making some easy money. Duh! The faceless man proceeded to tell me that he wanted me to take pictures of the water park with this strange device he handed me. It looked like a camera straight out of the movie Star Wars with its alien contours and large screen and bizarre color. When I flipped what I imagined was the power switch on, everything in the screen looked like a pixilated cartoon. I snapped some shots of my kids making weird faces, their tongues sticking out all over the place and their hands stretching their eyes and mouths into funny faces. It was all just too much. My kids can be a goddamn riot. It's true. Now, I don't know why I did this but I told my kids to stay put while I walked around the park and took pictures with the Star Wars camera. Leaving my kids without adult supervision was a really strange thing for me to do but I was dreaming and I thought they would be OK. Weird, huh? You can rationalize anything in a goddamn dream.

I walked around the water park taking pictures of people having fun and eating hot dogs and drinking goddamn sodas while their fat asses baked in the sun without a lick of sunscreen on. Time seemed to speed up a bit because I was power walking around the entire goddamn place. I must have covered the entire park in a matter of minutes and I must have taken thousands of pictures. I soon found myself in the outskirts of the water park, walking through a wooded area filled with deer and squirrels and birds and foxes and turtles. It was like I was in a goddamn Disney movie or something. All of the creatures were cuddling and shit and talking in high-pitched voices. It was a strange sight to see, very strange. It's true.

At the edge of the wooded area, I realized I was walking through my neighborhood and I had a group of old folks following me. They were decked out in these wild exercise outfits, neon jogging suits with matching headbands and fanny packs. You know, to put their Geritol and Aspercreme and shit in. They were cackling and hooting it up all over the goddamn place like a pack of elderly savages, having a good time and all. I remember telling them to keep it down because it was a quiet neighborhood. They just giggled at that, telling me I was a wet blanket. Crazy bastards! Old people can be crazy when they want to be with no regard for decency. I guess because they had nothing to fear anymore. Or they were senile. It's true.

I came to a house that was strangely out of place. It was a huge mansion in the middle of this modest neighborhood of small houses. The old folks continued on without me and I decided I had to check out this strange house that I had never seen before. The front yard was filled with all kinds of exorbitant bullshit like water fountains and bushes trimmed in the shape of animals and palm trees and gazebos and various sitting areas with barbecue pits and lawn furniture and hot tubs. It was a goddamn sight to see! Who would own a place like this in my little neighborhood? It was very strange indeed. It's true.

I soon found myself inside. I could hear a baby crying, nothing too serious I could tell (I'm a father, you know? I know these things when I hear babies cry). As I walked into this humongous living room, I found Grant the Rockstar sitting on the couch, still pierced in every orifice like before, tattooed all over his goddamn body, clad in black leather and denim, but wearing an apron around his waist like a maid would wear with lace and embroidery and shit on it. His hair still looked like it had been styled with a box of firecrackers, sticking up all over the goddamn place. But you know what? I was kind of glad to see him. Don't ask me why but I was. It's true. He turned around and saw me.

"Well, well. If it isn't the nerdy computer programmer who thinks he's some hot shit writer!" He hopped up and gave me a big bear hug. He squeezed the shit out of me.

"I am a writer!" I said. Boy, that really pissed me off. Who the fuck did he think he was? What an asshole!

"Whatever. How you doing buddy?"

"I'm fine. When did you move into my neighborhood?" I asked. I was really curious about that. How did I not notice this punk rock brat moving into my neighborhood?

"I've always lived here. But after my band The Assholes were put on the cover of the Rolling Stone, we blew up and I made a pile of cash. So I tore down my old house and built this rockstar pad. Isn't it fucking bad ass?!" He started playing air guitar and banging his head like a fucking idiot. "But, the stardom was getting to be too much so I told my band mates that I needed a break. And now I'm a dad!"

"*You* are a father?" I asked, flabbergasted.

"Yep! You can call me Papa Grant!" He started with the headbanging again, thrashing his head around. I thought his head was going to pop off his goddamn body. It's true. "Wanna see my kid?"

"Sure."

He led me over to a crib on the other side of the living room. It was a cute affair filled with stuffed animals and baby toys. I could hear the baby cooing and making silly baby noises. Grant leaned over and cooed back to the baby. He picked it up and handed it to me.

"Don't drop the little bugger. You got that?" The baby had the cutest face I had ever seen but its body was not quite right. The baby fit in the palms of my hands and had this body like a chinchilla or a squirrel or some type of fuzzy animal like that. But its face was a normal, cute, human baby face. I couldn't believe it. It was the strangest thing I had ever seen. It's true. "Cute little bugger, isn't it?"

"Uh, yes." The baby climbed out of my hands and was crawling all over me, its little baby claws gripping onto my clothes, its little animal tail wrapping itself around my arms and legs as it crawled all over me. It was a strange sight to see. It's true. "Is it a boy or a girl?"

"What?!" he blurted, pissed off and red in the face. "It's a boy, you asshole!" He was really mad and all and I felt bad for a quick moment. I knew that was rude of me to ask but what would you think if some fuzzy, squirrely, baby creature was climbing all over your goddamn body? I thought so.

"I'm sorry. He's adorable." I was really laying it on thick with that fib. It was the creepiest little thing I had ever seen. It's true. Grant grabbed his fuzzy, squirrely, baby creature and cradled it in his arms. He was a proud papa for sure. I could tell. "Can I ask you a question?"

"Shoot, nerdy man."

"You seem to have it so easy and I have it so tough. As a creative person, how do you do it?"

"What are you getting at?" he asked, laying the fuzzy, squirrely, baby creature back in its crib.

"Why does life have to be so goddamn hard?" That was it. That's why my dream led me to Grant's house. I had a realization in my dream that I was searching for something and that's what it must have been. Some truth, I was searching for some truth, even if it was from a crazy punk rock asshole with firecracker hair and a kid that looked like it was out of a bad horror movie.

"Life isn't hard, dummy."

"But..."

"No but's, you got that? Lighten up! Have some fun. Loosen those nerdy shackles. Have a drink. Get laid. Something." Just then, I could hear a voice from another part of the house, a female voice. "I'm in the living room, honey."

A woman walked into the living room and, just like the weird baby, she had a strange appearance to her. She had this large, rectangular head and her skin was wrinkly and bumpy like an elephant's skin but it was pink and dewy. She was all made up too with red lipstick and eye shadow and rouge and styled hair. What a family!

"How's the baby?" she asked, a little concerned.

"The little bugger is fine. This is Simon. He thinks he's a writer! Of all things, a writer. Isn't that funny? Ha!"

"I am a writer!" I barked back, pissed off again. I was steaming mad. Furious!

"Now, Simon," she said, sweetly, her big head leaning toward me. "If you're going to be rude, then I'm going to have to ask you to leave."

"Yeah!" Grant yelled, jumping on the couch and bouncing around like a goddamn idiot. He was jumping all over the place and his goofy looking wife was getting a real kick out of it. The baby too, the fuzzy bastard. They all started hooting and hollering and jumping around. They were a bunch of lunatics!

"Fine," I said and I walked out of their goddamn monstrous mansion.

"And don't come back. You got that, nerdy computer programmer?! Don't come back!"

It was all just too disappointing. I walked through their ridiculous front yard and I could still hear them hooting and hollering and jumping all over the goddamn place. They were a crazy bunch of lunatics living in my quiet neighborhood and I felt relieved to be out of their mad house. As I walked down the middle of the street, I remembered that I had left my kids alone and started running back toward the water park, trying to find my way, trying to get back to them in a hurry. I felt a real sense of urgency so I picked up the pace. I tried to get my pudgy body going but I couldn't get there fast enough. Before I knew it, a manhole cover slid open and I fell in, falling in darkness, falling like a bag of rocks into the void.

And then I woke up.

I tried to analyze the dream and make some sense of it all but I couldn't. It was all just too bizarre and surreal and strange. 'What did it mean?' I kept asking myself. Was there some hidden nugget of truth that my subconscious was trying to tell me? Or did the beer and Oreos create some kind of stomach disturbance that caused my brain to freak out and revolt in my sleep? I don't know. It was all just too much to take. It's true. All I knew was that I missed my kids. Maybe that had something to do with it. That had to be it, I was sure of it. Like I said, they say if you analyze your dreams they mean something. Well, that's what they say anyway.

11.

I tried to call Jessica several times but she never answered her phone or returned my calls. She was really starting to piss me off. I mean, who the hell did she think she was, wanting to move to Dallas and take our kids? It was all a goddamn mess. It's true. And I'm sure Sammie and little Jessica didn't appreciate it either. All of their little friends were here in Austin. Their school was here. Their life was here. Their father was here. I imagined that they would have no interest in moving to Dallas, away from everything they knew. But, then again, kids have no choice in the matter. They will do what they're fucking told to do and my kids were no different. They were good kids. It's true.

After getting the go ahead from my supervisor Rod, I realized I had one thing to do before leaving town. I had to go see my doctor. Weird, huh? Well, not really. I'm getting old, you know? It's true. This slightly pudgy, slightly balding "Adonis" isn't going to stay beautiful forever. Ha! Besides, everyone needs to go see their doctor every once and a while. It is a goddamn moral imperative. I made the appointment a couple of months ago after realizing I hadn't seen my doctor in quite some time, maybe before all my divorce bullshit. I had been compiling a list of ailments and weird goings-on with my body and health in general and I felt I really needed to discuss them with Dr. Todd, especially before leaving town. I call him Dr. Todd because his last name is so unruly and filled with dozens of unnecessary consonants that I'm not even going to waste precious keyboard strokes trying to spell it out for you. Just trust me, his last name is a goddamn Polish disaster. It's true. But Dr. Todd is a kind man with a caring way about him and I rather enjoy talking to him, even though I'm sure he will be examining my nutsack or prodding his finger in my poop shoot at some point today. Great. Just great.

Here, in no particular order, was the list of things that were bothering me over the last few years: constipation, left eye twitch, hemorrhoids, upset stomach, random headaches, weight gain, hair loss, weird dreams (duh!), knee pain, seasonal allergies, lower back pain, etcetera, so on and so forth. It was a pretty goddamn long list of ailments and nuisances but they were things that were really bothering me. I mean, especially for a writer, having distractions of the bodily nature can really put a damper on your creative spirit and literary output. Nothing is worse than a raging case of hemorrhoids to ruin a marathon writing session. You can't sit down for more than 15 goddamn minutes at a time when you have burning blisters poking out your asshole. It's true.

Anyway, I drove over to Dr. Todd's office. I pulled my car into the office building parking lot and parked in the back. The building was a pretty nondescript place tucked away behind a group of these massive oak trees in a decent part of town. Dr. Todd had his office here for years before I became his patient and I'm sure it would be here for years to come. On the outside, the building looked like one huge metal and glass box but on the inside, it was an elaborate maze of offices connected by a serpentine hallway that zigged and zagged in no justifiable way. If I didn't already know where his office was then it would be damn near impossible to find. I wondered if that was on purpose. Doctors do some sneaky shit like that sometimes. It's true.

I found his office after walking through the maze of hallways and entered quietly, standing next to the front desk. A nurse was sitting there, busy with something. She wore pink scrubs that had Winnie the Pooh and Tigger on them and her hair was long and blonde and styled in a way that reminded me of the TV sitcom moms from the 1980s. She didn't seem to notice me and I stood there for what seemed like a goddamn eternity while she scribbled on some forms on a clipboard. They must have been pretty goddamn important forms because she was carefully and intently filling in the boxes and checking other boxes and crossing her t's and dotting her i's and examining the hell out of that paperwork. Time really seems to stand still when you're waiting unnoticed for something. It's true. I decided to stop the madness and tap on the desk so she would notice me. I think I startled her. She about jumped out of her goddamn seat.

"Oh! I didn't see you there," she said, straightening herself, fixing her 1980s hairdo.

"No problem."

"I'm so sorry. And you are?"

"Simon. Simon Burchwood."

"And do you have an appointment this morning, Mr. Burchwood?"

"Yes I do. It's at 9:00am. And call me Simon. Mr. Burchwood is so formal."

She put down her important paperwork and typed something on her computer, mousing here and clicking around there. I couldn't quite place which 1980s actress she reminded me of but she reminded me of someone. Meredith Baxter Birney, maybe? I couldn't figure it out. I knew it was going to drive me crazy until I figured it out. It's true.

"Yes, Mr. Burch... I mean, Simon. I see you here in our system for a 9:00am appointment. Do you have your health insurance card?"

"No. I don't have insurance anymore."

"Oh. You don't have health insurance?"

"Is that a problem?" I asked, a little perplexed. Losing your job and losing your benefits really puts a kink in things, doesn't it? My benefits with the State of Texas weren't going to start for 90 days after my first day on the job which meant zero health insurance for me for 90 days. I decided right then and there that I was going to have to be extra careful over the next 90 days and not lop off a finger or smash a toe or get into a car wreck. I would be royally fucked then without health insurance if a major medical problem came up. It's true.

"I don't imagine... it will be a problem. Will you be paying cash?"

"Yes."

"OK. Wait one moment." She typed some more on her computer. She looked confused about something. Whatever it was, she didn't tell me. Figures. "Thanks Mr. Burchwood... I mean Simon. Have a seat in the waiting room." She flashed me a bullshit smile which told me she knew something I didn't know which probably meant I was going to be in serious trouble when the bill for this visit showed up in my mailbox. Shit! Or as good ol' Sammie would say: Shmit.

The waiting room was spacious with big, poofy couches and a coffee table covered with a mound of crappy gossip magazines. Here I was in a fine goddamn business establishment and they had a pile of bullshit celebrity magazines wasting space. Nothing was lower on the publishing scale of importance than gossip magazines. It's true. Well, I would imagine those novelty rolls of toilet paper with one-liner jokes printed on them may be lower but not by much. With all the fine literature in the world (including literary masterpieces by yours truly), why anyone would buy this crap about some actress' cellulite on her ass or some actor's worthless marriage to a costar or some TV celebrity's gay skeletons in his closet or some singer's drug-fueled rampage is beyond me. It was really a goddamn shame, a waste of dead trees. It's true. The only thing gossip magazines were good for was reading in the can because you didn't have to think too much while reading them. Thinking too much in the can will make for a long sitting.

As soon as I got myself comfortable on a poofy couch, a middle-aged woman entered the office, dragging an over-sized purse on the ground and holding the hand of her booger-eating little boy. He couldn't have been older than five years old. He immediately locked his beady eyes with mine as he waved a red lollipop in the air with his free hand like a magician's wand. I knew that little bastard was going to cause trouble. I could just tell. His mother released his hand, demanding that he be good, and he made a beeline for the coffee table. He slid a portion of the magazines off the coffee table and stuck his gooey lollipop on a copy of People Magazine, right on top of Oprah Winfrey's face. Bullseye!

"What's your name?" he asked me, shoving his index finger up his crusty nostril. I didn't respond at first, mesmerized at the tenacity of his nose digging. He was really going at it! I was speechless. "What's your name?" he asked again.

"Oh. My name is Simon."

"I have a friend named Simon. He has a dog that rubs his butt on the carpet."

"Matthew!" his mother barked, looking pissed and tired and stressed. The nurse giggled. "Sit down and be quiet."

Matthew the Booger Eater pulled his lollipop from the magazine, ripping Oprah's face off, and plopped on the couch next to me. He smelled of sugar and curdled milk and Lysol and chicken nuggets. He picked at the glossy paper stuck to his lollipop, perplexed on how it got there. His little beady eyes were as blue as an afternoon summer sky in West Texas.

"Mr. Simon?"

"Yes?" I replied, pulling my arms in close. He was nudging his way toward me, invading my personal space. It was kind of annoying. It's true.

"Do you know what 1 + 1 is? It's 2. Do you know what 2 + 2 is?" He looked at me with a seriousness seldom seen in adults. He looked as if he knew the answers to all of mankind's problems. "It's 4! Do you know what 4 + 4 is?"

"No. What is 4 + 4?" I asked.

"I don't know but when I find out I'll tell you. I like you mister," he said, jumping up from the couch, dancing a little jig, and shoving the pile of magazines around, some more sliding off the coffee table. The little bastard was starting to make a real mess.

"Matthew!" his mother snapped again, still stressed, still red in the face. It looked like her head was going to explode. "Be quiet!"

Matthew the Booger Eater looked down, ashamed for a moment. But that only lasted a second or two. He giggled and smiled and continued shoving the magazines around on the coffee table.

"Hey mister?" he whispered, obeying his mother's command to be quiet. "Did you know... that..." Suddenly, he stood upright, a look of concern on his face, grave concern. He was completely frozen, the way a cat looks when you grab it by its scruff. His eyes glazed over a bit as he stared off in the distance, his body tense. Then he farted, loudly, sending him into hysterics. I don't know what it is about farts that make kids go crazy but the sound of a good fart always makes a kid laugh. It's true.

"Matthew Broderick Jones!" his mother commanded. "Get over here this instant!" She hurried to complete her paperwork, annoyed that her son was acting like, well, acting like a five year old. What did she expect for him to do? Act like he was getting ready to meet the goddamn Queen of England or some shit like that?

He ran around the coffee table to me and pulled at my shirt, pulling me close to him. He cupped his hand to my ear, whispering seriously.

"I pooped in my pants a little," he said, standing upright, looking gravely serious again, as if he told me something that only my ears were meant to hear. He nodded an acknowledgment to me before his mother grabbed him by the collar and dragged him from the waiting room, pulling him quickly out the door. "Mommy, my lollipop! Mommy! I left my lollipop!"

And that was that of Matthew Broderick Jones the Booger Eater. I truly believe all children suffer from a mild case of Tourette syndrome and offer socially inappropriate remarks without a thought or care in the world. What else could it be that would allow them to talk about pooping in their pants to complete strangers without any shame or concern? It's true. Matthew Broderick Jones the Booger Eater was no different than any other little kid his age. Sammie once told me at a large family gathering, loudly in front of all his relatives, that his ding dong was like a water hose and that he "watered" his grandma's potted plants in the foyer of her house. He thought the plants could use a little "drink." He was very proud of his multi-purpose ding dong and his thoughtful deed. What a kid! I love him to death though. It's true.

Pretty soon the nurse stood up and called my name and I knew it was my turn to see Dr. Todd. She motioned for me to enter through a door next to the desk so I did, quietly closing it behind me after I went through. I followed her to a room at the end of the hall and when we got inside, she asked me to sit on the examination table. The paper lining covering the table crinkled and crackled as I sat my pudgy ass on it. It was kind of embarrassing how loud it was. It startled the nurse, who seemed to really be on edge for some reason. Every time I did something, she was startled. It was making me fucking crazy. It's true.

"Dr. Todd will be in shortly," she said, leaving abruptly, slamming the door. What a bitch! Did the fact that I didn't have health insurance bother her that much? How unprofessional! I decided right then and there that when Dr. Todd came in that I would discuss her unprofessional demeanor with him. When they were passing out bedside manners at nursing school she must have been asleep in her dorm room, hung over from a night of keg stands and promiscuous make out sessions with strange fraternity brothers. It's true.

The examination room was sparsely decorated, a few framed photos of the Texas coast on the walls, maybe of Port Aransas or South Padre Island or Galveston. There was a desk in the corner and that was pretty much it. Dr. Todd's decoration budget must have mostly gone to the waiting room and the poofy couches and the subscriptions to all the bullshit gossip magazines, obviously not to the examination room. But I did notice something curious on the desk. Next to a couple of glass containers with Q-Tips and tongue depressors in them was an ash tray. What a weird thing to see in an examination room. Now, I know in the old days that doctors used to smoke their asses off while giving you an examination but those days were long gone. The sight of a doctor smoking nowadays would no doubt send his or her patients reeling and mobilize them to file a class-action lawsuit or call their local news channel or some shit like that. I hopped off the examination table and opened the cabinet above the desk and lo and behold, there was a bottle of whiskey in there: Jack Daniel's Black Label Whiskey. I couldn't believe my goddamn eyes! What the hell was going on? It didn't matter because I heard some foot steps outside so I shut the cabinet and hopped back on the examination table, the paper covering the table crinkling and crackling all over the goddamn place. I did it so fast that I was short of breath like I had run a 40-yard dash or something. It's true.

"Mr. Simon Burchwood. How the hell are you?" asked Dr. Todd, extending his hand for a shake. He looked exactly how I'd remembered him, kind of like an 80s era Tom Selleck, moustache, tan, and all. He was a good-looking fellow. It's true. Lucky bastard. "Why are you out of breath, buddy?"

"Oh, I don't know. Nervous I guess."

"Nervous? That's ridiculous." He walked over to his desk and plopped on a stool, organizing some papers on the desk, pushing aside the ash tray. I wondered if he knew that I knew that he had a bottle of whiskey in the cabinet. I bet he did. "How are your kiddos?"

"Fine. I think. Their mother told me that she's moving to Dallas and taking them with her. I'm very upset about it."

"What?" He seemed really thrown by that for some reason. He started scratching his head like he had a really bad case of dandruff, scratching all over.

"That's what she told me the other day." I said.

"That's strange."

"Why is that strange?"

"Well..." he said, scratching his head some more. Boy, he was really going at it to, like a dog going after a tick. "She was in here recently, with your kiddos, getting a physical exam. She didn't mention anything about it. I asked her if any life changes were coming up and she said no. Strange indeed."

"Yes, strange indeed," I said, kind of sarcastically but he didn't notice. He was too busy scratching his goddamn scalp.

"What about you? Any life changes since you last came in?"

"Well, I did get divorced. You knew that, right?"

"No, I did not. Sorry to hear that."

"You didn't know that?"

"No, sad to say."

"And Jessica didn't mention anything about that either?"

"No, she did not. Strange." He picked up a clipboard from the desk and jotted down notes and checked boxes here and filled in squares there. He was very thorough, I could tell. "Please take off your shirt for the examination."

As I took off my shirt and exposed my fat gut I thought it weird that Jessica had been here recently (with the kids no less!) and hadn't mentioned any of these things to Dr. Todd, particularly since moving to another city with your goddamn kids is a pretty major fucking life change in my opinion. It's true. And what a strange coincidence that she was here too recently, with the kids, seeing Dr. Todd, just like me. It was all getting to be too much to take. I felt like I was on the verge of having a nervous breakdown, an A-class, full-on, mental meltdown. It's true.

"Have you quit smoking?" asked Dr. Todd.

"Sure, yes. Well, no. Pretty much."

"Pretty much? What does that mean?" he asked, pressing his stethoscope against my chest, then my back, then my chest again.

"Once in a blue moon, I'll have a cigarette. Is that so bad?"

"If you smoke, even one cigarette, then you haven't quit smoking."

"Oh."

"You need to quit by the time you're 40 or else it's impossible to quit. I can't help you after that."

"OK." What a crock of shit. Here I was being told to quit smoking by a doctor who had an ashtray on his desk in his examination room. Pretty goddamn ridiculous if you ask me. It's true. "I'll do my best."

"I'll give you some samples of nicotine gum when you leave. And how about the booze? Still drinking?" he asked, sticking one of those ear-thingies in my ear. What do you call them? Otoscope! It was like aliens were taking a peek into my brain. He was shoving that thing so far into my ear that my goddamn ear drums were ringing.

"I've never..."

"Simon?" he said, sitting upright on his stool, placing his hands on his sides. I had a feeling that a scolding was coming on. I could tell. "You and I both know you like to drink. No excuses, buddy."

OK, all right. I have a little bit of a drinking problem. Well, more appropriately, I had a little bit of a drinking problem. Shit, I don't know. It comes and it goes. There are periods in my life when I don't drink a drop of booze. Then there are periods in my life when I'm swimming in alcohol. What can I say? When I'm with my kids, I'm happy and I don't drink at all, not even a fancy-pantsy Pina Colada. But (and this is a BIG but) there are times when I'm alone and I'm reflecting on my divorce and I honestly wonder what the fuck I'm doing here at this point in my life. I never in a million years would have thought after marrying my true love that I would EVER be divorced. It's true. That's how I knew I was in love. The devastation after my divorce truly sent me into a tailspin and I still haven't recovered. Pretty stupid, huh? I guess most people would assume that I would go all bachelor-crazy and try to fuck everything that moves but that's just no fun at all after being in love. I mean, when you're a kid and you don't know what true love is then fucking every skank that comes you're way seems like so much fun. And it is, I guess, in a shallow, barbarian kind of way. But to someone who thinks a lot, and being that I'm a writer and all, there just is no meaning in a life where your ding dong does all the thinking and the doing. That's what makes us humans so special: the thinking, and the feeling, in addition to the fucking. I've never heard of no ostrich who thinks about its place in the universe or some goddamn ant eater who feels true love for another goddamn ant eater. If all you want to do is go fuck everything that moves then go live with a community of chimpanzees because that's all they do. It's that simple. But recovering from divorce, that's a pretty goddamn hard thing to do, it really is. I guess, in many ways, I'm really not as sharp as I think I am sometimes. If I was, then I wouldn't drink so much when I was feeling down. There have been times when I was pretty down, down in the dumps of self-pity and shame, and drank a twelve-pack of beer in one sitting. It's true.

"You're right, Doc. But I haven't had much to drink lately. I've been trying really hard. You have to believe me."

"Do you remember the time I saw you at the bar?"

"What time?"

"You told me some story about how you were going to New York, going to read from your book to some large group of adoring fans, at a Barnes & Noble in Manhattan. Do you remember?"

"Are you asking me if I remember seeing you at a bar or if I went to New York?"

"Does it really matter? Do you remember?"

"I remember... some things."

"OK. Do you remember seeing me at the bar that time?"

"No."

"You were drunk out of your mind."

"Oh."

"You were so drunk that your eyes were empty, blank sockets. You had completely checked out. Nobody was home."

"Yeah."

"I'm surprised, now that I think about it, that you made it home alive. And you don't remember that night?"

"No. I don't."

"Then, as your doctor, I'm telling you, get your act together."

"I will."

"Otherwise, you'll be dead. You want your children to be fatherless?"

"No."

"Do you want them to know you were a drunken suicidal degenerate?"

"Uh, no."

"Then take the nicotine gum, lay off the booze, and straighten up. You have a lot of potential to do great things. So do it. And put your shirt back on."

Oh, shit. Sometimes when your life is summarized into a few bad decisions it can make you seem like the ultimate loser. It's true. Think about all the bad decisions you've made in your entire lifetime, all of them. Do you have them all listed in your mind? I'll wait a moment while you dust off the memories of bad relationships, bad choices, bad jobs, all of it. OK. Now, how would you feel if someone plucked out a couple of choice boo-boos from your life and summarized where you are today because of them? What a pile of shit, right? It's enough to make you want to end it all because what's the point of being a loser? Maybe. But you know what? It did get me thinking. I *did* have the potential to be great. I knew that. Sometimes, you just have to take some constructive criticism and turn things around. Sometimes, you just have to take a good look at yourself, shake off the mistakes, and make another run at it. Life is too short to sit around like a sad bastard. It's true. I decided right then and there that I would take Dr. Todd's advice and turn things around. The time was now.

"OK. I'll do it," I said.

"Good. Let me get you some nicotine gum for when you have a craving to smoke." He went over to the cabinet and opened it. Right there, on the bottom shelf, was the bottle of whiskey. He pushed it aside, looking for the cigarette gum. I couldn't resist. I just had to say something. If he was going to be a judgmental bastard, then why couldn't I be a judgmental bastard? It's true.

"Hey Doc?"

"Yes?"

"What is that?"

"What?"

"Right there. That bottle?"

"Oh, this?" He pulled out the bottle of whiskey and turned red in the face. Boo-yah! Explain that, you self-righteous bastard! "Oh, it's nothing."

"Nothing?" I asked, confused. "Really?"

"You know, Simon. The best advice I can give you is do what I say, not what I do. Didn't your parents ever tell you that?"

"Sure."

"Good. The nurse will have your invoice on the way out. Have a good day." He placed the bottle back in the cabinet and closed the door. "Make sure to schedule an appointment for next year, same time."

"But..."

"Get out."

I left the examination room feeling like shit. Who was I to be a judgmental bastard? I mean, Dr. Todd was just trying to help me. He really was. I can see that now. But sometimes it's hard taking advice from someone who is obviously just as fucked up as you are. It's true.

12.

I made an executive decision that for this road trip to Dallas, I was going to rent a car. Not just any car, mind you, but a big ass, American-style, monolithic cruiser mobile. That's right, my friends. I rented a Cadillac. It's true. I had a couple reasons for doing this. 1) Whenever you take a trip outside of your hometown city limits, it's always best to go in style. Even though this really wasn't a vacation, per say, it's always a good idea to make a trip at least *seem* like a vacation, that way any chance of stress creeping in can be alleviated by the thought of "this is supposed to be MY vacation." 2) I was taking a road trip with a filthy bastard that I hardly knew at all, not even a little bit. I knew I was going to need the space from Snaggle. You know what I'm talking about with his pocket pool and his snaggly teeth and his hemming and hawing all over the goddamn place and his ridiculous fucking jokes? I had a good feeling I was going to regret inviting that snaggly bastard along but at least in a big ass Caddy, I would have some elbow room between me and him. If you haven't figured this out so far, my personal space is very important to me. Important I tell you! It's true.

The night before my trip, I stayed up late rummaging through my closet for some clothes as well as some promotional materials for my craptastic book *The Rise and Fall of a Titan*. I knew I had some of those things leftover and I wanted to take some along, just in case. You never know who you are going to run into on long trips and I had a habit of running into all sorts of folks: bartenders, stewardesses, waiters, taxi drivers, store clerks, old friends, you name it. You never know when you will be able to woo any potential new readers and fans. Anyone is a new fan waiting to be enlightened! It's true. Luckily for me, I found the motherload, a box full of all kinds of promotional crap. I found headshots (what a stud!), pamphlets, sample chapters, business cards, coupons for store discounts (although they expired LONG ago I decided to take them anyway), a HUGE pile of this promo dog shit. I had so much of it that I wondered if I was going to have room for any of my goddamn clothes. With all the embarrassing crap Jessica used to make me wear, I was hesitant to take most of the clothes I had in my closet. I decided right then and there that when I got back that I would buy myself an entire new wardrobe. She would make me wear shit like I was some goddamn GQ model or something. It was all a goddamn disgrace. It's true. New clothes for a new me was in order.

I got up the next morning with my bags packed and waited for the rental car company to drop off my big ass, American-style, monolithic cruiser mobile at my apartment. They had an option where you didn't have to go to the rental car place, they would just bring it to you, and that seemed like the right thing to do. They said they would drop it off at my place at 10:00am sharp. It was 10:05am. The bastards were late! A few minutes later, I heard a car horn outside and went to my balcony to see who it was. My beautiful big ass, American-style, monolithic cruiser mobile, painted metallic maroon with a white vinyl roof was waiting for me down below. It was perfect. A tall African-American fellow got out of the car and waved. A white van pulled up behind it and waited too. That must have been his ride back to the rental car place, I figured. I waved back, went inside, got my bags, and locked up. My road trip was about to begin. It's true.

Down in the parking lot, I dragged my bags behind me, waiting for the African-American fellow to come over and help but he stood there like a goddamn idiot, staring at the sky. He didn't make an effort to help me at all. I dragged my bags to the back of the car and that's when he moseyed over, taking his time like the day was his, not mine. He pressed a button on the key dongle and the trunk popped open. What a fantastic luxury mobile. And then he opened his goddamn mouth.

"You need some help, sir?" he asked, after I had plopped my bags in the trunk. What a piece of work, the lazy bastard.

"No. I got it."

He stood there staring at me, staring at me up and down like he knew me or something. I didn't know him from shit so I was kind of worried. Don't ask me why. I just was.

"Do I know you?" he asked, giving me the stink eye.

"I don't know. Do you like to read?"

"Sho nuff. I like to read Playboy, Penthouse, Jugs, whatever."

"No, I mean do you like to read *literature*?"

"Not really. Reading is for pussies," he said, laughing all over the goddamn place, slapping his knee and throwing his head back. He got a real kick out of that joke too, a joke at my expense. I didn't think it was too funny but he sure did. He was laughing and spitting and wiping his brow. What a numbskull.

"Maybe you recognize my face from the newspaper. I'm a writer. My novel *The Rise and Fall*..."

"I told you, reading is for pussies!" All of a sudden, he got really serious, gave me a look like he meant business. I about crapped in my pants. But then, out of nowhere, his pissed-off looked changed to a look of bewilderment. He blinked a couple of times, wiping his brow again, and looked me up and down. It was like he really knew me or something. Weird. "Do I know you from somewhere?"

"I don't think so."

"Yeah, I know you motherfucker. Come here!" He grabbed me in a bear hug that almost choked the breath out of me. It was like I was a long, lost relative or some shit like that. It's true. He squeezed me hard, picking me up off the ground. "I know you, homie. I saw you on the east side."

I stepped back a bit, puzzled, and looked at his name tag. It said "Marvin." I knew exactly who he was, unfortunately.

"Oh, yes. Yes, we've met."

"You were driving over to see that white bitch who say she give massages when she really gives blow jobs and shit. Weren't you?"

"Uh, no."

"I know you white people. Always paying for blow jobs and shit. I feel ya!" He raised his hand in the air for a high-five. I was hesitant to give good ol' Marvin a high-five but I did anyway. He slapped my hand so hard that it felt like a bolt of lightning shot up my arm. I knew my hand would be tingling for the next hour. It's true. "I ain't never paid fo no blow job but that's cool. You gots to do what you gots to do sometimes. We men, right?" He nudged me with his elbow and gave me a wink-wink, as if to say he knew my deep, dark, perverted secret. What a dipshit.

"I didn't go to see her for a... blow..."

"Don't be embarrassed, nigga."

"OK."

He smiled and slapped the car keys in my hand. Patting me on the shoulder, he then waved to the white van, indicating that his job was complete. "Don't get you self in any trouble now, you hear me? If you need any help, just call the 800 number in the car. Just ask for Marvin!" He walked over to the white van and hopped in the passenger seat. The van pulled up right next to me and good ol' Marvin rolled down the window. "Wait til I tell the ol' lady that I delivered a car to a honky writer. She'll think I'm talking shit. But Marvin don't talk no shit! Peace out, Tom Brokaw!"

The van tore off. Thank God! What a gas bag. That Marvin, he really did talk a lot of shit. He was delusional. What is it that makes people who talk a lot of shit think they don't talk a lot of shit? I thought that was very strange as I watched the white van speed off through the parking lot, not yielding to the speed bumps and the goddamn signs that said to DRIVE SLOW. If I never saw good ol' Marvin again then it wouldn't be soon enough. It's true.

I sat in my beautiful big ass, American-style, monolithic cruiser mobile and I have to tell you, it was fantastic! The driver's seat was a white, poofy monstrosity that was like sitting on a goddamn leather marshmallow. I could tell already that it was going to be a fantastic trip driving in this bad boy. I felt like a million bucks. It's true. There's something about luxurious American automobiles that make you feel like a goddamn important individual. What do you think the President of the United States drives around in? That's right, a Cadillac. What more do I need to say? The rest of the car cabin was decked out in leather and wood paneling and electronics galore and buttons and knobs all over the goddamn place. There's probably even a feature where I don't have to drive the goddamn car, just tell it where I'm going and it will drive all by itself. If this car didn't have this feature, then it should. Imagine the look on good ol' Sammie's face when I pull up in this car. I can hear him now. "Daddy, that's a shmancy shmar!" Ha! That kid just kills me. It's true.

I put the Caddy in drive and pulled a wad of paper from my pocket. On it, in an almost illegible chicken scratch, was directions to Snaggle's place. Strange as it may seem, he actually didn't live too far from me so the drive there would be short and uneventful. If he hadn't told me beforehand where he lived, I probably wouldn't have been able to make out what he wrote down on this piece of paper. His handwriting was a goddamn mess. It looked like a combination of Egyptian hieroglyphics, elementary school level cursive, and random digits and swirly thingies. His mother must be absolutely disgraced. It's true. When I was a kid, handwriting was a big deal. Learning cursive was a big deal. I received grades for handwriting on my report card and if you didn't write well, you were assumed to be retarded or worse, unrefined. Nowadays, no one gives a shit about handwriting. Everyone is too busy using their goddamn thumbs typing on their smart phones or their cell phones or their PDAs or whatever you want to call them. The art of handwriting has gone down the goddamn toilet. My kids don't receive grades for handwriting on their report cards like I did. Snaggle, since he's quite a bit younger than me, probably didn't receive grades for handwriting either, at least as far as I could tell. His handwriting was atrocious. It's true.

I quickly settled into my poofy driver's seat and turned on the stereo. Good ol' Marvin must have left his CD in the car because The Commodores started playing Brick House. It was marvelous! I turned the volume up, put the seat back, and cruised down the main road that cut through my neighborhood. Snaggle's apartment complex was on the other side of my neighborhood, not too far away, but far enough. As soon as The Commodores came to their funky climax, I arrived at Snaggle's complex. I pulled into the main entrance and headed for the back, where he told me he'd be waiting. The Caddy's ride was so smooth and comfortable that I didn't even feel the speed bumps as I drove over them. That's what I call American ingenuity!

At the back of the complex, right in the middle of the fucking parking lot, was Snaggle, standing in front of a pile of luggage. It looked like he had packed for a goddamn trip to Europe or something, several suitcases and duffle bags piled as high as he was tall. It was goddamn ridiculous. In front of the luggage pile, he pranced around kicking a hacky sack, his arms and legs flailing out of control all over the goddamn place. The way he tried to keep the hacky sack in the air, he looked like a gibbon having a seizure while wearing nerd's clothing. He was a nerdy, uncoordinated goof ball. It's true. I parked the Caddy next to his pile of luggage and rolled down the window.

"What gives with all the luggage?" I asked.

"I packed what I needed for our trip."

"But we're only going to be gone for a few days. What do you have in there?"

"Clothes."

"Clothes? In all of those suitcases?"

"Yeah, clothes. Oh! And some board games, in case we get bored!" He started hemming and hawing all over the goddamn place, laughing his nerdy head off. He thought he was pretty goddamn funny. "Oh! And a Linux server I started building last night. Oh! And some snacks and..."

"This isn't all going to fit into my trunk, you know? You really should only bring what you need. Do you really need to bring a Linux server?"

The minute I said that, his demeanor quickly turned from happy nerd to sad nerd. It was a sight to see. It almost looked like he was going to start crying. He was a sad bastard if there ever was one. It's true.

"Alright, I guess. I'll just bring my clothes."

I popped the trunk and he lifted one, very small duffle bag and placed it in there. The rest of his pile of crap he took back to his apartment, one by one, dragging them across the asphalt. It took him a good 10 minutes to get all of that crap back into his place. I thought of helping him but I quickly decided against it. That would have been an awful lot of unnecessary work on my part and I wasn't going to do any unnecessary work on my vacation. It's true. When he was finished, he hopped in the passenger seat. I could already smell his rank breath. A stench of peanut butter and pop tarts and coffee filled the car's cabin. I felt like I was going to barf. I took a deep breath, trying to hold the bile down. It was very difficult.

"Ready?" I asked.

"Did you know that Monarch butterflies migrate thousands of miles every year from Canada to Mexico and back?"

Goddamn it! He was already starting with his bullshit and I wondered if I was going to kill Snaggle before even getting out of the city limits. I also wondered if I was going to be able to handle this snaggly bastard's constant stream of goddamn trivia questions or his rank breath or his testicle juggling habit. It was all just too much to take. He looked at me with his goofy smile, his teeth jutting out from between his dry, cracked lips, and I realized for one quick second, that Snaggle was oblivious to his awkward demeanor and nerdy behavior. I felt bad for some reason. I decided right then and there to suck it up and make the best of it. I was going on a road trip to save my kids, for God's sake. I was going to be a hero! It's true.

"No, I did not know that."

And then we drove off, headed for Dallas.

13.

I-35 stretched out in front of us, an uninhibited highway cutting through the Texas country side. There was very little traffic, except for the occasional eighteen-wheeler, so there was plenty of room for my beautiful big ass, American-style, monolithic cruiser mobile to maneuver. The Caddy. I decided that my cool ride needed a name, a manly name. So without even a single suggestion from Snaggle, who was too busy digging into his nostrils with alternating index fingers and not-so-secretly flicking his boogers onto the floor mats, I christened the Caddy with the manliest of names: Clint. Clint the Caddy. The name Clint made me think of a lone cowboy, toughened by the sun and a solitary life, drowning unsuspecting desert insects with tobacco spit, arriving in little towns wearing crusty boots and jingly spurs, kicking everyone's asses yet uninterested in taking any names. It was a grand thought and the Caddy deserved a manly name like that. It's true.

Snaggle, on the other hand, was not manly at all. In fact, he was the anti-Clint, an awkward, nerdy, snaggly mess, with a face only a mother could love, if that was even possible. He also lacked the simplest of coordination skills that most of us take for granted, as I watched him putz around with the window button and air vents and the glove box, almost breaking everything he touched. I couldn't say this enough but he really was a goddamn mess. It's hard to believe that he was supposed to be some kind of computer programming genius, or at least that's what my boss Rod claimed. Rod would tell me these little asides about Snaggle, how he whipped out batch files in seconds that performed elegantly, how he would create applets in a matter of minutes that would save employees thousands of man hours, or how he would code scripts that saved the agency thousands of dollars. But (and this is a big BUT) if he wanted to toast a strawberry pop tart, then he failed miserably and almost burned the goddamn building down once. It's true.

For the first half hour of our trip, Snaggle was relatively quiet. Occasionally, he'd blurt out a goddamn trivia fact or two but for the most part, he sulked in his seat like a sack of moldy potatoes, which was fine with me. The less I had to listen to him the more likely I wouldn't have to kill him and dump his body on the side of the highway in the middle of nowhere (I'm just kidding, sheesh!). He just looked out the window, watching the rest stops, Dairy Queens, and gas stations go by. Then suddenly, as if he had been injected with adrenaline, he shot up in his seat and blurted out at the top of his lungs like a crazed bum.

"SLUG BUG!"

He punched my arm as hard as he could and scared the shit out of me! The punch sent a chain reaction to the rest of my body, my arms pulling the wheel back and forth, and I tried to control the car but I was driving all over the place like a goddamn idiot. My legs stiffened and stomped on the gas and brake pedals and poor Clint the Caddy screeched and bounced across the lanes almost crashing into the cement wall that separated our north bound lanes from the south bound lanes. If a State Trooper had been watching us, I guarantee that he would have pulled us over and given me a sobriety test. It's true.

"Hey?!" I said, giving good ol' Snaggle the stink eye. It's like he went crazy all of a sudden. "What was that for?"

"Don't you ever play Slug Bug?"

"What?"

"You have kids. Don't you play Slug Bug with them?"

"I don't know what you are talking about!" I really didn't know what the fuck he was talking about. He might as well have been speaking Pig Latin for all I knew. It's true. "All I know is that you never hit the driver while HE'S DRIVING!" I was really surprised that I lost my temper like that but what did Snaggle expect from me? I mean, I was already on edge from dealing with the stench of peanut butter and pop tarts and coffee reeking up Clint's cabin but goddamn it if he had to go all psycho and shit and start punching me while I was driving. It was enough to drive me insane. It's true.

"I'm sorry, Simon," he said. He sounded genuinely sorry. I could tell. It made me feel bad, believe it or not. He started sulking all over the goddamn place like a sad bastard and there is nothing worse than being stuck in a car on a long trip with a sad bastard. It's true. "I just thought it would be a fun way to pass the time. I used to play Slug Bug on long road trips with my family. It was fun."

"I see. Well, how about we play a game I like to play?"

"OK!" He perked up like a puppy that spotted a brand new leather shoe. He was all excited and shit, barely containing himself. "What's it called?"

"Mad Libs."

"Mad Libs? The game where you fill in the blanks and make silly sentences?"

"Yes." That's right, doofus, the game that was pure genius for literary inspiration. It's true.

"Well, OK, but that game isn't really any fun unless you're under 10 years old."

"Excuse me?" Was this nerdy bastard crazy?! I had to hear his explanation for this because he obviously was out of his goddamn mind.

"Sometimes you will come up with a funny sentence or two but otherwise the end result usually doesn't make a lot of sense."

"Well, then, what would you suggest for a game for us to play?"

"How about Trivial Pursuit?"

"I'm not playing Trivial Pursuit with you. You know everything about trivia."

"Well, then what are we going to play?"

"How about we play the silent game?"

And that was it. Over. Done. He sulked back down in his seat and stared out the goddamn window. Why wouldn't he want to play MadLibs with me? It was pure genius. There were practically hundreds of hours of writer's block I had to fight through and MadLibs was the only thing that ever got me through it. MadLibs got my writer brain going. It triggered my stifled, creative mind into action every time. It's true. How was I going to pass the next few hours with this snaggly bastard without MadLibs? It was enough to drive me crazy. If only my good friend Jason was here. He'd play MadLibs with me for sure, no doubt about it. But Jason wasn't here. He was back in Montgomery, Alabama with his goddamn whore wife. So after thinking it over, and realizing I was on a long trip with a coworker who volunteered to tag along, I decided to play nice and include him. It was the right thing to do. It's true.

"Actually, here's something we can do together. When I was a kid, there was a convenience store along this highway called Stuckey's. I used to love going to that store when I would go on road trips with my parents to my grandmother's house in Oklahoma. If we can find that Stuckey's, then I would be very grateful."

This perked that snaggly bastard up real quick.

"Aye aye, Captain!" he said, sitting up, peering out the window like a dog waiting for a squirrel to run across the lawn. It was a crazy sight to see. It's true.

Like I said, when I was a kid, I would go on these LONG road trips to my grandmother's house in Oklahoma City with my family. They were excruciating road trips where long periods of time would go by without passing anything of interest on the highway. Being that Texas is so goddamn large, you could go miles and miles without seeing anything but an old abandoned field with some emaciated cows or a rundown Dairy Queen that looked like it was built in the 1950s or junk yards filled with crushed cars and appliances. For a kid, this was a goddamn nightmare. It was the worst kind of torture. But the funny thing was, also during this time in the 1970s, there were a bunch of movies that glamorized the lifestyle of truckers and outlaws and they made it seem like traveling on these goddamn barren highways was a lot of fun. And when I was a kid, I soaked up these silly movies like a sponge. Who wouldn't want to drive a goddamn eighteen-wheeler with an orangutan or a chimpanzee or whatever monkey the movie studios could find to work for no money and get all the booze and bananas it could consume? It was a beautiful thing to an 8-year-old kid. It's true.

So, the thing was, there were these humongous convenience stores at the time called Stuckey's and my parents would stop there in the middle of fucking nowhere so we could go to the potty and buy some snacks and sodas or whatever. When you stepped inside one of these Stuckey's convenience stores, it was like stepping into a shrine for these truckers or outlaws or whoever was eluding the rascally sheriff or redneck constable or local kingpin cattle rancher or whatever fit the mold of an inept authority figure. Stuckey's had aisle after aisle of cowboy belt buckles and leather wallets and Buck Knives and CB radios and tools and pecan pralines and trucker gear and pop guns and ice cream. It was a little boy's goddamn fantasy extravaganza. It's true.

On these long road trips, whenever we saw the billboard signs for Stuckey's, I would start screaming my head off like a goddamn idiot and my father would turn his van off the highway and we would spend a good 30 minutes roaming around in these convenience store shrines to the trucker lifestyle. Now, when I was an 8-year-old kid, I didn't have a lot of money on my person but I did have a little Velcro wallet filled with a few dollars that I earned from doing chores around the house. I saved those few dollars for times like these when I knew I was going to need to buy a plastic six-shooter or a rubber tomahawk or a miniature screwdriver set or a plastic longhorn or some other worthless trinket that would drive my father absolute ape shit. He hated the fact that I would waste my hard-earned money on some bullshit piece of crap that was imported from China but I absolutely loved it. Stuckey's was a magical place to me when I was a kid. It's true.

For old time's sake, I thought it would be fun to go into a Stuckey's as an adult and see if the old magic was still there. About 15 miles north of Temple, Texas, the hope was still alive, sort of.

"Look! A sign for Stuckey's!" Snaggle said, hemming and hawing all over the goddamn place like a monkey that spotted a banana tree. "Right there!"

He pointed to a billboard on the side of the highway. Sure enough, it said Stuckey's was a few exits up the highway. But the sign looked like it was 30-years-old and had been neglected and battered and worn down by years of sitting in the Texas sun. I didn't get the best feeling from seeing that old, beat-up goddamn sign. But I had hope that I would be able to rekindle some of that childhood magic.

"Let's check it out," I said.

"It should be just a couple of exits up," Snaggle said. What a goddamn genius!

When we arrived at the exit, I felt the anticipation and excitement build in me like a geyser, ready to explode. All the memories from when I was a kid started to pour into my brain and that excitement I used to feel in my gut returned. It was a goddamn amazing feeling. Sometimes, things from your past can come back to the present and feel exactly the same, even as an adult. It's true.

I pulled Clint the Caddy off the pristine highway and sped onto the shitty access road, barely covered with asphalt and pitted with potholes and deep tread marks and covered with gravel. I didn't expect the access road to be in such crappy condition and I didn't anticipate slowing down like I really needed to. A dust cloud quickly engulfed Clint the Caddy, making it difficult for me to see where I was going. I slammed on the brakes and the steering wheel jerked from right to left. All of a sudden, Snaggle started screaming like a little girl, his high-pitched screech scaring the shit out of me and distracting me from the task at hand, which was not driving off the access road into a cow pasture or barbed-wire fence. Everything in the car caught air and popped around in the cabin, including Snaggle. He slammed his face against the dashboard then held his bloody nose, crying and sniffling and sneezing. I could make out a silhouette of a building that was shaped very much like the Stuckey's distinctively styled buildings so I continued in that direction, shit still flying, Snaggle still crying. When Snaggle decided he'd had enough, he screamed at the top of his lungs, triggering both of my feet to stomp the brake pedal almost through the floor board. We had arrived in style, I must say. It's true.

"Are you crazy?" he asked, almost in tears.

"I thought I handled that pretty well, all things considered," I said. I meant it too. It's true.

"Really?! Because we almost died!"

"Almost but not quite."

As soon as the dust cloud started to clear, I could see we had parked catty-corner across from Stuckey's and fortunately, we were the only car in the parking lot. That was good. Clint the Caddy would have crushed any cars in his path. I opened my door and turned to Snaggle, still weeping a little.

"Are you coming or not?" I asked. He gave me a sad look, a sad bastard look, the look a puppy has after you smack it on the butt for peeing on the kitchen floor. He wiped the snot from his nose and opened his door too.

We got out and stood next to Clint and as the dust completely settled, I could tell that something was amiss about Stuckey's. I mean, it looked pretty much how I'd remembered it: steep, high-pitch roof with the long over-hang but it was painted black instead of the bright neon colors I remembered. All the windows had been blacked-out and the front entrance, which once was as inviting as could be, was boarded up. Something was not quite right. It's true.

"I don't think this is a Stuckey's anymore, Simon," Snaggle said. No shit, Sherlock! For a computer genius, Snaggle sure was a goddamn knucklehead. "Look! There's a XXX sign that is not turned on. Right there." For once, Snaggle was right about something. At the front left corner of the building was a neon sign with three large X's on it, in the exact same spot where the Stuckey's sign used to be. It was a strange sight to see. It's true. "Stuckey's is now a porno shop!"

Snaggle started hemming and hawing all over the goddamn place like a jackass, slapping his knee and wheezing for breath. All of his laughing and cackling about made me blow my goddamn top except that the sadness I quickly felt took over any anger I had toward that snaggly bastard. I couldn't help but think that a precious little piece of my youth had been squashed by a fucking sleazy, smut peddler. Who in the hell in this shithole town would let a fine establishment like Stuckey's go under to only be replaced by a porno shop? It was a goddamn disgrace. It's true. I decided right then and there that I was going to go inside and find out what had happened to Stuckey's. It wasn't *that* long ago that this building was a Stuckey's. Someone inside would have the information I wanted. We walked around the side of the building and found the entrance at the back.

Inside, the porno shop was dark as night and cold as a penguin's penis and had a distinct smell that was somewhere between coconut-scented hand lotion and mildew. It was the smell of my youth's destruction, only to be replaced by someone else's filthy opportunism. It was pretty sad, if you ask me, pretty sad indeed. It's true. The aisles of candy and chips and the trinkets I so looked forward to rummaging through were replaced by aisles of adult DVDs, racks of slutty lingerie, and glass cases filled with dildos and anal probes and tubes of lubricants and magazines so filthy that apparently they needed to be encased in glass. It was a goddamn shame, a goddamn filthy, dirty, pornographic shame. Snaggle followed close behind me, his arms wrapped around his torso as if he was shielding his innocent little heart from being lured to the dark side. It seemed as if Snaggle had no idea of the existence of a dirty place like this but he recognized the sign as being a porno sign so I was sure that at some point in his nerdy life he had been in a porno shop. It wasn't like girls threw themselves at him on a daily basis. All snaggly, sad bastards needed something to jack off to. It's true.

In the far corner of the shop was a counter with a cash register on it, an ashtray with a lit cigarette in it, a beer bottle next to it, and a lava lamp, yet there was no clerk in sight. So I indicated to Snaggle, by tilting my head in the counter's direction, to follow me over there. He stepped close behind me, his arms still wrapped around his torso like vines on a flagpole. It was hilarious, like he didn't want to get the cooties or herpes or something. It's true. I leaned over the counter but didn't see anyone. I looked at Snaggle and he looked back at me, a little concerned.

"Maybe we should go," he said.

"I just want to ask a few questions then we can go."

"OK."

We stood around like a couple of dopes for a few moments in uncomfortable silence between the two of us, accompanied by the sounds of porno soundtracks and angry humping in the background. We, a couple of nerds from Austin in a porno shop in the middle of nowhere, were as out of place in there as two Eskimos trying to build an igloo in the Amazon. It's true. Eventually, some sounds came from the back of the shop, like someone tripping over something large and heavy, and a short chubby man in a military vest came to the front. He perched himself on a stool behind the counter and looked at us, up and down, up and down, like we were a couple of turds wearing human clothes. He put the lit cigarette in his mouth and took a swig from his beer. He tapped the ashes from his cigarette and crossed his legs in a very "I'm superior" manner. He really thought he was hot shit sitting there behind a counter, smoking and drinking, in a porno shop. It's true.

"What do you two faggots want? I don't have much gay porn here. You'll have to drive over to Juan's store if you want to watch two dudes butt fucking," the clerk said. He sucked on his cigarette some more like you would suck soda threw a straw. He inhaled a half-inch of cigarette with one puff. He had a name tag pinned to his military vest. The name tag said, "George."

"Oh, we're not looking for gay porn," I said, shaking my head.

"Well, you two look like a pair of butt-plugging homosexuals, that's for sure," he cackled. He smashed his poor cigarette into the ashtray and immediately lit another, sucking a quarter of its life in one drag. "You two look perfect for each other. Who is the pitcher?"

"Huh?" Snaggle replied, confused yet inquisitive.

"Which one of you faggots is the pitcher and which one of you is the catcher?" the clerk asked. He was starting to get on my goddamn nerves with all of his hateful, anti-gay slurs and his country boy inflection. I mean, Snaggle and I were in no way close to being in a same-sex relationship but if we were, I'd be mighty offended by now. Who did this guy think he was, anyway?

"I just wanted to ask you a couple of questions?" I asked.

"Oh shit! Are you a fucking reporter from the Temple Daily Telegram?" he asked, straightening himself up, fixing his hair and adjusting his vest. "If so, I'm ready for my 15 minutes of fame!" A slimy smile slid across his stubbly face. He was a real slimy bastard, I could tell. It's true.

"No, I'm not a reporter from the Temple Daily Telegraph."

"Then what the fuck do you want?" the clerk said. He was visibly irritated now, what, with his slimy smile turning into a curdled snarl.

"Did this used to be a Stuckey's?"

"Huh? What are you talking about?"

"This building. Did it used to be a Stuckey's?" I asked.

"I have no idea what you are talking about. As far as I know, this has always been The Adult Mega Mall."

"This was never a Stuckey's?" I asked, confused.

"No."

"Are you sure?"

"Yes."

"Really sure?"

"Look!" he barked, pulling a stubby revolver from his back pocket and slamming it on the glass counter in front of him. He slammed the counter so hard it almost cracked, tipping the beer bottle over and zapping the cord of the lava lamp. "Shit! Look what you made me do. I almost electrocuted myself."

"I'm sorry. I didn't..."

"If you two don't buy a pocket pussy or something, I'm going to shoot you faggots right in the fucking face. You go that?" he said, really mean and irritated and impolite. I was starting to think that he wasn't cut out to work in the service industry. His attitude was just terrible, the grumpy bastard.

"Simon," Snaggle said. "I think we should just do what the nice man says and get out of here."

"All right."

Snaggle reached into his pocket and placed some cash on the counter and said something about letting the clerk surprise him with a product of his choice. So the clerk took the cash and placed something in a paper bag and tossed it at Snaggle. We backed up together then turned around and walked out. I could hear his smoky cackle as the door slammed shut. Boy, I was never so glad to be out of some place than I was to be out of that dark, stinky porno shop. It was all just a goddamn shame. Sometimes, things from your past should just be left in the past. I mean, I was really hoping to relive visiting a Stuckey's but sometimes things are just not meant to be. Sometimes, your cherished memories should just stay that way, as cherished memories. If you try to relive them, then you could end up getting shot in the face by an anti-gay, redneck, porno store clerk wearing a military vest. It's true.

We quickly walked around the building back to the parking lot where Clint the Caddy was waiting for us. We hopped in and quickly drove off, only buckling our seatbelts once we were on our way up the highway. After getting a mile or so away from the creepy porno shop, I asked Snaggle what was in the bag. He opened the brown paper sack and pulled out something long, wrapped in loose cellophane. I asked him what it was. His answer was not very pleasant.

"It says it's a 12-inch Black Thunder King Dong Dildo with a wall-mount suction cup," he said, a tinge of fear in his voice. The goddamn thing was like the size of a small baseball bat. It was huge! It's true.

I asked Snaggle to throw it out of the window. He did. I watched it in my rearview mirror, bouncing around on the highway like a perverted pogo stick, until it vanished underneath an eighteen-wheeler.

14.

Waco. Do I have to say much more? If there was a bigger shithole in the entire state of Texas, then I have not been there. It is everything you can imagine it to be and worse, much worse, a small town trying to put on its big-boy pants and not realizing it had no business putting on big-boy pants. It's true. I spent a little time in Waco when I was in high school. I had a friend whose big brother went to Baylor University. He used to write home to us about how much fun he was having with Baylor, going to parties and hanging out at his fraternity and meeting chicks and drinking beer and this and that and whatnot. We didn't realize from his letters that he was really full of shit and that none of this stuff we were imagining was anything close to reality. The first time we went to visit his brother in Waco was a shock to us. What we encountered was closer to Little House on the Prairie than Animal House, an ultra-conservative university in a small town stuck in a 1950s segregationist mentality and a Baptist stranglehold. It was a goddamn disappointment, for sure. If anyone tells you that Waco is a pleasant town, then they are full of shit too. Mark my words. You'll be sorry if you ever stay one night in that shithole. The only thing worth doing there was grabbing a fast food meal on the way through or taking a dump at a dingy gas station, which sounded like a good idea to me. So we decided to stop and do both.

At the first exit I could find, I pulled Clint the Caddy off the highway and eased onto the access road. We passed a bevy of the usual fast food chains: McDonald's, Wendy's, Kentucky Fried Chicken (or KFC, as they call it now, to hide its southern origin), Pizza Hut, Taco Bell. They were all shit and not very appealing to me at that moment but close to the intersection coming up was a monstrous gas station / restaurant combo convenience stop that looked interesting. The sign had two parts: one that said CHEAP GAS and another that said El Pollo Loco (which is Spanish for the crazy chicken. Genius!). I decided right then and there that that was where we would take a break. I pulled Clint into the parking lot and found a spot by the entrance.

"What are we doing?" Snaggle asked.

"I thought we'd get a bite to eat and take a potty break."

"I'm not hungry."

"Don't you need to tinkle?"

"Tinkle?!" Snaggle started hemming and hawing all over the goddamn place, slapping his knee and jerking his head back and forth like a goddamn idiot. Here we were just an hour and a half from Austin and he was already getting on my last goddamn nerve. It's true. "I haven't heard the word *tinkle* since I was 5 years old."

"Sorry. I'm used to saying that because of my kids."

"Well, I don't have to go to the bathroom and I surely don't have to *tinkle*."

"Well, I do. Time for a break."

"OK. I'll get some Skittles. I love Skittles!"

Inside, we discovered an oasis of junk food the likes of which I had never seen before, row after row of candy, salty snacks, and refrigerators full of sodas. It was a goddamn sugar nightmare. The sight of all the shitty snacks sent Snaggle into a frenzy, his hand shoved in his pocket, his testicles receiving a battering that I hadn't seen since before we left Austin. Just what that bastard needed, more sugar to coat his decaying snaggle puss. It's true. Snaggle dove into the first candy aisle searching for his beloved Skittles. I decided to see what I could get to eat from El Pollo Loco.

The restaurant was in a cozy nook at the back of the convenience store. The smell of roasted chicken permeated the store like a delicious fog, a light smoky curtain hanging behind the counter where the cashiers were waiting for their next hungry customers. There were a few empty tables for patrons and a standing bar where a crew of Hispanic day-labor workers were devouring their meals before having to go back to cutting lawns or roofing houses or paving streets or whatever they were hired to do at a pay rate that was too low for the amount of hard work they had to endure. Hispanic workers got the short end of the stick. Where would the great, prosperous State of Texas be without the massive labor force of unsuspecting Mexicans that were taken advantage of by Anglo businessmen? These poor guys were getting fucked by the Man. It's true. But these Mexican guys here sure knew how to eat. They were stuffing their faces with chicken and rice and beans and tortillas and looked like they didn't have a care in the world on their sun-baked faces. I guess maybe these guys didn't have it so bad after all. If they did, then they would have look like sad bastards. They were anything but sad bastards. They were happy as can be eating their lunches.

I stepped up to the counter and surveyed what they had on the menu. Behind the counter stood a short, stocky black woman that looked like she was no taller than five feet and weighed about 300 pounds. She looked like a bull dog in a skirt. She was a sight to see. It's true. She didn't look too happy to be there, standing around and looking off in the distance like she was waiting for her shift to be over. On her stained shirt was a name tag. It said, "Consuela." I thought that was funny. She didn't look Hispanic. Maybe she was Puerto Rican. I wasn't about to ask. It looked like she could rip me in half with her bare hands if she wanted to. It's true. She glared at me while I looked at the menu.

"Wha' choo want?" she asked, putting her hands on her bulldog hips.

"What's good?"

"Everything. Wha' choo want?"

"What's your specialty?"

"Specialty?" she asked, sighing like the life had been punched out of her. She became visibly irritated. "We don't got no specialty unless you think chicken is special. That's what we gots. Chicken. You want some chicken?"

"Sure. What does it come with?"

"It comes with what I give you." She slapped some chicken and rice and beans on a plate and flung it on the counter. She looked satisfied tossing my plate like that. A little smile appeared on her bulldog face. She sure was pleased with herself. "That'll be five bucks."

I gave her the money and she shoved it in the cash register. She returned to where she was standing before, looking off into the distance. I felt compelled to say something to her. I regretfully did.

"You could be a little nicer, you know? It's all about good customer service." I really believed that too. There is nothing better than good customer service. It can make someone's day. It's true. She stepped to the counter and leaned toward me. She gestured for me to come closer. I did, a little.

"Mister, if you had my job, you wouldn't be nice to nobody either. Got that?"

"OK," I said. "I'm sorry."

"Just be glad I didn't spit in yo food. Enjoy yo chicken, white boy."

And then she walked into the kitchen. Spit in my food? What a goddamn disgusting thought. It was almost enough to make me toss my lunch plate in the trash but I was getting pretty hungry. And the thought of eating the junk food crap in the convenience store made my stomach turn. I decided to take a chance and eat my chicken. We still had a couple of hours before getting to Dallas and I didn't want to starve on the way. Besides, that roasted chicken sure smelled pretty damn good. I was convinced that the hot oven would have incinerated any cooties that good ol' Consuela could I have put on it. I was sure of it.

I found an empty spot along the bar and quietly ate my food. Snaggle was nowhere to be found. He was either knee deep in a sugar buzz or taking a dump. Either way, I knew I had at least a few minutes of quiet time and I intended to enjoy it. As I ate, I had a feeling that I was being watched. You ever have that feeling? It's a really creepy feeling like the air around you stagnates, making the hairs on your neck stand up. I looked around and saw a young woman standing in front of a beverage cooler, staring at me, or at least it looked like she was staring at me. I looked behind me to see if maybe she had made eye contact with one of the Mexican guys but they were all busy finishing their meals, not paying attention to her. I looked back at her and pointed at my chest, as if asking, "Me?" She nodded and began walking toward me.

She was a sight to see. She had short, pitch black hair that looked like a tornado had styled it and goddamn piercings all over her face. She was wearing a ripped t-shirt, a skirt, and combat boots. And instead of a purse, she had a messenger bag draped over her shoulder. The closer she got to me, the more I could tell that she was rather young (maybe in her early 20s) and that her pin-cushioned face was strikingly beautiful. Any woman that felt compelled to stick jewelry in a face like that must have had some issues, major issues. It was kind of like throwing darts at the Mona Lisa. It's true. She came right up to me, standing on the other side of the bar.

"Hey," she said.

"Hi."

She stood there for a few moments, looking at my food then looking at me. She was absolutely stunning, in a sour, punk rock kind of way. She exuded strength and fragility all at once. It was strange.

"Where are you headed?" she asked, glancing at my food.

"Dallas. Why?"

"Is that good?" she asked, grabbing my fork, poking at my food, and taking a bite.

"It's good."

She took a few bites and dropped the fork. I guess she didn't agree about the food.

"I need a ride to Norman but Dallas works for me. Can I tag along?" she asked.

"Well, I don't know. I'm kind of in a hurry and I have another passenger with me."

Just then, out of nowhere, Snaggle appeared, a massive bag of Skittles in one hand and his other hand deep in his pant pocket, giving his testicles another go. That bastard was shameless. How anyone could play pocket pool in the company of strangers was beyond me? But he did it. The sour girl looked down at his hand in his pants and started giggling. She giggled like what he was doing with his filthy hand was cute. It's true.

"Hi. I'm Ryan," Snaggle said, pulling his hand from his pocket and extending it to the sour girl for a shake. She pinched his hand with the tip of her thumb and index finger, as if she was picking up a hairball or some dried disgusting thing, and she shook it daintily. The touch from her fingers turned Snaggle into a blubbering mess.

"My name is Gina. Are you riding with this guy?" she asked, pointing at me.

"Yeah, that's Simon. We're going to Dallas for a funeral. His grandma died."

"Oh, I'm so sorry," she said, turning to me. She had a genuine tone of condolence in her voice. Too bad they didn't know my grandma was still alive and kicking, probably drinking scotch right now and smoking a goddamn cigarette. It's true.

"It's OK. Thanks though."

"I was just asking Simon for a ride. I'm trying to get to Norman, Oklahoma but Dallas is a good step for me. It gets me a little bit closer."

"Sure, you can come with us," Snaggle said, happy as can be. I couldn't fucking believe it! Who did he think he was inviting her along on MY trip? What an inconsiderate, snaggly bastard. I was beginning to regret bringing him along in the first place with his inconsiderateness and his pocket pool and his maddening trivia knowledge and his rank breath and his sugar frenzies. It was enough to drive any sane person insane. It's true.

"Wait a minute. I don't know if we have any room for another passenger," I said.

"Room?" Snaggle blurted, hemming and hawing all over the goddamn place, spittle flying from his mangled teeth. "That Cadillac has plenty of room."

"I'll help pay for gas. And all I have is my bag here," Gina said. I felt like I was being ganged up on. It was a very uncomfortable position to be in. But she gave me a sweet look and I thought maybe she'd keep Snaggle busy so he wouldn't bother me and the idea began to sink in that maybe it wouldn't be so bad having her tag along to Dallas.

"All right," I said, relenting. "But when we get to Dallas, I'll have to drop you off somewhere. I do have to go to a funeral, you know?"

"Deal," she said. "Let me wash up before we go." And off she went to the ladies' room.

I turned to Snaggle and gave him an eat shit look that would have burned a hole through a wall.

"What?" he asked, looking down and kicking his feet like he was kicking around an imaginary tin can or a soda can or some kind of can.

"Why did you invite her along without asking me first?"

"I don't know but she's hot!"

"That's beside the point."

"Who wouldn't want her to ride with us?"

"Uhhh..." I didn't know how to respond to that. I really didn't. Besides, she offered to help pay for gas and Clint the Caddy wasn't necessarily the most fuel-efficient vehicle in the whole goddamn world. It all made sense in a snaggly, idiotic kind of way. I felt I couldn't win. It's true.

"It'll be fun, Simon."

"I guess," I said, pushing my plate of food away. "I need to go to the bathroom before we go."

"I'll be waiting in the Cadillac," he said. He skipped away, probably to pay for his pound of goddamn Skittles, and I made my way to the men's room.

Inside, the men's room smelled like bleach and turds and some kind of moldy stank that made my stomach turn. It was all I could do to keep myself from vomiting all over the goddamn place. I found any empty urinal and began to relieve myself and I thought of how I was going to have to be vigilant about the lie my road trip was based on and to keep my story straight for my two weirdo passengers. It was almost too much to take. I closed my eyes as the urine drained from my body and all I could think about was seeing my sweet children's faces and hugging them and kissing them and bringing them back to Austin. I was in a dilemma for sure now that I had a couple of knuckleheads riding along with me. For some reason, I thought that it would all work out and that everything would be fine. Snaggle was a big boy and I was certain that he would understand once everything played out the way I had hoped. Plus, I knew I would be dropping Gina off at the first convenient place. It was all going to work out, I thought to myself. It would be just fine. It's true.

I must have been in a deep place of contemplation because I didn't realize that the urinal was clogged and before I could react, the stinky toilet water was spilling out from that filthy bowl and was draining on to my pants and shoes. The cold, dirty water snapped me out of my state of contemplation and all I could say was, "Shit! Shit! Shit!"

Or as my son good ol' Sammie boy would say:

Shmit.

15.

Recently, I considered changing things up for my next book and writing something completely different than I've written in the past. As I mentioned before, I thought of writing a memoir that was 100% fiction. That seemed to me to be a pretty entertaining project but I also considered writing a children's book. It's true. So, the thing is, I've read a LOT of children's books with my kids and they are all complete crap. With a few notable exceptions (they are all quite old and considered classics but I'll get to that later), every book given to my children as gifts or whatnot were terrible, absolute, abysmal hack jobs. I mean, who thinks writing a book about a mother explaining to her daughter that she is a lesbian is a great children's book? What author thinks writing about coping with "grumpiness" will inspire your kids? Reading these types of books to my own children was enough to make me want to blow up a Barnes & Noble book store with a handful of grenades and a box of TNT! It's true. Where were the Dr. Seusses of our time? Nowhere, I tell you. Dr. Seuss didn't write rhymes about why mommy and daddy got divorced or couplets about Little Johnny Smith growing prepubescent moustache hairs on his upper lip. It was all just a goddamn shame. Dr. Seuss is turning over in his grave this very instant, no doubt.

To me, Dr. Seuss wrote magical books. They were filled with immense imagination, wicked humor, fantastic artwork, and valuable lessons. You know what other book I liked? *Eloise*. That book not only made my kids laugh but it cracked me up as well. Little Eloise was a riot, running around the New York Plaza Hotel without any supervision whatsoever or her parents around to tell her to do her chores or worrying about school work to be done. She liked to hang around the guests of the hotel who smoked and drank too much and wise-cracked to Eloise about things they thought she wouldn't understand but that girl was a lot smarter than any of them could ever imagine. It was a brilliant children's book. Compared to the dreck in stores now, *Eloise* was a goddamn masterpiece. It's true. I'm still considering writing a children's book. Little Jessica and Sammie Boy would be so proud of their good ol' dad, don't you think? Anyway, it was something I was considering.

As soon as we left the monstrous gas station / restaurant combo convenience stop, I realized pretty quick that Snaggle was outmaneuvered by our new travelling companion and was given the short end of the stick in the seating situation. She single-handedly destroyed the Snagglepuss in a game of "Rock, Paper, Scissors" and declared the front-passenger seat hers and banished the stinky bastard and his pound of Skittles to the back seat. It was nice having a female passenger in the front with me even though she was covered from head to toe in leather and piercings and every punk rock accessory available at the nearest outlet mall. She was like a female version of Grant the Rockstar except a lot less spastic and a lot sexier. I had considered giving her a nickname too, something like "Pin Cushion" or "Porcupine" or "Hellraiser" or "Cactus Face" or some other ridiculous name to match her otherworldly, prickly goth appearance. But after thinking about it more and more, the name Gina seemed to suit her just fine, short and sweet just like her. It's true. The only annoying thing, so far, about our new passenger was her propensity to fuck with the radio / CD player. The minute she got in the car, she was poking buttons here and pushing things there and pretty much making herself a real nuisance. Literally, after five minutes, I considered throwing her out on the side of the highway. It's true.

"What are you doing?" I asked.

"Trying to find something good to listen to," she said, jamming more buttons then rummaging through her backpack for something.

"What do you want to listen to?"

"Punk or hip hop or reggae or ska. Something good."

"I see. I can't help you there."

"That's obvious."

"What does that mean?"

"Nothing," she said, pulling a CD from her backpack. "Here we go."

She put the CD in and some midtempo reggae music started playing. Bob Marley. I could tell. I may be a nerdy writer masquerading as a help desk tech but I know Bob Marley when I hear him. He had the voice of a goddamn angel. It's true. I could see Snaggle in the rear view mirror, bobbing his head to the music, popping Skittles into his grotesque mouth, looking out the window, quiet for once. A smile appeared on Gina's face. She seemed content.

"Simon, do you know who this is?" Snaggle asked. That was the end of the silence.

"Bob Marley."

"Did you know Bob Marley died from melanoma?" he asked, popping candy in his mouth like it was the last bag of Skittles on Earth. "He was only 36 when he died."

"I knew that," Gina said. "He was so young. Did you know he performed at a massive concert just a couple of days after being shot?"

"Yes! I did know that. And did you know..."

"All right, you two," I said, putting an end to the goddamn madness. If I hadn't of stopped it, then I would have had to listen to trivia bullshit all the way to Dallas and I wasn't going to stand for it. Listening to two idiots banter back and forth in a question and response frenzy was just too much to take. It's true. "If you're going to barrage me with trivia then you both might as well sit in the back seat together. There is plenty of room back there."

"Well, look who put on his grumpy pants today?" Gina said, punching me in the arm. She was really starting to get on my last goddamn nerves. It's true. "We're just trying to pass the time. Why don't you tell me about you guys? What do you two do for a living?"

"We're computer techs," Snaggle said, rudely interjecting from the back seat. "Oh, and Simon claims to be a writer but I've never heard of his books."

"You're a writer?" Gina asked, looking at me, surprised.

"Yes, I'm a published writer."

"How fucking cool is that?!" she said. And in an instant, she didn't seem to be such a babbling bore anymore. It's funny how telling people that I'm a writer sparks some kind of strange fascination in them, like I'm some kind of alien or something. It's true. Deep down inside, people have this weird sort of reverence for writers. It's the strangest thing. It's not like it's the most difficult thing in the world to do. You just write down a bunch of words, words, words and hope you make some semblance of sense in the end. Policeman. That's a hard job. Soldier. That's hard too. School teacher. Fuck, the hardest of them all. But a writer? Ha! She still gave me this weird look like something about me was different than five minutes before. "Did you write something I would know of?"

"My novel *The Rise and Fall of a Titan* was published last year but it didn't do very well."

"But you wrote a motherfucking book. That right there is something to be proud of." She was right about that. I was very proud of that book even though it hit bookstores like a goddamn cement turd. I was kind of ashamed of its dismal sales performance but I was also proud to have published it. There was something to be said for starting and then finishing a book, a small something. "You should be proud of yourself."

"I am, I guess."

"You guess? Can I get a copy?"

"I'm sure I have a copy somewhere I can give you."

"Cool. Will you sign it for me?"

"Can I have a copy too?" Snaggle asked.

"Maybe," I said, ignoring him. "Sure, I'll sign it for you. What do you do for a living?" I asked Gina.

"Nothing now. I'm a student. I go to the University of Oklahoma in Norman. I'm studying journalism."

"So you're a writer too?" I asked.

"Yes, but not like you. Writing fiction is a whole 'nother animal compared to writing news articles. It's apples to oranges."

"Well, my book wasn't all fiction. It was based on reality."

"Like a biography?"

"Sort of, I guess. Fictionalized biography, maybe."

"That's still fucking cool. Published. Cool."

We all sat there in silence for what seemed like an eternity but it was a good silence, the kind of satisfying silence that comes after a group has come to a consensus about something very meaningful and important. As an added bonus, I didn't have to listen to these two knuckleheads babble about some trivial bullshit. It was nice but I knew it wouldn't last too long. I was sure of that. It's true.

"Do you think you'll get a job at a newspaper or something?" Snaggle asked, his mouth full of half-chewed Skittles. He was spitting that shit all over the goddamn place.

"Maybe. I hope so. I don't know. Sometimes, I really feel like I don't know what I'm doing. It's like my life just moves forward and I'm just going with it. It's almost like I have no control. I guess I'm hoping I'll eventually gain control and steer my life in the right direction. But right now, it seems like everything is just so hard. Why does it have to be so hard?" Bingo! There it was again: the question, the question of all questions. I was starting to come to the conclusion that this was a universal question that was much bigger than anything I could comprehend at the moment. Here I was asking myself the same thing and then coming in contact with people asking me the question that I didn't have an answer to. What the fuck? I felt like someone was playing a trick on me, like God or something. It's true. "Does it get easier when you get old?" she asked.

"Old? Do you think I'm old?"

"I'm sorry. I didn't mean to offend you."

"How old do you think I am?" She turned to me and examined my face, looked at my hands, looked at my clothes, really looked me up and down. It was like she could see right through me. How embarrassing! "Be honest, now."

"Hmmm, I'd say... 45."

"What?!"

"Am I close?" she asked, retreating a bit from her answer.

"You're WAY off."

"By how much? Five years?"

"More."

"Ten years?"

"Less."

"How old are you?"

"I'm not telling you now. 45? Really? Geez."

"I'm sorry. I didn't mean to offend you. You said to be honest."

"It's OK."

Snaggle was cackling from the backseat, slapping his knee and flopping around like a goddamn idiot. He was laughing so hard that his candy spilled out of the bag onto the floor but he didn't care. He thought that was some funny shit. It wasn't funny to me at all. It's true. But you know what *was* funny (get ready because this is some funny shit!)? His hemming and hawing abruptly turned into belly-aching and I could hear him slowly start to grunt and groan and moan. I peered in the rearview mirror and Snaggle was gripping his stomach, wrapping his arms around his midsection. He had a distressed look on his face and as he moaned and groaned about something, it appeared as if he was going to barf.

"Are you OK?" Gina asked, turning around to check on the Snagglepuss.

"I think I'm going to be sick."

"Do you need for us to pull over?" she asked.

"Yes. Fast!"

"Simon?" she asked.

"I heard him."

Luckily for Snaggle, I saw a sign for a rest area that was coming up so I put the pedal to the floor and quickly got to the exit and parked. The rest area was completely deserted except for us, which was convenient. If Snaggle was going to throw up his pound of Skittles, then it was better that no one else was around. I could just imagine the smell that goddamn mess was going to make. It was going to be disaster of biblical proportions. It's true.

"I'm going to help him," she said, getting out of the car and opening the back door for Snaggle. He eased out, hunched over and gripping his stomach, and she walked next to him to the rest rooms, his other arm draped over her shoulders. I watched them until they vanished into the building where the rest rooms were.

Peace and quiet.

I finally had some time to myself. I was pretty sure Gina was going to regret helping that filthy bastard, especially when the techicolor vomit started flying, but I didn't care. He deserved it for stuffing his face with that crap. I was just happy to have a moment to myself. As I was sitting there in the air-conditioned car, I noticed a plaque mounted outside. It was one of those "historical marker" plaques, the ones that tell the history of the place you're looking at and explained why it was designated historical in the first place. Apparently, this land used to belong to a big shot rancher named James "Tex" Smith, a rich bastard who had a lot of money and had a lot of cattle. Supposedly, he wanted to donate this land to the State after his death in hopes that his name would be eulogized into posterity. It appeared his wishes came true.

I imagined what it was like back then in the late 1800s when good ol' "Tex" was alive, probably riding a horse around so he could rope some cattle and living in a humongous log cabin-type ranch house with a wife wearing a bonnet and a bunch of dirty-faced children wearing bonnets or suspenders or whatever. Everybody wore white and brown clothes in the Old West. Maybe he had an oil-drilling rig and a water-well and an outhouse with a copy of the Bible in it in case anybody wanted to read scripture while taking a shit. I imagined the Waco Indians (the town Waco was named after an Indian tribe called the Waco, dummy) surrounded his property and demanded that he trade bottles of fire water for bushels of corn and threatened to rape his daughters if he didn't oblige. I was having a good ol' time thinking about this old-timey shit. Not a lick of it was true but it sure was fun thinking about it. I even thought it would make a fine novel if I would put my energy into it. I was sure of it.

There was one thing I knew to be absolutely true about James "Tex" Smith. I knew this to be an absolute *fact*. When he was writing his will and explaining how he wanted to donate his land to the State of Texas and have that land turned into a goddamn state park or historical place or whatever, he DID NOT imagine in his wildest dreams that his land would be turned into a "rest area." If he had any inkling of an idea that his property would be turned into a place where people pulled off the highway to take a shit or throw their cigarette butts on the ground or spank their kids or barf their Skittles into the toilet or let their dogs whiz on the trees or buy donuts out of a vending machine or whatever, then he never, I mean NEVER, would have donated his land to the State. He would have given his property to his children like most normal human beings and gotten over himself and his desire to have his name permanently attached to a place in history. It's true.

After my imaginary fun was over I realized that those two knuckleheads had been gone for quite some time and feared, believe it or not, that Snaggle was in serious trouble. So I decided right then and there that I would go check on those two knuckleheads in case I needed to call an ambulance or something. I turned off Clint the Caddy and locked the door after getting out. I made my way to the building where the bathrooms were, still noticing that there was no one else around but us and I thought that to be quite strange. As I got closer to the rest rooms, I could hear a strange sound coming from the men's room, kind of like someone's mouth was being muffled. I hesitated at first, fearing that if Snaggle was barfing that a chain reaction would start and I would barf as well, but I went in anyway.

Inside, I could hear some whispering from one of the toilet stalls. I couldn't make out what they were saying but I did hear something like, "Just let me see it" and "No, no, no." I tip-toed to the stall and noticed there were definitely some people in there. All I could hear was whispering and muffled noises. I placed my hand on the stall door and pushed it open and you will not believe what I found. Snaggle was standing there with his pants down with Gina kneeling in front of him, his ding dong in her hand.

"Oh shit!" I screamed and ran out of the men's room. I was so shocked by what I saw that I actually cursed out loud and that was something I NEVER do. I could hear Gina calling to me as I ran.

"Simon! Simon! It's not what you think!"

But what was I supposed to think? I ran to Clint the Caddy, opened the door, and jumped in, locking the doors again. I covered my face with my hands and wished that I was anywhere, and I mean *anywhere*, far away from these two filthy bastards. I tried to think of what my options were. Could I leave them stranded here and go to Dallas by myself? Or could I suffer in silence as they rode along with me? I didn't know what to do. As I mulled it over, I heard a tapping at my window. Gina was standing there, her hair sticking up all over the goddamn place, the sunshine reflecting of the piercings in her face, and she looked rather concerned and embarrassed at the same time. She kept tapping at the window, asking me to roll my window down but I shook my head no. I didn't want to talk to her. I was in absolute shock. It's true.

"Simon," she said, leaning close to the window. "It's not what you think."

"What should I think?" I said.

"Please open the door so I can explain."

"I don't want you to explain anything. It was pretty clear."

"No, it was not."

"I'm not stupid, you know?"

"I know. Just, please, roll down the window."

I looked at her and it really did seem like she was sincere. I unlocked the doors and she walked around the car. She got in the front seat and closed the door. She sighed.

"Where is he?" I asked.

"He's in the rest room. He's embarrassed."

"How could you do that?"

"What do you think I was doing?" I looked at her and gave her a *really* sarcastic look. "That's NOT what I was doing."

"Then what were you doing?"

"Look, I helped him into the restroom and he thought he was going to puke but after sitting in front of the toilet for a little bit, nothing happened. He stood up and said he was feeling better and then he put his hand in his pocket and started doing that thing he does..."

"Playing with..."

"Yes, playing with himself. So I asked him why he did that in front of people. And he told me he had this problem, this itching, burning problem. So..." she said, hesitating.

"And?!"

"And I offered to look at it for him. Told him I had several brothers and they always had some kind of issue that I helped them with because they were too embarrassed to talk to my mom or dad about."

"OK."

"And your poor friend... he has the worst case of jock itch I've ever seen. His rash is something fierce."

"Jock itch? You were examining him and found jock itch? Really?"

"Yes."

"That's hard to believe."

"It's the truth."

"Uh huh."

"It really *is* the truth."

Just then, I could see Snaggle shuffling out of the building, a look of complete shame on his face, a look like a pet dog has when its owner discovers it peed on the new sofa. He slowly made his way to the car then got in the back seat. The three of us sat there in uncomfortable silence for a bit. It was awkward as hell but I looked at Gina and she indicated for me to confirm her story with Snaggle. So I did. I looked in the rearview mirror.

"Jock itch?" I asked.

"I guess so."

"And that's why..."

"I guess so."

"And you believe her?"

"I guess so."

The shame in his voice confirmed to me that her story was true. So I decided to start the car and move on. I knew it was going to be uncomfortable in Clint the Caddy for a while. We had at least an hour to go before getting to Dallas. The image of the two of them in that stall was burned in my brain like a cattle brand on the butt of one of Mr. James "Tex" Smith's cows. I tried to redirect my thoughts to my happy place but it just didn't work. My happy place had been destroyed to smithereens. It's true.

16.

When I first met my ex-wife, she was not the maniacal, heartless, psychotic bitch that she turned out to be when we got divorced. She was quite lovely back then and had a sweetness about her when I first met her that I could only attribute to one thing: excellent parents. When I was introduced to her parents Roger and Selena, I was awestruck with their generosity, kindness, and graciousness. They truly bent over backwards to make me feel comfortable in their home. As I got to know them over the years, I learned that they weren't that way with just me or other folks they initially met, they treated everyone that way ALL the time. They were special and, in contrast to my own parents, were family members that I bonded with on a very deep level. Jessica, the kids, and I spent lots of time with them and we all went on family vacations together, celebrated holiday gatherings together, and even turned a basketball game on TV into an event that the whole family enjoyed. They were a lot of fun to be around. So it goes without saying that they were utterly destroyed when they heard the news that Jessica and I were getting a divorce. That was one goddamn depressing day. It's true.

So when I turned Clint the Caddy off the highway and pulled into the area of Dallas where Roger and Selena's neighborhood was, I felt a rush of nostalgia wash over me. I had spent so much time at their house that I had an emotional attachment to this part of Dallas and this particular highway exit. I used to associate this exit with imminent fun. Now I felt a sense of dread. I had not seen them since the divorce and wasn't really sure how their reaction was going to be to seeing me in Dallas, unexpected, on their front porch. But I wasn't there to rekindle old feelings. I was there to get my kids and take them home. I was sure they would understand that. If there was one thing they knew about me, then it was how much I loved my goddamn kids. It's true.

The only little detail I hadn't figured out yet was how to explain to Snaggle that our destination wasn't about my grandmother's funeral. I also didn't foresee picking up a punk rock girl with hair like a porcupine and a propensity to examine men's genitals for minor rashes and infections. I was knee-deep in a pile of shit that I could see had the potential to turn into a goddamn disaster. But if there was one thing I learned after taking that trip to New York (or did I?) was that sometimes you have to just go with the flow, let things happen the way they are going to happen. Sometimes, and I mean sometimes, things don't turn out as bad as you think they are going to turn out. It's true. Just when I got in the right headspace, Snaggle had to ruin it all and start blabbing from the backseat.

"Are we almost to your grandparents' house?" he asked. That snagglepuss fucker just had to ruin everything by opening his goddamn mouth and I mean EVERYTHING. I was really starting to regret bringing him along. It's true. "I need to go to the bathroom."

"I do too," Gina said, squirming in her seat.

I looked at the two of them and realized they would pee their pants moments before getting to my ex-inlaws' house so I found a convenience store at the corner of the entrance to their neighborhood. I parked out front and the two of them ran inside to go to the bathroom, hopefully not together. I imagined those two knuckleheads cramming into a dirty bathroom stall for another "examination" of Snaggle's infected private parts and I cringed at the thought. They were a real pair of goddamn idiots. It's true. But I had time to think of another lie to cover my previous lie before they came back out. I racked my brain for something, anything to tell them and I came up with the best I could in the short time they were gone. When they got back in the car, I let them have it.

"I have to make a quick detour before going to my grandparents' house. Is that OK?" I asked. They both said they didn't mind and that was that. My goddamn disaster was quickly diverted, for now. It was a small victory but a victory nonetheless. It's true.

I pulled Clint the Caddy out of the parking lot and found their street a couple of blocks down. Everything looked exactly the same as I remembered. Massive oak trees lined the street, climbing 50 to 60 feet into the sky, and intertwining their branches overhead like a leafy canopy over the quiet neighborhood. It was a sight to see, something straight out of a Norman Rockwell painting or some shit like that. The majority of the residents were still the original owners of these immaculate homes, moving in soon after the houses were built in the 1950s and living their lives there, peacefully and quietly, into their retirement, after all their children had grown up and moved on to their boring careers and their boring apartments somewhere else far, far away, only coming home for Christmas or Easter or Thanksgiving. It's true. I eventually found my ex-inlaws' house. It looked exactly the same as I remembered. Exactly. I parked on the street out front.

"Is this where we are going?" Gina asked.

"Yes," I said.

"It's beautiful."

"Yes, it is."

I turned off Clint the Caddy and we, a gang of assholes that had traveled all the way from Austin and Waco to Dallas on the pretense of a lie about a dead grandmother and a funeral that was not going to happen, made our way to the front door. Our trip was truly the most ridiculous road trip in the history of the goddamn world. It's true. I rang the doorbell and we waited silently. The front door creaked open, just a tad, and a pair of old eyes peeked from the crack. It was my ex-father-in-law, I could tell. Roger had these deep blue eyes and the fuzziest eyebrows of any man I had ever seen. His eyebrows looked like two exotic, grey and white speckled caterpillars making-out on his forehead. It's true. He stared for a moment or two before saying anything.

"What do you want? I don't need a newspaper subscription!"

"It's me." I said.

"If you're selling something, I'm not buying," he said, getting irritated.

"Roger, it's me, Simon. I'm here to..."

"I said, I don't want to buy anything!"

"Roger, who is it?" The woman's voice came from the living room. It was Selena. I could tell.

"It's a bunch of goddamn Mormons or Jehovah's Witnesses or... or... Catholic sons of bitches. They want our money, damn it!"

"All right, Roger, I get the picture," Selena said, appearing at the door, opening it more, putting her arm around Roger. "I'm sure these lovely people are not..." And then she saw me. She froze for a minute, staring in disbelief. But her kind nature didn't allow her to stare too long. She was naturally sweet that way. It's true. "Simon, what a surprise."

"Hi Selena," I said, somewhat embarrassed.

"What brings you to Dallas?"

"With all of these fucking vacuum salesmen too!"

"Roger!" she said. She placed her hand over his mouth, muffling his next profane outburst. "You'll have to excuse my husband. He suffers from dementia."

"Is it getting worse?" I asked.

"Yes, much worse. And who are these lovely people?" she asked, looking at Snaggle and Porcupine, my retarded companions.

"Oh, this is Ryan and Gina. Ryan is a coworker and Gina is..."

"A student," she said, completing my sentence. She had a sweet tone in her voice that sugar-coated her odd appearance. If she didn't have all of that shit stuck in her face, she wouldn't be so bad looking. Under all of the goth accessories was a pretty girl hiding from something. I just didn't know what she was hiding from. It's true. "I'm a student at the University of Oklahoma."

"Good for you, sweetheart. Well, Simon," she said, pulling the door wide open. "Why don't you and your lovely traveling companions come in for some coffee or a cold beer?"

"Is it Miller Time?!" asked Roger.

"Yes, dear. It is Miller Time."

"Great! Where is my Mavericks Koozie?"

The three of us entered their home. It was as lovely as I remembered. Selena led Roger to the couch where he plopped down in his favorite spot, a place at the end of the couch with a divot in the seat cushion in the shape of his ass and a worn-out armrest. He zoned in to what was on TV: Golf. The three of us sat down and watched Roger. What a character! All of a sudden, it was like we didn't ring the door bell and he didn't cuss at us and call us Mormons or salesmen or sons of bitches or whatever. His dementia seemed to have a tenuous stranglehold on his personality. It's true. Selena asked us if we'd like coffee or beer and our orders went as follows: I had coffee, Gina asked for a beer, Roger got a beer in his Mavericks Koozie, and Snaggle asked for a goddamn Coca-Cola (of course). The bastard couldn't go five minutes without coating his busted choppers with some kind of sugary treat. He was addicted to sugar! Selena brought over our drinks on a tray and sat down with us. She had a sweet smile on her face and seemed genuinely happy to see us, or me, that is.

"It is nice having some company. Roger can be a... hand-full, sometimes," she said, sipping from her coffee cup. "I don't get much time to myself to enjoy the company of others."

"He's sweet," Gina said, giggling.

"If cussing like a sailor is sweet, then Roger is a piece of strawberry pie with whipped cream on top," Selena said, also giggling. Roger was oblivious to the conversation. He stared at the TV like it was a portal into another dimension. He was mesmerized. It's true. "He can be a challenge. But, you know, I married for better or worse and unfortunately now is the time for the worse part."

"I don't think I'll ever get married," Gina said, lowering her head and running her fingers through her hair. It was an obvious softball comment tossed at Selena to respond to. Gina the Porcupine was shuffling her feet in a ghee-whiz fashion. It was a goddamn sight to see, a blatant ploy for attention. It's true.

"Why dear, every girl wants to get married. Didn't you dream of picking out your wedding dress when you were a little girl?" Selena asked, sipping her coffee.

"No. I played in the dirt with the boys."

"Well, even Tomboys want to find true love. Right?"

"Yes, ma'am," Gina said, smirking.

"Now, my sweet little Jessica always dreamed of getting married. It was something she talked about ever since I can remember, ever since she was a little girl. When she was four or five years old, she would line up all her dolls in her room and have a wedding ceremony for her Barbie and Ken dolls. It was the cutest thing. She would put Ken in this fancy little tuxedo and her grandmother made a little custom wedding dress for her Barbie, one that was made from silk and lace. She would dress her Barbie and do her hair and go on and on about honeymoons and happily-ever-afters. What can I say? It unfortunately didn't turn out that way," she said, glancing at me quickly then back to her cup of coffee in her hand. "I'm sorry, Simon."

That was the first time I heard Selena apologize for my divorce and it hit me in the gut like a sack of potatoes. The wind was knocked out of my sails. It's true. I didn't know what to say.

"Can you tell me how you and your husband met?" Gina asked Selena. She was genuinely curious, I could tell. Snaggle, on the other hand, didn't give a shit. The only thing he cared about was his goddamn Coca-Cola. He was slurping on his drink like it was the last Coke in the goddamn world.

"Oh, what a great story," she said, a sparkle appearing in her smile as she placed her hand on Roger's knee. Her touch disturbed Roger's attention from the TV. He was a tad perturbed by that. It's true. "We met at a dance."

"A dance? Like a high school dance?" Gina asked.

"No, when I was a girl, a teenager that is, we used to go to these dances. I guess they were at night clubs or town halls or whatever you call them. I'm not sure what you call them but all of my friends would go with our parents. All the kids from my neighborhood would go and get together, the boys on one side and the girls on the other side while the parents sat at their tables near the bar. Our parents would watch us dance and that's where I met my husband, Roger." She patted his knee with her hand, smiling affectionately at him. He didn't smile back. He just stared at the goddamn TV. "We were just teenagers but he was SO handsome! Do you remember, sweetheart?"

"Remember what?" he asked.

"Meeting me at the dance?"

"What dance? I don't like to dance?!"

"You used to love to dance with me. You were such a good dancer, darling."

"Dancing is for morons," he said, annoyed. It was obvious that this memory eluded him. He had no idea what she was talking about. It was a sad goddamn sight to see. It's true. "Dancers are morons. Morons!"

"Roger!" she said, embarrassed to no end. "Excuse my husband. He doesn't mean what he says. Anyway, that's where we met and we fell in love and the rest is history."

"That's a nice story," Gina said, smiling.

"Oh, that's enough about me. What brings you all here to Dallas?"

"We're going to a funeral," Snaggle said, snapping out of his sugar daze.

"A funeral? Who died?" Selena asked.

"Simon's grandmother," Snaggle said. And that was that. The cat was out of the goddamn bag. I knew it was going to be hard to keep the cat in the bag but leave it to good ol' Snaggle, fucking things up like only he knew how to do.

"I'm so sorry, Simon," Selena said, patting my knee. "It's always hard when a family member passes on. Doesn't she live in Oklahoma City?"

The "cat" was in full escape-mode now. There was no looking back. Snaggle sat up with a confused look on his face. Porcupine noticed him too. It was all turning out to be a goddamn mess. Hiding lies upon lies always leads to disastrous results. Just keeping your lies straight was a monumental task in itself. I was royally fucked. It's true.

"Yes, ma'am, she does."

"Then you just stopped by on your way through Dallas?" she asked.

"No, actually..." It was now or never. I had to fess up to my real motivation. I knew Snaggle would be upset being that he was a sensitive son of a bitch and I didn't know Porcupine from shit so I didn't really have to explain myself to a goth hitchhiker with low self-esteem. But it was all getting to be too much to handle and I knew it was time to just tell the truth. So I did. "...I came here to get my children."

"Little Jessica and Sammie?"

"Yes."

"But they are not here. They should be in Austin."

It was at this point that Snaggle got up and stormed his nerdy ass out of the house. Porcupine looked pretty confused and, seeing that I was in a pretty personal dilemma, decided to make her exit too. Either she was going to comfort Snaggle or give him a testicular cancer exam out front. Anyway, they were both gone and I was there to finally resolve my own personal issue. It was one of those defining moments. It's true.

"Look, your daughter told me she was moving to Dallas and bringing the kids with her so I assumed she would be here. I couldn't think of any place else she would go. She relies on you guys for support."

"I couldn't agree with you more about that but I spoke to her yesterday and she was still in Austin at her new apartment. Why would you think she was in Dallas?"

"Like I said, she told me she was bringing the kids here."

"Well, Simon, I love my daughter to death. You know this. But she does have a tendency to not tell the truth. Or say things to mislead people. I love her deeply but she does have her issues."

"I see."

"Why didn't you talk to her first before coming here?"

"She wouldn't return my calls."

"And you REALLY thought she'd be here?"

"Yes."

"There's nobody here but us chickens, you bastards!" Roger blurted out. At that moment, that outburst was one of the funniest things I'd ever heard. I almost started to laugh my ass off. Almost. It was just all too sad to laugh at though. I realized I was a pretty pathetic loser at this point. A real fucking loser. It's true. "We're just chickens! Cockadoodle do!"

"Yes, Roger. We're chickens," she said, patting his knee. Then she turned to me with a very concerned look on her face. I could tell she felt really sorry for me. "Look, all I can say is that you need to go back to Austin and talk to her. Work it out."

"Will you call her for me? Put in a good word? I love my kids dearly. The thought of not seeing them just kills me."

"I know you're a good father. I'll talk to her. I promise." She stood up and pulled me toward her. She wrapped her arms around me and gave me a big hug, a tight "I love you" kind of hug. It was nice. Honest. It's true. "I wish the two of you had not gotten a divorce but all I can do now is support the both of you. You're the parents to my beautiful grandchildren."

"Thank you," I said. And that was that. I thanked her for the coffee and the drinks for my friends and wished her good luck. I said goodbye to Roger but he didn't give a shit if I was coming or going. All he cared about was watching golf on goddamn TV. So I decided right then and there that it was time to leave. I said goodbye to Selena and left.

Out front, Snaggle and Porcupine were sitting in Clint the Caddy, staring off into space. I knew it was going to be uncomfortable in the car but at least I knew the truth was out there and that I could deal with it. Sometimes, it's best just to tell people the truth. The whole truth. It's true.

I got in the car and sensed the tension but as soon as Snaggle started to say something, I raised my hand for him to zip it and drove off. We drove passed the well-manicured yards and drove under the overarching oak tree canopies and drove off to somewhere, anywhere. It was getting too late to drive back to Austin so I figured we had to do something. I just didn't know what.

17.

Lies are a funny business to get into, and it seems us dumbass humans have a propensity to lie, even though we know it can get us into a lot of trouble. We all lie about something or another at some point in our day, all day, every day. If someone tells you that they never lie about anything, then they are lying to you. It's true. Even I have lied about some things, lots of things actually. I'm not proud to admit that but it's the truth. A couple of years ago, I laid a doozy of a lie on my kids. I had to. See, they had this hamster that they named Harry Houdini like the magician. They named him Harry Houdini because he always escaped from this glass aquarium-type thing without any evidence of where he escaped from. That little fucker would be there in his glass house, running in his hamster wheel, working off some of his hamster food, and the next minute he would be gone. He just vanished. So we would look high and low throughout the house and we'd always find him in the strangest of places like the pantry or in the laundry room. One day, when the kids were still at day care, I got home early from my shitty job and that little bastard had escaped and eaten some ant bait that I had under the kitchen sink. There he was on the kitchen floor dead as dead could be, his little hamster legs sticking straight up in the air like he was reaching up to Jesus Christ, a trail of ant bait leading to him from the cabinet under the sink. So before the kids got home, I ran to the nearest pet store and bought another little bastard that looked just like Harry Houdini (or at least I thought he looked like the original Harry Houdini). Anyway, when my kids got home with their mother, they didn't notice the difference. The new Harry Houdini ran in the hamster wheel just like the original Harry Houdini and he escaped from his glass home with the same skill and dexterity as the original. It was a remarkable switch-a-roo on my part. It's true.

One day, good ol' Sammie boy came up to me with the new Harry Houdini in his hands and he started asking me all of these goddamn questions like why did Harry all of a sudden have a small white spot on his stomach and why did Harry have one ear that stuck up and the other laid down and why did Harry seem to be fatter all of a sudden? Kids are very observant and very inquisitive about stupid shit, you know? It's true. So I told him something or other about how Harry was getting older and things change about people or animals when they get older. And that little son of a gun believed it. He never asked me another thing about his goddamn hamster. There really would have been no point for me to tell him that the original Harry committed suicide by stuffing his face with ant poison. That would have traumatized my little boy and his big sister to no end. So I lied about it and that was that.

When I told my boss Rod that my grandmother had died and I needed to go to her goddamn funeral, I didn't think it would turn into this dark cloud hanging over my trip to Dallas. I just thought it would be an easy way to get out of work. Boy, was I wrong. I had no idea at the time when I told the lie that Snaggle would convince me to tag along or that we would pick up a goth hitchhiker in Waco or that they would both be with me when I went to my ex-inlaws house so I could get my children. But things have a funny way of not working out the way you think they will. If I had known these two knuckleheads would have been with me, then I would have told a completely different lie. I would have come up with something that was foolproof. It's true. What that lie would have entailed, I have no idea. I'll get back to you on that one.

Anyway, like I said, it was getting too late to drive back to Austin so after a quick pow-wow between the three of us, we all decided it would be best to get a good night's sleep and decide what to do in the morning. It seemed to me that Snaggle and I would be heading back to Austin and that Porcupine would find another sucker to hitch a ride with or get a cheap bus ticket or something, anything to get her to Norman, Oklahoma. What a shithole, Norman, Oklahoma. Norman made Waco look like a goddamn mega-metropolis. It's true. And all of the Sooner bastards that went to school there, what a bunch of goddamn idiots. Porcupine must have stuck out like a sore thumb in the little redneck, shit-stained town. And I'll tell you this much, there aren't any famous writers from Norman, Oklahoma. No way, no how. Just saying.

When we got on the highway from my ex-inlaws neighborhood, I immediately saw a Holiday Inn so I parked Clint the Caddy out front and made my way inside to see about getting a room for the night. Snaggle and Porcupine stayed behind in the car, probably to give each other colonoscopies or breast exams or whatever, the filthy bastards.

The lobby for the Holiday Inn was remarkably nice with a high ceiling that went up all three stories and glass elevators reaching to the ceiling. The remnants of a low-cost happy hour were scattered about, plastic cups here and bar napkins there, some of those little plastic swords scattered on the floor. The cleaning crew was most likely gone for the night, an underpaid crew smart enough to know that tomorrow was another day and there was no point working harder than they should. It's really difficult to care about your work when you only get paid minimum wage to clean up after some stingy, goddamn travelers who could give two shits about cleanliness and courtesy. It's true.

Standing behind the reception desk was a VERY tall woman, looking mopey and disinterested, straightening her name tag in case someone cared to look at it. The name tag said, "Lydia." Lydia was at least 6 foot five, lanky, and at some point in her recent adolescence was probably a so-so center on her unranked high school girls' basketball team. She was literally the tallest woman I had ever seen in person in my entire life. I had to remind myself in the morning to lookup in the Guinness Book of World Records who the tallest woman in the world was because I had a feeling Lydia was pretty close, if not taller. It's true.

"Hi. Welcome to Holiday Inn. How can I help you?" she asked, her voice drained of all life. Have you ever seen the look on a cat's face that had endured a life of physical abuse from the family dog? Lydia had that look on her face. She looked like life had given her a one-two punch. She looked defeated.

"Can I get a room, please?"

"How many guests will be staying in the room?"

"Does it really matter?"

"Well, if you have more than one guest with you, then I would need to ask you how many beds you would like. One or two beds?"

"Do you have a room with three beds?" I asked. I know that may seem like a stupid question to you but there was absolutely no way I was going to share a bed with either of those filthy bastards in my car. I was positively sure that both Snaggle and Porcupine had some kind of venereal disease or, at the very least, cooties. It's true.

"No, sir. The rooms either have one king size bed or two full size beds."

"Well, that just won't do," I said, frustrated.

"I take it you have three guests in your party?"

"Yes."

"Then you could either get two rooms or we have roll-out beds that you can get for an additional charge..." Lydia had this droll voice like the actress Annie Potts. Remember her from the movie Ghostbusters? She was the woman who the Ghostbusters hired as their receptionist who didn't, at first, believe that ghosts existed and she had this monotone voice that sounded like the hum a photocopier makes during a large print run. Absolutely irritating. It's true.

As I stood there, about ready to scratch my eyes out, I didn't realize that someone was standing behind me until I heard the sound of pocket change and keys and Skittles being tossed in a pant pocket. And you know what that means, don't you?

"Simon, did you know that all vested state employees have their own American Express business card?" Snaggle said, his hand giving his balls a rough and tumble, right in front Lydia and myself. She had a look of disgust on her face. It's true. I was utterly embarrassed.

"Really?"

"Yup."

"And why would YOU have a state-issued American Express business card?"

"In case I have to go buy computer parts."

"I see."

"But I never use it. Ever."

"And?"

"We should use it now and get a suite or something."

"A suite?"

"Why not?" For one, brief, infinitesimal moment, the snaggly bastard had something there. Why not? The eternal question. There was no way I would get in trouble for Snaggle's indecent proposal. It was his state-issued credit card, not mine. Why not turn lemons into lemonade, as my grandfather used to always say to me. "I'll just tell Rod someone stole my credit card. He won't care."

"Let's do it," I said. I turned to Lydia. "We'd like a suite, please."

"We don't have any suites, sir," she said, snickering. "We have one room size with either one bed or two beds."

"Fine. We'll take a room with two beds and a roll-out bed."

Lydia began furiously typing away at her computer, filling in information, asking me things she didn't know, typing some more. She was on a mission to get back to being by herself, probably to hide in the office and carve things into her bare legs. That's what young women do, you know? When they are miserable and they hate their lives and their parents and their selfish boyfriends, they carve shit into their bare arms and legs for attention. It's true. She eventually completed her typing and handed me a couple of electronic room keys and thanked us for staying at her crappy hotel.

"Where's Gina?" I asked.

"She said she needed something from the convenience store and would meet us at the room."

"When a young woman with... spiky hair comes in, can you tell her what room we're in?" I asked.

Lydia the Depressed Giant nodded, turned around, then quickly vanished into the office behind the reception desk. That would be the last I ever saw of Lydia the Depressed Giant. I wasn't going to miss her, not one bit. Fortunately for me, Snaggle had loaded our bags onto one of those hotel carts that valets use to lug your shit around in expensive hotels. But there were no valets at this crappy Holiday Inn. Snaggle was MY valet. I motioned for him to follow me and the dumb bastard grabbed the valet cart and pushed it behind me, broken front wheel and all. It rattled and clanked like it was going to disintegrate into a million pieces. It's true. We were looking for room 325, our luxury little room for the night.

We found the closest elevator, stepped inside, Snaggle pulling the beat up cart behind him, and I pushed the number "3" button. The doors slid shut.

"I've never stayed the night in Dallas before," Snaggle said, one hand holding the cart steady, his other hand plunging into his pocket for his tortured testicles. If that bastard didn't quit tossing his nuts, then he was going to give himself nut cancer. It's true.

"Yeah, it's going to be a blast," I said, sarcastically.

"We'll *make* it fun."

"Whatever you say, buddy. Nothing about this trip has been fun."

The elevator dinged when we reached the third floor. After the doors slid open and we entered the hallway, it was clear there weren't too many guests there that night. The hallway was pretty barren and absolutely quiet, the kind of quiet you encounter at a wake in a church. As we walked down the hall, the most noise we heard was from the broken front wheel on the valet cart, shaking back and forth as Snaggle pushed it. It sounded like the goddamn wheel was going to fly off, sending our luggage crashing to the floor. But for some reason, that thing held itself together until we found our room. Room 325. I slid the electronic key in the lock and after a few failed attempts, the door unlocked and I opened it. Inside, it was the lap of goddamn luxury. All that was in there was one king size bed, a chair, and a small dresser with the crappiest TV I had seen in years, the perfect complement to the crappy Holiday Inn. It was fucking pathetic. It's true.

"Only one bed? Where are you going to sleep?" I asked Snaggle. He looked confused yet excited. As far as I could tell, he didn't really care. He was just glad to be away from home.

"I get the roll-out bed!" he said, propping the door open with the valet cart and unloading our bags, tossing them on the floor without a care in the world.

Down the hall, I heard the elevator bell ding and some heavy footsteps running in our direction. It was Porcupine with a case of beer under one arm and a carton of cigarettes under the other. She was ready for something. What she was ready for, I didn't know.

"Is this where the party is?!" she asked, barging into the room. "What the fuck? Only one bed?" she asked.

"Ryan called the roll-out bed."

"Then it looks like you get the floor, Simon," she said, jumping on the bed then sitting down, her party supplies in front of her. She took off her shoes, tossed them on the floor, and made herself at home. "Who wants a beer?"

"I do!" Snaggle said, jumping on the bed and plopping down right next to Porcupine. "I told Simon we should have fun."

"Well, I want to thank you boys for showing me some hospitality. I really appreciate you giving me a ride this far and letting me stay in a nice hotel rather than sleeping in an alley somewhere. Let's make a toast," she said, ripping open the case of beer, the cans spilling out on the comforter.

"A toast to what?" I asked, sitting on the bed. The three of us sat there in a circle on that king size bed like a group of junior high kids getting ready to have a slumber party, only I never had a girl at any slumber party I had when I was a kid. That would have been an outright, blasphemous, goddamn thing to do as a 12 year old boy. Even though girls were our objects of affection, they were never allowed in our private boy clubs at that age. My good ol' buddy Jason would have had a heart attack back then. Actually, he probably would have a heart attack right now. Even though Porcupine had a bizarre way of dressing, she really was a beautiful girl. It's true. "Actually, I'd like to apologize for..."

"Apologize? For what?" Gina asked.

"For not being honest about this trip."

"I can't believe you lied to Rod about your grandmother. He's going to flip his lid!" Snaggle said, laughing and hemming and hawing all over the goddamn place like a goddamn idiot. As far as I could tell, he was a goddamn idiot. It's true.

"How is Rod going to find out about it?!"

"Boys? Boys?! Cut it out," Gina said, placing her hands on both of us as if to separate two wild dogs. We were the furthest thing from two wild dogs. We were two nerds from Austin, Texas. "It really doesn't matter, now does it? So let's enjoy the evening, get drunk, and figure out our next steps in the morning." The three of us raised our cold, cheap beers and pressed them together in the air. "To unusual friends!"

"I'll drink to that," Snaggle said.

We opened our beers and took big gulps. I wasn't much of a drinker but if there was a night ripe for drinking, it was this one. It seemed Snaggle and Porcupine were both lushes, each going at their beers like they were cans of water. They were cackling and screaming like two little girls, each covering their mouths to keep their beer from spewing from their faces as they made little asides to each other. Snaggle, in his own nerdy way, was quite flirtatious with Porcupine. But as far as I could tell, besides the jock itch diagnosis at the rest stop, Porcupine was not really reciprocating the nerdy flirtation. She seemed to think Snaggle was funny but that was about it. I thought he was pretty goddamn funny. He was one of the most awkward human beings I had ever met in my entire life. How could that NOT be funny? It's true.

"OK," Gina said, straightening herself up. "I'd like to get to know the two of you a little bit better. I really don't know you at all, which is weird since I'm here with you in this hotel room." She started giggling all over the place. The beer must have been getting to her. "But don't even think of any funny stuff. I'm a black belt, you know?" Snaggle couldn't contain himself. He started hemming and hawing and laughing like a goddamn hyena. Beer shot out of his nostrils like a geyser. It was a sight to see. It's true. "Tell me something about yourself, some kind of secret, something personal."

"OK. I'll go first," Snaggle said, straightening up, tossing his empty beer can over his shoulder. "First, I need a new beer." Gina handed him a beer and he opened it, taking a quick gulp. His face started to turn bright red. "I've masturbated in the rest room at work."

"Oooh!" Porcupine and I responded, loudly and in unison. I felt a tinge of disgust shoot through my body. That was a rest room I used quite frequently. Was I sitting on a toilet that this disgusting bastard had jacked-off all over? The thought turned my stomach.

"Ryan, that was... unexpected," Porcupine said, sipping her beer.

"You said tell a secret, something personal."

"Well, I didn't think you'd go THERE quite yet. You're not even drunk yet."

"I'm getting drunk though," Snaggle said, snorting and cackling. He sure was a goofy bastard. I'm not sure what kind of sick son of a bitch would admit to something like that out loud but he sure did. He was absolutely shameless. It's true.

"Ok, Simon. It's your turn," Porcupine said, lighting a cigarette.

"I don't think this is a smoking room," Snaggle said.

"Who cares. Simon? You're up."

"Can I have a cigarette?" I asked. I hadn't smoked in quite a while but it sure looked good to me. That's what drinking alcohol will do, make me want to smoke. It was a disgusting filthy habit but there was a part of me that loved to smoke. Cigarettes once had a hold on me. They are addicting as all hell. It's true. Porcupine handed me a smoke and lit it. I took in the first drag and felt the smoke seep into my lungs. The nicotine quickly shot through my veins. An old demon was awakened. "I don't know what to say."

"Oh, come one," Porcupine said.

"Yeah, I said something personal," Snaggle said.

"I know. Something quite disgusting, I might add," I replied.

"Just give us one secret. Please?" Porcupine asked.

I racked my brain for something personal to say. I sorted through years and years of memories in my brain like a file system, flipping through scenes running all the way back to my early childhood. I didn't have much to share that I would have considered a secret. I mean, I'm a writer. Most writers write about themselves, even about personal shit. I felt like I was an open book. But I wasn't about to confess something like Snaggle did, the filthy bastard. I mean, all guys jack-off in inappropriate places but I'm not going to admit to that with a young woman in my company. But I did think of something rather personal and felt it was a good fit to share.

"OK. I cheated on my taxes last year."

"The room was dead silent, not a peep was said for a few moments.

"Simon, everyone cheats on their taxes. That's no secret," Porcupine said.

"Yeah, what's that all about?" Snaggle asked, a little perturbed.

"Well, that's all I got."

"Boring!" Porcupine yelped. She tossed her empty beer can on the floor and opened another. I had to admit, there was something in me that really enjoyed being around Porcupine. She was fun. She was free. She was... a lot of things. Most of all, she was interesting. There are not a lot of interesting people in the world. Most people are pretty fucking boring. It's true. But not Gina. She was anything but boring.

"All right, you two. Are you ready for my secret?" Snaggle and I both nodded, inching inward in the circle a bit, our attention fixated on Gina. "Come in closer," she said, putting her arms around our shoulders. Her voice lowered to a slight whisper. "I have three nipples," she said. Our mouths dropped open, hanging there, mesmerized. "But if you think I'm going to show you guys, you're fucking crazy!" she barked, smacking our foreheads with her hands, sending the two of us backwards onto the bed.

The three of us laughed hysterically and continued to drink into the night. We drank until my memory faded into darkness, the kind of darkness that comes from heavy drinking and smoking, a deep sedation that was welcome and very much needed on my part. It's true.

18.

I woke up with the worst hangover in the history of all hangovers. There was a banging in my head that didn't cease to stop no matter how much I squeezed it or how much I rubbed it. The pain was almost unbearable, the kind of pain that puts drastic measures into your mind. For the life of me, I couldn't remember the last time I drank and smoked that much in a few short hours but Snaggle, Gina, and I ripped through that case of beer and half of that carton of cigarettes like we were on a mission, a mission to kill boredom and cluelessness. Staying in a crappy hotel in an unfamiliar place will do that to you, bring on the boredom. And we killed it all right. It's true.

I sat up in the bed in total darkness except for a sliver of light poking through the curtains, waxing and waning in the slight opening of the curtains brought on by the motion from the air conditioner, wheezing moist air into the room. I felt around blindly in my vicinity on the bed but found nothing so I stood up and tip-toed to the curtains. I opened them slightly, letting in a little more light. It was bright outside and the sunlight desperately wanted to come into our crappy room. And to my horror, the light shone on Snaggle's half-naked body. He was draped over the end of the bed, limp, his torso on the bed, his legs on the floor, his pants down around his ankles, his arms crossed on his chest. He looked like a drunk mummy with his arms crossed like that. And to my poor eyes' misfortune, the morning light revealed that he *did* have the worst festering goddamn rash I had ever seen, the kind of rash that would make a leper wince with disgust. It really looked terrible. For a quick moment, I felt sorry for the poor bastard. He must have been in a lot of pain or at least some major discomfort. It's true.

But I could only take so much of looking at my coworkers diseased private parts so I tossed a pillow on him, hitting his stomach, waking him up abruptly. Of course, he realized instantly that he was half-naked and screamed like a little girl, running as fast as he could to the bathroom. All that nerdy racket woke Gina up. She had fallen asleep in a chair, curled up like a house cat. She rubbed her eyes then stretched her arms.

"What was *that* horrible sound?" she asked.

"That was Ryan," I said.

"Ryan? It sounded like a little dog getting run over by a car then being dragged for a block or two."

"Like I said, *that* was Ryan."

"What happened?"

"I have no idea. All I know is that I opened the curtains and he had his pants around his ankles."

"Lucky you," she said, snickering. "We partied like rock stars. Killed that beer."

She got up, stretched, and walked to the bathroom. She knocked on the door, asking Snaggle if he was OK. He said something or another about being embarrassed or ashamed or some shit like that. She laughed and banged on the door some more, asking him to come out. He eventually did. He made his way back to the bed, embarrassed, sitting down at the end with his face covered.

"I'm sorry. I must have tried taking my clothes off. I like to sleep in the nude, you know?"

"I didn't know that," she said. "But thanks for sharing."

"We drank a lot," he said. "A *whole* lot!"

"Yep."

"What's for breakfast?" he asked, smacking his gums. "Do they serve breakfast here? Waffles with LOTS of syrup sound good."

"I saw something about an all-you-can-eat breakfast buffet when we checked in last night."

"Sounds perfect," he said, zipping his pants, straightening his shirt. "Then what?"

"Who knows," I said. "Probably go back to Austin."

"I have to find a ride to Norman. But first, a shower."

She went into the bathroom and closed the door, leaving me with the snaggly bastard with the diseased nutsack, sitting on the bed with his hands in his pockets, doing what he did best. I was surprised I survived that long with Snaggle. I was also surprised that I hadn't killed him by that point or abandoned him at a remote rest stop or pushed him out of Clint the Caddy while we were going 70 miles per hour or some shit like that. My tolerance for him was wearing pretty thin. I think that if Gina wasn't with us, then I would have done one of those things by now. He deserved to be left stranded somewhere. It's true.

I decided against taking a shower myself even thought that's what I normally would have done. I'm not much for walking around smelling like a stinky bastard but sometimes your current circumstances overrule what you would normally do. Sometimes, weird circumstances make you do all kind of weird goddamn things. It's true. So instead, I started to gather my things together, getting my bag in order, thinking about going home. My trip had turned out to be a real bust. I drove all the way to Dallas with two goddamn knuckleheads because I wanted to get my kids and they weren't even *in* Dallas. They were at home somewhere in Austin, probably watching a movie, eating chicken nuggets, and enjoying their time with their mother, not even knowing that I was on a mission to get them. It was a sad goddamn state of affairs. It's true. Snaggle gathered his things too including, surprisingly enough, his bag of Skittles. I couldn't figure out why he still had some left at the pace he was going, shoving fistfuls of candy in his mouth whenever he had the chance. He was a fiend for sugar.

After a short moment of silent packing, Gina emerged from the bathroom, fresh and clean from her shower. Her hair laid flat on her head, not her usual spiky hairdo, and she had removed all the shit from her face with the exception of a pair of earrings. She looked like a normal goddamn human being for once and a beautiful one at that. It was a pleasant surprise.

"Are you boys ready to grub?" she asked, tossing her towel on the floor. "Let's go!"

We found the valet cart in the hallway and tossed our things on it. Snaggle pushed the rickety thing to the elevator, its wheel still broken. We took the elevator down to the first floor and found the lobby / dining area full of travelers. Where did all of these goddamn people come from? I assumed the crappy hotel was empty because I didn't hear a peep from anyone last night. Clearly, I was wrong.

I gave Snaggle the car keys so he could take our things to the car. Gina and I sat at the last empty table. The hungry travelers were swarming the all-you-can-eat buffet, piling their plates with everything they could get their grubby hands on: pancakes, waffles, eggs, bagels, donuts, bacon, muffins, everything. This buffet was a cheap bastard's wet dream and these cheap bastards were taking full advantage. Gina stood up and asked me if I wanted anything. I told her I wanted some coffee and watched her invade the throng of hungry travelers. Unlike everyone else, she didn't pile a mound of food on her plate. She came back with two pieces of wheat toast for herself and a cup of coffee for me. I wondered momentarily as she was setting the things on the table if she would ever be attracted to a pudgy, slightly balding guy like me. I felt a tiny smile stretch across my face and she noticed it, giving me a perplexed look.

"What?" she asked.

"Nothing," I said, prepping my coffee. I like my sugar with coffee and cream, as they say, my one sweet indulgence. It's true.

"You looked at me funny."

"I didn't mean to. Sorry."

Out of nowhere, Snaggle appeared with a stack of waffles a foot high and a bowl of syrup to pour over his mound of breakfast. His poor teeth were begging for mercy at that very moment. Those poor incisors and molars were in for a world of hurt. It's true.

"Waffles!" he chirped, shoving fork-fulls drenched with syrup into his mouth. It was fucking disgusting.

"Hey, slow down!" I said. "You're going to choke yourself." He replied with nothing more than a groan.

"So what's the plan, boys?" Gina asked. I sat back in my seat, looked at her, then looked at Snaggle. It hit me right then and there. I knew exactly what I wanted to do. It's funny how inspiration hits you like that, just out of nowhere, right out of thin air.

"Well, after all this talk about my grandparents, I think I want to go visit them in Oklahoma City," I said.

"What?!" Snaggle said, sitting up, food stuffed in his snaggly mouth. "You want us to go to visit your grandparents after all?"

"Well, I want to go visit them. And I can drop Gina off in Norman since it's on the way." Gina looked at me, shocked.

"But what about me?" Snaggle asked.

"I think you should go back to Austin."

"How am I going to do that?"

"I'll buy you a bus ticket."

Snaggle sulked while he slowly chewed his breakfast. He looked like a sad bastard, what, with his droopy face and full mouth and greasy nerd hair. He was a sight to see but I wasn't about to spend one day further with that disgusting jackass. I was determined to send him on his way.

"But what about our vacation?"

"It was never a vacation," I said, sipping coffee. "I think I need to go visit my grandparents, by myself."

After that, he didn't say another goddamn word to me. Not one single word. We finished up our breakfast and hopped in Clint the Caddy and still not a word from Snaggle. I drove up the highway a bit, found a bus station, bought Snaggle a ticket, and helped him get on the bus. Inside, he found a seat by the window and just looked at me and Gina like a stray dog, his face sad and weepy and shit. The bus roared to life and slowly pulled away and then he was gone. The snaggly bastard was on his way home. And I was on my way to Oklahoma with Gina.

19.

When I was a kid, I used to spend a couple of weeks every summer at my grandparents' house in Oklahoma. My mother, the kind soul that she was, probably needed a break from me (although she never *actually* said that to my snot-nosed face) and arranged a time with my grandparents when she could drive me up and leave me there with them. I always looked forward to this road trip to Oklahoma for a couple of reasons. 1) Stuckey's convenience stores. I already mentioned those shrines of craptastic awesomeness to you. And 2) Cooter's Big Burger Drive-In. Cooter's Big Burger Drive-In was this drive-in burger joint where you could park your car and order food and eat in your car. Now, anyone with half a brain would say to me, "What is so special about that? You can go to a Sonic anywhere, goofball." And I would reply, "You don't know what the fuck you're talking about, smarty pants." Cooter's Big Burger Drive-In was the real deal, not a corporate, fast food rip-off. Cooter's Big Burger Drive-In was outside of Ardmore, Oklahoma, a little shithole town that was frozen in time, a place right out of the 1950s that evolved untouched into the early 1980s. Cooter's had these humongous billboard signs with a cartoon of Cooter on it wearing a big ol' cowboy hat and he had this big ol' hamburger in one hand and a big ol' cigar in the other hand. I always thought that was kind of strange, him having food in one hand and a stinky cigar in the other. That didn't make much sense to me because it seemed to my little boyhood mind that those things didn't go well together but he had a big grin on his face like he was as happy as a clam getting ready to stuff his face with that big ol' burger and that was enough for me. It's true. Whenever I would see the billboard signs for Cooter's, usually about 10 or 15 miles before the exit, I would start screaming to my mom.

"Mom! Mom! Can we go to Cooter's Big Burger Drive-In? Please?! PLEASE!" I would say, like the little brat I was.

"OK," she would always say. My mother had an affinity for Cooter's Big Burger Drive-In because she went there when she was a teenager. And I loved it too. It was a bonding experience for the two of us, mom and son on a long car trip in the middle of nowhere. It's true.

So when the exit would come up, she would pull her car off the highway and we would drive in and find a place to park. There would be teenage girls rollerskating around in 50s outfits, poodle skirts, pink sweaters, and their hair pulled up in 50s hairdos. And there would be teenage boys in 50s greaser get-ups, their hair slicked back, jeans rolled up at the bottom, and tight t-shirts on with cigarette packs rolled up in their sleeves, standing around their cars, looking cool and cruising for chicks. It was a goddamn sight to see. It's true. And I loved every second of it.

We would park our car and roll down the windows and the 50s music would blast from the speaker under the menu signs in each parking space. The menu was a cornucopia of food that had the least amount of nutritional value whatsoever but was what a lot of people refer to as comfort food, which means every goddamn thing in sight was deep-fried and served with ketchup. I always ordered a cheeseburger with fries and a vanilla milkshake while my mom always ordered a bacon cheeseburger with onion rings and a chocolate malt. It was absolute heaven, even for Oklahoma. There's something about eating greasy, fried food in a car that makes children happy. Maybe it had to do with the fact that most times, eating in the car was frowned upon by my parents but for this one time, I was allowed to gobble down the greasiest, messiest, most delicious meal I'd ever had. It was a little on the magical side. It's true.

So as we got closer and closer to Ardmore, I related this story from my childhood to Gina, telling her every detail about the food I ate and the people I would see hanging out and working at Cooter's. She didn't seem all that impressed with my childhood memories but she nodded and smiled and went along when I asked her to keep an eye out for the billboard sign. She was being a real goddamn trooper and I appreciated that. I knew one thing for sure though. When we did see that sign for Cooter's Big Burger Drive-In, I was going to haul ass off the highway, find the first parking space, park Clint the Caddy, order my favorite meal, and I was going to face-fuck that hamburger. It's true.

"Ardmore isn't too far away," I said. "I'm sure we'll see the sign soon."

"I'm looking," she said.

"Are you going to get something to eat when we get there?"

"No, I don't think so."

"Why not?" I asked, startled. After all of my stories about how great Cooter's was, how could she NOT want to at least try the food? Weird girl.

"I'm a vegetarian."

"A vegetarian? How do you survive in the South by being a vegetarian?" That was a very honest question on my part. Everything, and I mean everything, in the South was prepared from something that used to moo or oink or cluck. That was just the way it was. It's true.

"It's very difficult," she said. "But I make do."

"You could order some fries or onion rings."

"Uh, but those are fried with the rest of the food with meat in it."

"Oh, right. Well, a milkshake doesn't have meat in it."

"A Cooter's milkshake probably has meat in it." We both laughed hysterically. There's one thing I could say about Gina, she had a sense of humor on her. She was sharp as a tack. You must be sharp as a tack to be able to hitchhike like she was, across Texas to Oklahoma, through towns that weren't particularly known for hospitality towards a college girl with weird hair and goth clothes and shit stuck in her face. I was really curious as to why she was hitchhiking in the first place. That was something she never mentioned to me or Snaggle. Well, maybe she told Snaggle while she was giving him a prostate exam in the highway rest stop but she never mentioned it to me. I was pretty goddamn curious at this point. It's true.

"So," I said. She turned and looked at me. "You never told me WHY you were hitchhiking to Norman."

"I didn't?" she asked.

"No, you didn't."

"I just thought it would be more interesting that way."

"More interesting?"

"I thought it would be more interesting than taking a bus or a plane. And safer. I have something with me that I didn't want to take on a bus or plane."

"Really? What do you have?" Now I was curious, really curious. What did she have with her that she didn't want to take on a bus or a plane? I was curious as hell. It's true.

"I can't tell you."

"Why not? You're in MY car, you know?"

"I know. I just can't tell you. OK?"

"OK." That was really fucking annoying. Who the fuck did she think I was? Her personal taxi driver? She was really starting to annoy the shit out of me with her snide comment and her mystery package and all. I was really starting to regret bringing her along now. What if she had drugs in her bag? Or a bomb?! I started to feel uneasy and a little disturbed. She was becoming a liability. It's true.

"Tell you what. I'll tell you once we get to Norman. OK? It really is no big deal. It's just personal. That's all."

"OK."

I was really starting to regret a lot of the choices I had made over the last few weeks, few months even. It didn't seem like I was making the right choices about anything really. Not one goddamn thing. In fact, I would have to say since my divorce, almost nothing had gone my way. It was a pretty sad goddamn state of affairs. It's true. I was becoming one of those sad bastards that I liked to make fun of. You know the type? Pretty much everyone I came in contact with, the whole lot of them, all sad bastards. And I didn't want to be like everyone else. I wanted to be a famous writer! But it seemed as more time went on, the more fucked up I was becoming. Who would bring their nerdy, testicle juggling coworker on a road trip with them to a funeral that was never going to happen? Who would pick up some strange hitchhiker in Waco and have her tag along to the house of their ex-wive's parents? It was sad to think that the answers to these types of questions always pointed to dumbass decisions on my part. It's true. It's fucking unbelievably true.

"Tell me about being a writer," she said, steering away from the topic of her secret stash.

"There is no greater profession than being a writer. It's my dream."

"But you had a book published, right?"

"Yes, but it didn't do very well. I want to write GREAT books. I want my name to be remembered alongside Hemingway, Steinbeck, Vonnegut, Bukowski, the greats. I want to be great."

"You will be one day," she said, looking out the window. "I can tell."

"It doesn't seem like it's going to happen any time soon. My life has been so hard lately. Why does life have to be so hard?"

"Life is just hard. That's the way it is."

"There has to be a better answer than that."

"I'm sure there is. But what do I know? I'm just a college kid. I don't know anything."

Right when she said that, I saw a sign on the side of the highway that said, "Ardmore. Next exit." I realized I hadn't seen the sign for Cooter's Big Burger Drive-In. I became frantic. Did we miss the sign while we were bullshitting? Did we pass it without seeing it? It was another unfortunate event in a long series of unfortunate events. It's true.

"I didn't see the sign. Did you?" I asked.

"No, we must have missed it."

"I'll exit at the next one. I remember Cooter's being around here somewhere."

When we got to the exit, I pulled off the highway and onto the access road but the only thing I could see was an outlet mall, a big, massive tan-colored building with department stores and shoe stores and luggage stores and shit like that. And the only restaurants around were corporate, chain restaurants like Applebee's and Red Lobster and Chili's. Cooter's Big Burger Drive-In was nowhere to be found. For all I knew, it had vanished under the urban sprawl like the other relics from my past. I decided right then and there that I was going to get to the bottom of this. I had to know if this great place still existed. It was an imperative. It's true.

"I'm going to ask someone if they know where it is," I said, turning Clint the Caddy into the outlet mall parking lot. "Someone here has to know. Cooter's is famous!"

The parking lot was a massive black eye in front of the outlet mall, the rows lined with thousands of minivans, pickup trucks, SUVs, and the like. Dozens of families streamed out in each row, pulling baby strollers from their vehicles, gathering their diaper bags and their purses and whatever other shit they felt was a necessity for their day walking around the outlet mall shopping for useless shit they didn't need. It was a goddamn sight to see, all the people walking like herds of zombies. Since the parking lot was practically full, I had to find a spot in the back as far from the mall as physically possible. We had a long trek ahead of us, a long torturous trek. It's true.

"Do you think you could park any farther?" Gina said, the sarcasm not lost on me. I smiled at her, annoyed.

We made our way to the mall. As we walked, I thought of asking some of the families if they knew where Cooter's Big Burger Drive-In was but most of the families we passed didn't seem like they were from Oklahoma since some spoke Spanish or some had Midwestern accents and some just looked plain old lost. I mean, there is just no point in asking tourists for directions. That's like asking a bum if you can borrow a quarter, absolutely worthless. It's true.

The outlet mall was like a modern-day fortress. The outside of it was completely walled in. The entrances for the stores were on the inside of the complex. All the people were corralled into a single entrance and then once you were on the path to the first section of stores, it was almost impossible to get out without passing the rest of the goddamn stores. The herds of zombies looked in the store-front windows, their eyes glazed over, their minds filled with fantasies of owning designer shoes at rock-bottom prices. It was an absolute goddamn nightmare. It's true. I turned to Gina, stunned.

"I don't know who to ask," I said.

"We should ask in there." She pointed to the Food Court. That seemed like a fine idea.

Inside, the Food Court was packed. All the tables were filled with more families, kids screaming and tossing their food on the floor, parents with their heads weighing heavy in their hands pretending their kids didn't exist, grandparents oblivious to the rest of the world. We found a burger place called McSkippy's, got in line, and waited for our turn at the counter.

"If anyone knows, they will," Gina said, giving me a supportive smile. I could only hope that what she said was true.

I watched all the families at their tables, stuffing their goddamn faces with crap, looking miserable. Man, what a bunch of fucking losers. I wondered why they would come here to spend their family time. It seemed to me that there were a lot better places to spend time with your children than in a Food Court at a goddamn outlet mall. Little kids don't care about Puma shoes and Gap jeans and Gucci purses and shit like that. Kids just want to play outside and get dirty. These poor little bastards had to suffer because their parents wanted better belongings than their neighbors had. It's true.

After 10 minutes or so we got to the front of the line. The teenage boy behind the counter looked happy to serve me, a big white smile stretching across his pimply face. He had a name tag on his shirt. It said, "Little Wing."

"Welcome to McSkippy's. What can I get for you?" he asked, his voice like a little bird's song.

"Your name is Little Wing?" I asked.

"Yessir."

"Do you know that Little Wing is the name of a Stevie Ray Vaughn song?" I asked, seeing if the little guy had any idea about the origin of his name. He shook his head.

"Actually, sir, Stevie Ray Vaughn's version is a cover of the original Jimi Hendrix version."

"I see. Well, I'm from Austin, Texas. I only know of the Stevie Ray Vaughn version. Are your parents hippies?"

"No, they are Chickasaw Indians."

"Oh."

Gina tapped me on the shoulder, pointing to a man that looked like he was a supervisor or a manager or an assistant manager or some shit like that. He was giving me and Little Wing the stink eye. I didn't want the little fellow to get in trouble. He seemed like a sweet kid and all. It's true.

"Would you like to order some food?" Little Wing asked.

"No, I'm actually looking for a place called Cooter's Big Burger Drive-In. Do you know where it is?"

"I'm sorry, sir. I've never heard of it."

"You've never heard of Cooter's Big Burger Drive-In? That's impossible."

"No sir."

At this point, the supervisor or manager or assistant manager or whatever he was walked over. I heard some grumbling and groaning coming from the line behind us. I could feel some tension in the air, the kind of tension that comes from keeping hungry, fat bastards from eating their beloved fast food crap. The manager had a name tag on his shirt. It said, "Skip." He didn't look very happy. He probably hated his job, what, with the shitty pay and long hours and no respect from teenage employees who would rather be anywhere but at work. He was probably suicidal too. It's true.

"Is there a problem, sir?"

"No, I was just asking Little Wing here if he knew of a place called Cooter's Big Burger Drive-In."

"Oh, Lord," Skip said, his head rolling back in an Oh-My-God fashion. The impatient fat bastards grew restless and being that Skip was probably concerned about burger sales and weekly sales targets and all kinds of corporate pressures to sell as much crap as possible, he kindly asked me to step aside and said he would come out from behind the counter to talk to me. He did and this is what he said. "I'm sorry to say that Cooter's Big Burger Drive-In is no longer around."

"No, no! What happened?"

"Well, I don't know for absolutely sure what happened but I can tell you what I know."

"OK."

"Well, Big Cooter passed away about 15 years ago and he left the drive-in to a slew of family members including Cooter Junior and a bevy of relatives, siblings, cousins, you name it. After trying to run that place the best they could, they eventually ran that place into the ground, sad to say, through a slew of bad business decisions and on account of Cooter Junior's horrendous cocaine habit."

"Oh no."

"Oh yes. The family fell into squabbling and in-fighting and after a few years, they sold the property to an outlet mall consortium and this fine establishment was built on the very ground where Cooter's Big Burger Drive-In thrived for so long. It has been both a good and bad turning for me personally."

"How so?" I asked.

"Well, I worked plenty of summers at Cooter's Big Burger Drive-In. Good times, good times. So I was really sad to see them tear down that place. But, I did get a job here at McSkippy's and eventually became a manager. So some good did come out of them selling the place and tearing it down."

"I see. So, you're not the Skip in McSkippy's?"

"No, that's just a weird coincidence."

"Thanks for your time," I said.

We walked out of McSkippy's, leaving behind Little Wing the Chickasaw boy who was named after a Jimi Hendrix song and Skip the unhappy manager / ex Cooter's Big Burger Drive-In employee and all the miserable, fat bastards waiting for their crappy, mushy hamburgers. We walked out into the throng of zombie shoppers, slumping along from store to store. All I wanted to do was to get on the highway and get away from that goddamn place but Gina said she had one place she wanted to run into really quick. It was probably some goth boutique or lingerie store or teenage teeny bopper clothing store or something so I decided to sit on a bench near the entrance and waited for her.

The hundreds of people walking by hypnotized me, their feet shuffling with a mannered, plodding cadence. I found myself in a contemplative mood and I thought about not only Cooter's Big Burger Drive-In but all of the other places from my youth that I loved so much: Tyrone's BGP Convenient Store, Dan's Watering Hole, Stuckey's, and now Cooter's. I realized that even though my fond memories of these places were very present in me that time wasn't so kind to them. Time had a way of bulldozing over the things you loved and that made me really sad. I was the saddest of all the sad bastards, sitting on a metal bench in a shithole town called Ardmore at a goddamn outlet mall that was placed over my favorite drive-in restaurant like a tombstone. I couldn't think of a worse place to be. It's true.

After 10 minutes or so, Gina came walking back to where I was waiting. She had a perplexed look on her face.

"What's wrong?" I asked.

"I went into that book store over there and asked them about your book. They said they'd never heard of it."

"That's weird," I said. "Let's go."

"Wait! So I asked them to look it up in their computer. I asked them to look up, *The Rise and Fall of a Titan*. They said there wasn't a book by that name in their system."

"That's very strange. Can we go now?"

We walked out the exit. Gina continued on.

"So, then I asked them to look up your name and they didn't find anything with your name either. Why is that?"

"I have no idea. Maybe different stores have different systems. Who knows?"

"Well, I thought that was strange. How could they not have any books by the *best-selling author*, Simon Burchwood?"

"We are in the middle of nowhere, you know?"

"Yes, that is true."

And that was it. Then we left.

20.

The drive to Norman was pretty quiet. We didn't talk much except for an occasional question or two from Gina about my book. You see, before we drove away from that goddamn outlet mall, I opened the trunk of the Cadillac and pulled out all the promotional crap I had for my book, the headshots, the pamphlets, sample chapters, all of the business cards, all of the bullshit I had been lugging around on this abysmal trip. That pile of crap made me look like a real goddamn professional, you know? It's true. Unfortunately, I didn't have an actual copy of the book. I had sold or given away all of the copies I had in my possession long ago but there was enough stuff there for her to read that kept her busy for most of the way to Norman. Thank God for that. I was getting kind of tired by that point of having meaningless conversations about this and that and why this and why that and blah blah blah. It was enough to give me a goddamn migraine headache. I did take a peek every once and a while at what she was reading. She really seemed to be into those sample chapters. She was engrossed in those pages, slumping in her seat, her feet up on the dashboard. What can I say? I wrote a real page-turner! It's true.

After reading all of the written stuff, she pulled out a headshot of me, a fine photograph taken by the world-renown French Canadian photographer Jacques Partee. When it was time for me to have a headshot made for the promotional material for my book, I initially had the bright idea of having my kids take a photograph of me. That wasn't the smartest idea in the goddamn world. The photos good ol' Sammie boy took were absolute crap. Bless his heart. He tried his best. But the best from a five year old is not much to write home about. He would yell out, "Shmoto! Shmoto!" as he ran around, snapping shots of me angrily trying to get him to stand still and follow my directions. After that fiasco, I decided to look in the classifieds for a professional photographer. I found an ad Jacques posted that claimed, "Un photographe de magnifiques!" I was sold. He sounded like a real goddamn professional the way he plopped in a little French into his ad. It's true. I contacted him and he came to my house the next day.

Jacques showed up at my house wearing a beret and a scarf, telling me this and that about how he was going to make me look like a star, asking if he could check out my backyard for natural light, etc. He had a midget assistant in tow, a little fellow named Francois. The two of them examined my backyard, tiptoeing around the dog poop left there to dry in the sun. They found a spot in the corner of my backyard and setup their equipment, erecting these contraptions for reflecting light that looked like white umbrellas with legs, hanging lights from the tree limbs above, laying down extension cords to power everything. The midget scurried around, performing the tasks Jacques barked at him in French, all the while Jacques was giving me directions in English as he went into great detail about how his family immigrated to Canada in the mid 1700s and created an extremely successful business trapping furry animals and selling their pelts for tons of money. It was a pretty bizarre afternoon and all. But, I will say this, that French Canadian bastard took some great photos. He was a goddamn professional. It's true.

"Why do you look so serious in these photos?" Gina asked, holding up one of the headshots for me to see.

"I wanted to look professional."

"You look kind of constipated in this one." She held up one that was my favorite. I thought I looked rather fantastic in that shot. She seemed to disagree. She was a real goddamn critic. It's true. "You should have smiled more. You have a nice smile when you do smile."

"I was following directions from my photographer. He thought I looked regal."

"Regal?" She started laughing and cackling all over the goddamn place. She was getting a real kick out of that on my expense. "Sorry. That just sounded a little funny."

"Ha ha. Very funny."

"Can I have one of your business cards?" she asked.

"Sure."

"This is your cell number here?"

"Yes."

"So I can keep in touch with you?"

"Of course. And you can check out my stuff on my web site. Become one of my patrons, if you want. Writers need patrons, you know?"

"I don't know about being a patron. I'm a poor college student. How about we just be friends?"

"I would like that."

She smiled and looked out the window. As we approached the exit for Norman, Oklahoma, she pointed to this gigantic building, a pink and teal gargantuan casino called The Riverwind Casino. It looked like a Vegas nightmare gone awry with a tall neon sign that jutted toward the sky, animated advertisements flashing and dancing and beckoning suckers, luring gamblers with promises of 10-times payouts and the opportunity to cash their paychecks right there. It was a redneck's nightmare and an Indian tribe's dream come true. I imagined all of the local white folks draining their savings in that hellhole while the Indian owners sat in the back, counting and sorting the White Man's hard earned cash, smoking cigars and drinking scotch. It was a funny goddamn thought. It's true.

"I worked there last summer," she said. "I was a cocktail waitress. I made pretty good money."

"Did you see anybody win a jackpot?"

"Sometimes. Mostly no. The customers sure were determined though. Sometimes, my customers would get so drunk that they would leave me their payout slips by accident. They'd give up hundreds of dollars while stumbling out to their cars or taxis. Sometimes, I would find them crying."

"Crying? Why?"

"Because they had just lost all of their savings."

"Oh."

"But I did meet this cool guy while I was working there. He was an Indian Shaman. He had a little business behind the casino where he would tell people their futures, their fortunes."

"How did you meet him?"

"He would come into the casino with a stack of business cards. He'd drink rum and cokes and walk around handing out his cards. He belonged to the tribe that owned the casino. They didn't mind him looking for business. He'd watch the old ladies put their money in the slot machines. If they were losing, then he'd tell them to go to his shop and see him and he'd tell them when they would win next."

"Was he right?"

"All I know is that I was telling him one time that I was hard up for some money. I went to see him at his shop and he told me that the next day, I would have some good luck then he blessed me. So before I went on my shift the next day, I put a $20 bill in a slot machine and I won $1,000! I couldn't believe it."

"Wow! That's crazy."

"It sure was."

I pulled Clint the Caddy off the highway and turned east to go to Norman. It was just a few minutes away. As we got into town, Gina pointed to some places where she liked to hang out near the university, a couple of punk rock bars, a thrift shop, a record store. It seemed like she lived a typical college life, going to school, hanging out with her friends, getting drunk at punk shows, barely making it. All in all, it was a pretty simple life compared to my goddamn life, one without kids and salaried jobs and divorce and bills and all the shit I had to deal with. To tell you the truth, I was a little envious of her simple life. She didn't see it that way but I sure as hell did. She couldn't see the forest for the trees or however that stupid saying goes. It's true.

She pointed to a side street where her apartment complex was and I turned and pulled into the parking lot. She told me to make lefts and rights and we found her building in the back, a dumpy two story building that probably could tell a lot of good stories if it could talk. I parked, got out, and helped her get her things out of the trunk.

"Well, Simon, thanks for the ride."

"You're welcome."

"I'd invite you up but my place is probably pretty messy. My boyfriend isn't very clean."

"Boyfriend?"

"Yes, boyfriend."

"You never mentioned you had a boyfriend."

"Does it really matter?" she asked, giving me an inquisitive look. She sure was beautiful for a goth girl that liked blasting her hair into a spiky mess and sticking jewelry all over her face. If I wasn't so old, then I might have asked her out on a date or something. If I wasn't slightly balding and kind of pudgy, then she might have actually found me somewhat attractive. If she didn't have a boyfriend, then she might have considered it, at *least* considered it. Boyfriends have a way of ruining things for single men like me. It's true. "Well?"

"Maybe."

"You're cute and sweet. Keep in touch. You never know what the future holds."

She hugged me tightly then placed her hand on my face. She pulled me towards her and kissed me on the cheek. Then she walked away. I watched her walk to her building and climb the stairs. When she got to the top, she waved at me. I waved back then yelled out to her.

"What's in your backpack?"

"What?!" she yelled.

"Your backpack? You never told me what was in your backpack. The personal thing? You said you'd tell me when we got here."

She stood there for a second, a smile stretching across her face. She waved again, turned around, went into her apartment, and closed the door behind her.

I got back into Clint the Caddy and drove away. I knew that mystery was going to bother me until the end of time. It was already starting to bother me. Women have a way of doing that to you, bothering you with their goddamn mysteries. Women are real mysterious creatures. It's true.

* * *

As much as I was looking forward to continuing this trip by myself, I have to admit Clint the Caddy was uncomfortably quiet. I guess I had gotten used to those two knuckleheads yapping it up and cackling and hemming and hawing all over the goddamn place, annoying the shit out of me with their incessant chatter and mindless banter. Sometimes as much as quiet solitude sounds like a peaceful place, the stillness can be maddening, even in a moving vehicle. I mean, I turned on the radio to try to quiet my restless thoughts but that didn't help. That only made things worse for me. So I decided right then and there that I would fight through the madness and just get to my grandparents' house. Norman wasn't too far from where they lived, 30 minutes at most. I tried to make the best of it. It's true.

Even though it had only been a few hours since I dropped Snaggle off at the bus station and left Gina at her apartment complex, I was starting to worry about them both. Would Snaggle make it home back to Austin OK or would he get raped in the bus restroom by a six foot four Mexican with a cobra tattoo on his left bicep and a Jesus tattoo on his right bicep? Would Gina get into a fight with her boyfriend because she caught a hitch in Waco, Texas with two strange men, one of which she gave a testicular cancer examination? I couldn't say one way or the other. All I knew was that I missed the goofy bastards. I missed them a lot. It's true.

Fortunately, I wasn't on the highway for more than 15 minutes when I got close to their part of town. It was closer than I remembered. Their neck of the woods had aged somewhat gracefully, giving way to corporate retail stores and chain restaurants like any other goddamn metropolis yet it was also apparent that some traditions had kept hold. You see, Oklahoma City was a military town and a capital city, therefore a lot of veterans lived there. And since they were from an era our country had endured that was much more intense than what my generation lived through, they were pretty adamant about keeping the status quo, which meant golf clubs and officers clubs and VFW clubs and whatever. They wanted us to know that they fought for something important and they wanted to be recognized for it. And they wanted to relax and chill out in their old age. It's true. I found the exit for their neighborhood and took it.

Once off the highway, I went a block or two or three and found the street that would take me to their house. I turned into their section of the neighborhood and brought Clint the Caddy to a crawl. I wanted to absorb the scenery. Most of the houses were built in the 60s and 70s and with the exception of an occasional satellite dish strapped to a chimney or a modern coat of paint, all of the houses looked like they had been frozen in time. It was a real sight to see. It's true. My childhood memories rushed into my mind and I had flashes of several summers gone by, memories of running around outside in this neighborhood, looking for other kids my age. The lawns were still manicured. The driveways filled now with SUVs and pickup trucks and Lincolns.

A turn here and a turn there and I found their home. I parked in the street out front and took it all in. I had finally arrived, all by myself. It had been years, several years too long, since I had seen my grandparents. In fact, I hadn't spoken to them in quite some time either. I was quite ashamed of that but it was my goddamn divorce's fault. I lay blame where blame is deserved. Divorce has a way of doing that to you, throwing you into a hole of despair, covering you, smothering you from the rest of the world, separating you from your loved ones. It took a long time for me to dig out of that hole. That fucker was pretty deep. It's true.

I turned off the engine, got out of the car, and walked across the crunchy Bermuda grass to the front door. I pressed the door bell. As I remembered, the door bell rang a few bars of the song Dixie Land. A smile stretched across my face and for a brief moment, I felt like I was 12 years old again. My grandparents always expected me when I was coming for my visits and they would wait for me in the den by the front door, usually with a bowl of candy or a plate of brownies or some sweet treat to greet me with. I held onto a small bit of hope that they would be waiting there for me with some sweet treats nearby. The door slowly opened and a little, old woman peeked out from behind the door. She had a kind, gentle face but it wasn't my grandmother's kind, gentle face. I didn't know who the fuck this old woman was opening my grandparents' door.

"Can I help you?" she asked. She looked at me like I was a vacuum salesman or the UPS man or some shit like that. It's true.

"Uh..." I said. I was speechless. I was caught off-guard by this strange, little old lady. I thought for a quick second that maybe I was at the wrong house. I stepped back and found the street number by the door. It was the correct number. "I'm looking for my grandparents. I know it's been a long time but I'm pretty certain this is their house."

"Well," she said, opening the door some more. "Are you looking for the Paulsons?"

"Yes, I am." Paulson was my mother's maiden name, you dummies. She took the great name Burchwood when she married my dad. She was a Paulson until she was 25 years old, 25 years too long. It's true. "The Paulsons are my grandparents."

She opened the door and invited me in. I immediately noticed that the house didn't smell like I remembered it. Like I said, my grandmother usually had something delicious in the oven. The house now smelled like mothballs, urine, and that sour old-people smell. It was absolutely disgusting. It's true. It took a lot of courage for me not to pinch my nose in disgust in front of this old lady. I had a hard time breathing without wanting to vomit. That was really tough. She guided me to a sofa in the den next to a coffee table with a bowl of hard candy on it. The candy was covered with dust. She sat in a chair across from me.

"I'm surprised you don't know this but your grandparents moved to the nursing home down near the military base."

"What?!" I asked. Nursing home? Near the military base? Did I just step into The Twilight Zone? What the fuck?! "When?"

"Oh, let me see. My grandchildren bought me this house about a year ago so I guess they moved there... about a year ago."

"Why?"

"I'm sorry dear. I do not know. But I remember them telling me at the closing that they were getting old and rundown and they didn't have anyone to take care of them. They just had themselves. But they needed help. So they sold this house and moved to the nursing home together."

"Where is the nursing home again?"

"Here, dear. Let me write it down for you." She slowly got up and hobbled to the kitchen. While she was gone, I had the pleasure of inhaling the house stench, trying my hardest to keep the bile down. It was horrendous, absolutely disgusting. She came back with a piece of paper in her shaky hand. "Here you go. I wrote down the address for you."

"Thank you," I said, standing up.

"Would you like some hard candy?" she asked, lifting the dusty candy bowl.

"Oh, no thank you. I really have to go."

"Well, I'm glad you stopped by. You know, I rarely get any visits from anyone anymore. My grandchildren bought me this house but they never come to see me. They are too busy with their own lives to worry about their old grandmother. It's a real shame, you know?"

"Yes, I know."

"Are you sure you don't want a cup of coffee or some tea? I can make some hot tea for you."

"I appreciate that but I have to go see my grandparents. I came all the way from Austin and I don't have much time."

"Well, that's very sweet of you. I'm sure they will be glad to see you."

She walked me to the door. I opened it and the fresh, clean air came in. I walked to my car as I heard her say something about coming to visit again but I knew I would never be visiting that house again. Never.

Like I said, my divorce put me in a hole so deep that I didn't even know how deep I was in it. So deep, apparently, that life had passed me by. I felt like a real asshole. How this ever could have happened without me knowing was a real goddamn shame. I was a really shameful, goddamn, worthless bastard grandson. It's true.

21.

One of my favorite memories involving my grandfather (in addition to sitting with him and his buddies listening to their advice about life) was playing golf with him during my summer visits to Oklahoma. Now here's the thing: Golf, to me, is one of the most goddamn boring sports I have ever played in my ENTIRE life. But, when I was a kid, playing golf with my grandfather meant spending time with my grandfather and I enjoyed spending time with him. My grandfather had this sweet, affable demeanor that was impervious to the hyperactive, annoying, and often detestable nature of a young child around the age of 10 or 11. I mean, I love kids, don't get me wrong but kids can also be annoying little fuckers and I was no different. I was a hyperactive kid with boundless energy and a propensity to get bored quite easily but that didn't faze my grandfather one bit. He always had shit to do, errands or card games or bowling games or golf games or chores and he always invited me along with him. I liked that. In contrast, my father was a workaholic and had quite a few hobbies to take up his time when he wasn't working and there wasn't a place for me plus I didn't care much to join in helping with the hobbies he enjoyed. I liked playing games and my grandfather did too, even if it was goddamn golf.

I remember during one visit that my grandfather asked me if I wanted to learn how to play golf. I didn't know just how boring golf was at age 10 but the invitation was enough for me. My grandfather had an old women's set that had rather short clubs and he sized me up to them and they seemed to fit my arms' length quite nicely so he called the golf course and reserved a spot for us. We hopped in his little old Ford pickup truck, throwing our clubs and a cooler of beer and sodas in the back, and we drove across town. On the way, I would always take these cassette tapes that I had, cassettes of God-awful music from the 80s, and he didn't mind that I took control of the pickup truck stereo and played this music while we rode to the golf course. He always got a kick out of the goddamn crap I played and would tell me how funny the music sounded to him. "You call that music?" he would say, laughing. I mean, how would Quiet Riot or Michael Jackson or Van Halen or Journey or any of the other crap I played sound to a man in his early 70s who had survived the Great Depression and World War II? It sounded like shit to him but he let me play it anyway. He was sweet that way. We would haul ass in his little truck, my crappy music playing, the windows rolled down, the hot Oklahoma wind blowing through the pickup cab, all the way to the course.

When we got there, he gloated to all of the other retired officers about how I was his grandson and that he was going to teach me to be the next fucking Jack Nicklaus. They would all laugh and toast and drink beer together while I chugged root beer and putzed around the club house, looking at golf gear and shit. When he was finished with his buddies, the two of us hopped into a golf cart and zoom around the course. He always let me drive and got a kick out of watching me destroy that golf cart. When we reached the tee box, he showed me how to swing and let me go at it until I hit a decent shot, all the while giving me mulligan after mulligan, never letting my shanked shots get me down. When it was his turn, there was always a loud crack and the ball would sail WAY past my ball. We'd hop in the cart and zoom after them, a beer in his hand, a big smile on my face.

Later that that week, after quite a few shanked balls and quite a few beers and sodas, we pulled up to a hole with a rather short fairway to the green with an insanely low par like 2 or 3 or some shit like that. He leaned over to me and said, "Now, Simon, you got a pretty good swing on you now and that fairway is pretty short. I imagine you can hit that sucker right on the green, yessir. You can do it," he said to me. He smiled and patted me on the back and gave me a little shove. I sized up that ball, extending my arms the way he taught me, gripping the club just like he showed me, and I gave him a glance. He nodded and that was all he had to do. I knew, deep in my little heart, that if he said I could do then I could do it. So I stared that ball down, lifted my club, and swung hard, missing the ball badly. He told me not to worry about it and to try again. He placed a new golf ball on the tee and smiled at me. So I setup again. I imagined hitting the ball on the green in my mind. I closed my eyes and swung hard. I heard the ball crack and watched it sail through the air, high above, shooting to the clouds. When it came down, it landed about two feet behind the hole. I jumped and cheered for joy, dancing a little jig in the tee box. But then he patted my shoulder and pointed to the green, stunned. The ball started to roll backwards toward the hole. It inched and inched its way down the incline and plopped into that unsuspecting hole. With a mulligan to aid me, I had scored a hole-in-one. I was elated. My grandfather beamed at me. He was rather proud of his good ol' grandson. It's true.

The funny thing was, he wasn't really my grandfather. He was my step-grandfather. My grandmother had remarried after her first husband, my natural grandfather, died of a heart attack at a young age. But for all intensive purposes, he was MY grandfather. I didn't know any different. He was good to me and I knew it. I loved him with all of my heart.

My grandmother was a pretty unique person in her own right. She was an independent sort that probably didn't fit well into the mold of the 1940s and 50s and 60s, doing what she damned-well pleased and not caring what others thought of her one bit. I remember vividly that she liked to cuss and drink and smoke in front of me because that was what she liked to do in front of anybody, whether young or old, friend or stranger. That was her thing. When I would visit, she threw these parties for her friends and they would all come over and smoke and drink and cuss and play cards, hooting and hollering all over the goddamn place like a bunch of senior party animals. It was a stark contrast to my parents who didn't do any of that, no smoking, no drinking, no partying, no card playing. She was a very social creature and my grandfather appeased her. He was a social creature too although he didn't smoke. His first wife had died from cancer from smoking but he didn't seem to mind that my grandmother smoked, at least I never heard him say anything about it. He was cool like that. It's true.

When I would visit, my grandmother made a point of setting me up with girls that were the granddaughters of her friends, girls that were too young to date no matter how you looked at it, and so was I. She would always tell me, "My friend so and so has a beautiful granddaughter. She would be good for you," she would say to me. I remembered my ten-year-old mind being puzzled by that. "Good for what?" I would think to myself. "Good for a game of Battleship?" This particular summer, the hole-in-one summer, she told me that she had arranged a goddamn movie date with me and a girl named Samantha. Samantha was a ten-year-old girl who was the granddaughter of a neighbor down the street. She was blond and supposedly cute, whatever that meant. The only thing ten-year-old boys thought were cute were small cups of bubble gum ice cream from Baskin Robbins Ice Cream shops. Girls were yucky. It's true.

My grandmother would tell me to get gussied up, which meant putting on shorts, a t-shirt, and Reebok tennis shoes. She drove me to the theater in her big ass white Oldsmobile with a big ass back seat like a couch. She pulled up to the movie theater and there little ol' Samantha was, looking something like a young Jodie Foster, in her shorts, t-shirt, and Keds tennis shoes, standing next to her grandmother. After an awkward introduction to her grandmother, the two grandmas bought us tickets and shoved cash in our hands, pushing us into the theater, then probably off to bowl a few games or drink scotch or whatever it was grandmothers did while their grandchildren were on a "date." I didn't know Samantha from shit but we were both kids with wads of cash in our pockets in a movie theater by ourselves. We bought all of the junk food we could hold, large popcorns, candies, sodas, whatever, and found seats in the back of the theater. It was a strange thing being unaccompanied by adults but we managed, shoving food in our little faces while watching the previews. We both had ants in our pants so sitting for too long wasn't an option. We ran around the theater like wild animals, playing Asteroids in the lobby, running in and out of the other movie theaters without a care in the world. It wasn't a date. It was an excuse to act like little brats and we did it like pros.

When our grandmothers finally showed up, they were drunk, three sheets to the wind, scotch in their tanks, laughter in their hearts. They asked us how our date went. Samantha and I looked at each other and giggled. If a date meant acting like heathens on a sugar high, playing all of the video games, and not watching a bit of the movie, then I guess you could say we had a great date. But if what they really meant was if we kissed and made plans to get married when we were 18, then they were WAY off. Nothing could have been farther from the truth. It's true.

Those were good times. Good times. The best. Now, the thought of my grandparents selling their house and moving to a nursing home just killed me. Absolutely slayed my heart and soul. It's true. They were a fun couple, no doubt. I wasn't sure what to expect at the nursing home but I prepared myself for the worst. How good could living in a nursing home be good? Not good, I tell you. Sounds like a bunch of shit to me. I couldn't imagine they would be drinking and partying and playing cards like I remembered them doing when I was a kid. I couldn't imagine at all what they would be doing. What the hell were they thinking?

***

The nursing home was worse than I expected. When I walked in, the smell of stale urine and misery and lingering death and heartache and loneliness was in the air. It was a miserable smell. Mostly, I could sense the sadness of dying alone. Old folks were usually put in these places because they became too much for their families to bear or they had absolutely no place else to go with no one to help them. It was a sad state of affairs. It's true. My grandparents, on the other hand, moved here of their own *free will*, at least that's what the old lady living in my grandparents' home had me believe. It was absolutely hard to believe that anyone would move here of their own free will. Something serious must have gone wrong. Why didn't anyone tell me? It was a goddamn mess. It's true.

At the reception desk sat a chubby, middle-aged woman wearing pink scrubs, reading a gossip magazine, looking bored to death. Rolls of body fat were giving the cotton fibers of her outfit a run for their money. I could sense that she hated her job. Her evenings were probably filled with drunken binges and packs of cigarettes inhaled into her lungs, the only way she could cope with a job that constantly had death waiting in the next room. She was just as sad and miserable as the place she worked. It's true. She had a name tag on her pink blouse. It read, "Myrtle." I decided to give Myrtle something to do.

"Can you tell me where the Paulsons' room is, please?" I asked. It seemed at that moment I was disturbing her. She abruptly dropped her magazine and started typing something into her computer. She was pissed, I could tell.

"They are in room 325. Third floor, out the elevator, to the right," she said, picking up her magazine, drifting back into oblivion.

"Thanks."

"Mmm hmm."

"Can you tell me where the elevator is?" She pointed behind her, not looking at me. What a bitch! Hospitality was not in her job description. It's true. "Thanks."

Behind the desk was a sign with an arrow and the word "Elevator" on it, pointing toward a hallway to the right. I followed its direction. The hallway seemed like a mile long, stretching the full length of the building, no doubt. I could see the elevator way at the other end of the hallway, the long walkway lined with elderly folks slumped in their rickety wheel chairs, babbling to themselves, slobbering about this or that or something unintelligible. As I walked down the hallway, they noticed me as I walked by, extending their hands to touch me, calling me Jack or Phil or Steven or some shit like that, hoping or imagining I was their son or grandson or nephew coming to get them out of this shithole. It was a goddamn shame. It's true. A little part of me felt sorry for them and wanted to extend my hand back but I knew deep down that would be cruel. I wasn't who they thought or hoped I was and I had my own grandparents to see so I kept on.

Halfway down the hall was an old lady slumped over in her wheelchair facing the wall, her torso laying flat on the top of her skinny legs, her head hanging over her knees like it was about to pop off, mumbling something. She looked extremely uncomfortable. Who in their right mind would sit like that? Right then and there I decided to ask her if she needed help or at least to be turned away from the wall. I knelt down next to her, placing my hand on her shoulder, and I whispered to her.

"Do you want me to turn your wheel chair around?"

My touch must have startled her because she started yelling, cussing and screaming all over the goddamn place, cursing the goddamn floor. She surprised the shit out of me, enough to make me jump back and question why I did that in the first place. I decided to leave her be. It was for the best. It's true.

I hurried to the end of the hall and got in the elevator. I pushed the number three button and the doors closed, sealing off the stench of the hallway. The elevator smelled of bleach and Lysol, the floor stained with splotches of red and brown. I didn't know what was worse, the stench of the hallway or the stench of disinfectant. Both were pretty goddamn tough to take.

When the elevator dinged at the third floor, I got out and immediately looked for room 325. Room 325. Room 325. Why did that sound so familiar? I found room 325 halfway down the hall. I slowly peeked in and found my grandfather sitting in a twin hospital bed, propped up, watching golf on a TV mounted to the wall on the other side of the room. He had a big goddamn smile on his face, the kind of smile I remembered he had when we went golfing together when I was a kid. He looked as happy as a goddamn clam. It's true. The window curtains were open, the sunlight pouring in. The room was sparsely furnished with a few family photos and a chair in the corner. Another twin bed sat next to his, the sheets and blanket tightly tucked in, and it looked unused. A photo of my grandmother sat on a table between the two beds. I thought for one quick moment to walk away and leave him be. He did look pretty happy sitting there watching golf on TV but I wanted to see him. So I went in.

"Hi grandpa," I said. He looked at me with a surprise looked. He was genuinely surprised to see me. It's true.

"Well, I'll be. If it isn't good ol' Simon. Simon Burchwood. What are you doing here, my boy?"

"I came to see you and grandma."

"Well, I'm glad you did. It's been a long time. Your grandmother will be pleased to see you."

"Where is grandma?"

"Oh... she's off getting her sponge bath. She really loves her sponge bath. It's the high point of her day, she tells me. She loves her sponge bath like a duck loves floating in a pond." That made me chuckle. Good ol' grandpa. He always had these little sayings, comparing people to happy animals and shit like that. He got a real kick out of saying those little sayings. He was really inventive too. It's true. "I imagine she'll be back shortly."

I found a stool sitting next to some monitoring equipment and pulled it next to his bed. I sat down and patted him on the leg. His leg was as skinny as could be. It was like patting a bare bone.

"I was pretty surprised to learn that you two were here. Why did you sell your house and move here?"

"Well, my boy, your grandparents are old if you didn't know. It was getting pretty hard to take care of ourselves with our arthritis and our bad hips and our shakes and whatnot. Getting old is a tough business."

"But why move here? It seems so depressing?"

"Depressing? Ha! They do everything here for us, bring us food, wipe my ass, change our clothes. It's fantastic!"

"I see."

"We needed some taking care of. We didn't want to burden nobody. We just want to be taken care of and die with some dignity."

"Die with dignity?"

"Simon, my boy, everyone dies. That's just the way it is. You should know that." Well, of course I knew that. Everyone knows that. It's just a hard thing to admit to yourself when someone you love says a goddamn thing like that. That's a pretty miserable thought. It's true.

"Grandpa, can I ask you a question?"

"Of course, my boy. Shoot."

"Why does life have to be so hard?"

"Hard? Life isn't hard. Life is a piece of cake. That's it."

"I don't understand."

"Everybody has ups and downs. There's always bumps in the road. But the road keeps going until the end and when you look back, none of those bumps matter. They're just bumps."

"I see." I did kind of get what he was saying but I guess it's hard to see the philosophy in it when I had huge bumps in my road. I had bumps the size of goddamn mountains. It's true.

"Boy, all I can tell you is to enjoy the things you do, enjoy time with people you love, don't spend any time doing things that make you unhappy, because that's all there is. You can sit there and make yourself unhappy. But there is no point in doing that."

"Thanks grandpa."

"And remember what I told you. Brush your teeth. That's the best advice I can give you. The food here is God-awful but at least I can chew it all by myself. There's nothing worse than not being able to chew your own food."

He turned his head to the TV and watched the golf tournament. The smile returned to his face, that big happy smile. He seemed content, even living in this goddamn place. It's true.

"I think I'll go check on grandma."

"You do that, boy. I'm going to watch this Tiger Woods choke. He's playing like a dog turd on a sidewalk. Worthless"

"OK, grandpa."

I walked out of the room to look for a nurse or someone to tell me where my grandma was. At the other end of the hallway was a desk with a different chubby nurse sitting behind it. She was also reading a goddamn gossip magazine, her feet propped up on the end of the desk, sitting there without a care in the world. She also had a name tag on her pink blouse. It said, "Bertha."

"Can I help you?" she asked, annoyed. Why was everyone in this place annoyed? It was starting to get on my nerves.

"Hi. I'm looking for my grandmother. My grandfather said she's getting a sponge bath."

"Sponge baths. My *favorite* part of my day," she said, sarcastically. "What is her name?"

"Her name is Mrs. Paulson."

"Did you say Mrs. Paulson?"

"Yes, ma'am."

"Mrs. Paulson ain't taking no sponge bath unless dead people get sponge baths around here."

"Excuse me?"

"Mrs. Paulson died a few weeks ago. She's buried at the military cemetery. Didn't you know that?"

"No, I didn't know that." I didn't know whether to cry or punch Bertha in the fucking face. She had just dropped some information on me that I wasn't prepared to hear. In fact, I was in absolute shock. This trip was turning out to be one big goddamn nightmare. It's true. "How did she die?"

"In her sleep, I think. I don't know for sure. You want me to find out for you?"

"Uh, no thank you."

"I can find out for you, if you want."

I just walked away. I didn't want her to find out anything for me. In fact, I wanted Bertha to take a big flying leap off of a tall building for all I cared. I walked back to my grandfather's room and looked in. He was still happy, a big smile stretched across his face, his thumbs twiddling, his hopes of Tiger Woods choking evident as he watched. I decided right then and there that I needed some time to myself so I left. I walked down the hallway toward the elevator, Big Bertha calling to me about finding out stuff. I ignored her and got in the elevator and went down to the first floor.

I walked past all the old people slumping in their wheel chairs. I walked past Myrtle and her goddamn gossip magazine. I walked out the front door and found Clint the Caddy sitting in the parking lot. I got in and covered my face with my hands. Tears poured from my eyes, snot poured from my nose, and I sat there alone and cried like a baby. I cried and cried and cried like a goddamn baby. I cried for what must have been 30 minutes. It was the hardest cry of my entire life. It's true.

Piece of cake, my ass.

Then I drove away.

22.

Death. What a pile of shit. I mean, no matter what you do with your life you're going to just end up in the ground or cremated or stuck in a mausoleum or some shit like that. I guess that's why I've always wanted to be a writer because at least a writer's work can live forever. It's true. Look at Plato or Shakespeare or Dante or Twain. Those bastards lived a long time ago yet their work still influences people today. Even recently deceased writers like Hemingway and Miller and Bukowski and Vonnegut are influencing people as we speak even though those dead bastards are pushing up daisies, as Johnny Cash would say. See, singers too are immortal although I can't sing for shit. I'll stick with writing, thank you very much.

Anyway, I thought about what my grandfather said and it did make sense to me. I should be enjoying life and not making myself miserable because of it. I should be writing and spending time with my kids. I should get in contact with good ol' Jason and spend time with that messy bastard although he's probably divorced by now. At least we could be miserable divorcees together, right? And Snaggle. That goddamn nut juggler can be so annoying but he did seem to have some good qualities too. Maybe we could be friends when I got back to Austin. Maybe. And Gina. I was really starting to miss Gina. In our short time together, that punk rock goth girl with shit stuck in her face and hair exploding toward the sky turned out to be a beautiful, thoughtful, young woman. Who knew when we saw her at the convenience store in Waco, tempting fate by hitchhiking, that she would turn out like that? I had no idea. It's true.

I toyed with the idea of visiting the military cemetery and seeing where my grandmother was buried but I quickly decided against that. I was going to take my grandfather's advice seriously and only do the things that made me happy. Sitting in some dirty old military cemetery staring at my grandmother's tombstone lined up next to thousands of other dead soldiers and their dead spouses didn't sound like something that would make me very happy. So that idea was out the window! No more unhappiness for me. I was going to enjoy the things I did, enjoy time with the people I loved, and not spend any time doing things that made me unhappy. My new mantra. It's true. So basically that meant getting the hell out of Oklahoma and getting back to Austin, Texas, my home, the place that made me happy. That was going to be a LONG drive. For a brief moment, I thought it sure would be nice if I could use a transporter like in the sci-fi TV show Star Trek, what, so I could be zapped instantaneously back to Austin without having to drive for seven goddamn hours. Now THAT would have been nice, zipping across Texas as particles like Captain Kirk and Spock getting zipped down to some strange planet instantaneously. It's true. But there was no such thing as a transporter. All I had was Clint the Caddy and I had to make due. Clint was a pretty nice ride though, even though he wasn't a transporter. It wouldn't be THAT bad.

It was getting late and I didn't want to drive all that way back to Austin in the dark so I decided right then and there that I would stay one more night. One more night in Craplahoma? Sheesh. Why did it have to be so goddamn late? I would stay one more night, get a good night's rest, get up, have a massive southern breakfast with eggs and biscuits and bacon and pancakes and coffee, then drive home to find my children. That sounded like a goddamn splendid idea. It's true.

As I drove down I-35, the only places to stay the night were these cheap ass motels, places that looked like they were infested with bed bugs and fleas and ticks and lice, rooms that probably smelled like cheap sex and body odor and cigarettes and bleach, and only coffee served for breakfast with no food in sight. The last thing I wanted to do was to stay in some miserable motel on the last night in Craplahoma. It sounded like a goddamn nightmare to me. But after only a few minutes on the highway, something appeared on the horizon, a place that beaconed in the darkening sky, beams of light shooting towards the moon, a neon glow filling the air: The Riverwind Casino. It appeared like an oasis in the middle of some goddamn desert and it called to me like a pool of cold water calls to a dehydrated traveler. And boy, was I feeling emotionally dehydrated. I was pretty sure the casino had a hotel, not a motel, but a fancy hotel next to it or near it or behind it. I was absolutely sure of it. It's true.

***

I pulled Clint the Caddy off the highway and turned toward The Riverwind Casino and wouldn't you know it? There was a massive hotel right next to that massive goddamn casino. Those Indians must really be sticking it to the white man with their fancy casino and fancy hotel and fancy tax breaks and fancy amnesty from goddamn everything else us poor bastards have to endure from our government. Those goddamn Indians really had it made. It's true. The rest of us poor bastards had to pay income tax and sales tax and abide by laws and shit like that. What a rub. I once heard my grandmother tell me that I had some Cherokee Indian in me. She claimed that my great grandmother was half Cherokee so that would make me... hmm, let's see. That would make me 1/32 Cherokee Indian. Do you think they would let me join their Indian gambling racket and stick it to the man? I didn't think so either. Fuck.

I drove past The Riverwind Casino and pulled into the parking lot for The Riverwind Hotel. It was a fancy goddamn place and rose into the sky five or six stories and was the same friggin' pastel colors that the casino was painted. It was the casino's goddamn ugly twin. It's true. The parking lot was full and there were all kinds of drunk gamblers stumbling around this way and that, some looking happy and some looking stripped of their pride. I bet they lost all of their savings. I bet they were scalped by those sneaky Indians. It's true.

I parked Clint in the check-in lane at the front of the hotel and went inside. The hotel's lobby was massive, lined with marble on the floor and walls, sparkly chandeliers hanging from the ceiling, goddamn slot machines everywhere the eye could see. It was like I was already in the casino. I could hear the sound of coins dropping into imaginary metal catchers, clink clink clink! And cigarette smoke was everywhere. It hung in the air like a nicotine fog. It was enough to get you high from contact alone. It's true.

The reservation desk was empty except for a few clerks standing behind it. They all looked somewhat Indian except for this one kid who looked like he was straight out of a western movie. He had long, straight black hair pulled back in a twisted braid and the striking, angular features of a Native American and some beaded bracelets on his wrists and some turquoise and silver rings on his fingers, quite a few of them. I was expecting his name tag to say Sitting Bull or Screeching Hawk or Fighting something or another but it said, "Phil." Stereotypes are such bullshit but everyone is guilty of them every once and a while. I was guilty. It's true. I approached Phil.

"Good evening, sir. Are you staying with us this evening?" Phil asked. He had the whitest teeth of anybody I had ever seen. It was amazing. They sparkled like goddamn pearls.

"Yes. I don't have a reservation though. Do you have any rooms available?"

"You are lucky this evening. We do have a room available. Would you like it?"

"Yes, I would. How many beds does it have?"

"How many guests do you have?" he asked. He sure was being kind of snoopy. What did he care how many guests I had? Why was everyone in the goddamn State of Craplahoma asking me how many guests I had?! I tried to remain calm.

"Just me."

"The room we have available has a single king-sized bed. Will that be OK?" he asked.

"Sure." I wondered if Phil knew Little Foot or Little Wing or whatever the fuck his name was, the kid that worked at the burger joint at the outlet mall. Little something or other was a Chickasaw Indian and this casino was owned by the Chickasaw Nation and it only made sense that good ol' Phil here was probably a Chickasaw Indian too. I just had to ask. "Can I ask you a question?"

"Sure."

"Do you know a kid named Little... What was his name? Little Wing! Do you know a kid named Little Wing?"

"I don't think so," he said, typing some things into his computer.

"Are you sure? He's a Chickasaw Indian too, like you."

"Well, sir. Where are you from?"

"I'm from Austin, Texas."

"OK, sir. Then that would be like me asking if you knew a guy named Steve in Austin."

"I see."

"The Chickasaw Nation is quite large."

"OK." Well, the bastard didn't have to be SO rude about it. I mean, I was just curious that's all. The Chickasaw Indians must not have a goddamn sense of humor. It's true. Little Wing didn't have a sense of humor either, the little bastard. Sheesh. "I'm sorry. I was just curious."

"Can I see your ID?" I showed him my driver's license and he continued to type at his computer, unfazed by my question or anything else. He must have had his job down pat. He was typing up a storm. "OK, Mr. Simon Burchwood. We take credit cards or cash. How will you be paying?" I slid him my credit card and paid for my room and he finished typing whatever he was typing and he slid me my room key. Then he gave me a strange look. "Your name sounds really familiar? I know your name from somewhere," he said.

BINGO! He must have read my book or read a review about my book or maybe read an interview with me on a book blogger's web site or in the local newspaper or something like that. It had been a while since someone had asked me about my goddamn book. There were times that I really thought that book was a goddamn disastrous failure but maybe I did have some fans somewhere, even as far away as the Chickasaw Nation all the way in Craplahoma. Crazy! I had some butterflies in my stomach, I was that excited. It was a fantastic feeling, for once.

"Well, maybe you've read my book. It's called *THE RISE AND FALL OF A TITAN.*"

"No, I don't think that's it. I don't read books."

"You don't read ANY books?"

"No, books are boring. I thought maybe you were a radio personality or a news anchorman. Maybe not. Your name still sounds familiar."

"No, sorry."

"Well, Mr. Burchwood. Have a fantastic stay at our hotel and good luck! As a token of our appreciation, here's a player's card with $10 of credits, redeemable at the casino or here in our lobby."

"OK. Thanks."

Books are boring? What the fuck was this world coming to? It was a goddamn nightmare, I tell you. It's true. I had briefly considered a career in radio or television but I realized pretty quick back then that I had a terrible speaking voice. My speaking voice is the absolute worst. It's all scratchy and pitchy and not very manly. I knew I should stick with writing, even if nobody in the world seemed to read anymore. Being a writer was a goddamn dying breed. It's true.

***

After I gave the valet my keys to Clint the Caddy, I walked back in through the lobby and the maze of slot machines. There were all types of white folks sitting there, sliding their slot machine credits away, some of them playing two or three machines at one time. It was a crazy sight to see. The amount of money going down the gambling toilet was staggering. Those Indians really had it figured out, the lucky bastards. It's true.

I found my way out of the money pit and stepped into an elevator at the other side of the lobby. My room number was 325. What was up with that number? It was following me everywhere in the last week. Strange, very strange indeed. I went up to the third floor and looked for my room. I found it halfway down the hall.

Inside, my room was as sparse as could be. I guess the Indians spent all of their money on the casino and went cheap with the rooms. Cheap bastards! I was expecting some grand affair but it wasn't any fancier than the motel room I got with Snaggle and Gina. Gina. Oh, Gina. I couldn't stop thinking about Gina. I wondered what she was doing at that moment. Was she with her boyfriend? Was she unpacking the backpack with the mysterious contents? Was she thinking about me? I doubted she was thinking about me. Who would think about me? Nobody, I tell you. Nobody. I unpacked my bag and made myself at home.

I sat on the bed and turned on the TV. It was one of those old crappy tube TVs, not a new fancy shmancy flat-panel TV like you would expect in such a fancy shmancy hotel. I flipped through the channels and found a station that explained how to play the various games in the casino, Black Jack, Poker, 21, Roulette, Craps, even how to play the slot machines, if you can believe that crap. Who needs instructions on how to play the slot machines? You'd have to be a pretty dumb bastard to NOT know how to play those retarded machines. All you do is push the button and lose all of your money. It's that easy. It's true.

As I was unpacking my things, pulling my clothes and toiletries out, I noticed my cell phone indicator light flashing. I must have missed some calls or received a text and didn't know it. Maybe Jessica was texting me to ask why I was in Dallas at her fucking parents' house. Or maybe it was my kiddos sneaking their mother's cell phone into their room to send me a text message. Good ol' Sammie boy does that every once in a while, that cutie pie. He's a sneaky little bastard sometimes. It's true. But when I went through the call log and the text messages, most of them from creditors or telemarketers or other people wanting money from me, I saw a number with an Oklahoma area code. It was a text message. It simply said, "Hi. What are you doing? Gina."

I quickly responded, "Sitting in my hotel room. What are you doing?"

A few minutes later she said, "Waiting for my boyfriend. Thinking of you."

Yowza! Thinking of me? Why was she thinking of me? That was weird and quite unexpected. "Why don't you come to my hotel. I'm staying at The Riverwind Hotel. Room 325."

"I can't," she said. "I don't have a car."

"I can come get you."

"No, you can't. My boyfriend would get mad. Text me tomorrow. OK?"

"OK," I responded.

And that was it. I saved her phone number into my address book, took my clothes off, put my flannel pajamas on, and got into bed. I closed my eyes and thought of sheep jumping over a wood fence. They were cute sheep, white and fuzzy, flying through the air, dozens of them, and they put me to sleep.

23.

When I woke up in the morning, I did my usual morning routine to cover up the stink that had adhered to my body overnight from the hotel bed. I couldn't place what the stink was but I could smell it on my hands and arms and wherever. It was all over me and must have been some special Native American deodorizer or some shit like that. So I took a scalding shower and scrubbed myself really good, then dried my hair, put on deodorant, splashed on my favorite cologne, plucked a few nose hairs, popped a zit on my nose, brushed my teeth and gargled with Scope (I changed from Listerine because it burned my mouth too much), and dashed on some talcum powder. Like I've said before, what separates us humans from the apes and monkeys of the world is the stink-covering gene in our DNA. Unless you're a bum and down on your luck or the unfortunate type like my old friend Jason who was a goddamn pig, you're supposed to cover up your stink. That's what we humans do. It's true.

I got dressed and packed my bag and decided that the best thing to do on a Sunday morning was to have a big southern breakfast with eggs and biscuits and bacon and pancakes and coffee before my drive home. I figured I'd take my grandfather's advice and enjoy myself, what, with work Monday and my life back to normal with Jessica being a bitch and hiding my kids from me and bills and more bills and this and that and the other shit. It was all a goddamn mess. It's true. But that was tomorrow and this was now and the idea of stuffing my face with some delicious pancakes and hot coffee sounded very appealing so I left my stinky room and made my way downstairs. Surely there was a breakfast buffet or hotel restaurant or a diner or something. I was sure of it.

The hotel lobby was no different than the night before. The cigarette fog still lingered and the slot machines were still clink clink clinking and the sirens were still blaring and whirling and the chatter from the old white folks was as frantic and busy as if the day had never turned to night then back to day. It was a 24 hour gambling frenzy. There wasn't a single window in the entire goddamn place except for the sliding front doors. Being in there was like being stuck in some time-altering machine where the world outside kept moving but the world in there was booze, booze, gamble, gamble, smoke, smoke and if you were lucky then a little win here and there. I wasn't up to gambling at that moment because I knew, more than anything, that I was having the absolute worst luck in the entire goddamn world. My luck was absolutely abysmal and there would have been no point of me shoving any of my money into any of those goddamn slot machines. My money would just simply vanish into thin air. I was sure of it. My mind wasn't on money anyway. I could smell pancakes and that was all that mattered.

I followed the smell (which was stronger than the cigarette smell if you can believe it) and found the hotel restaurant where they had setup a massive breakfast buffet and all of the drunken gamblers were lined up looking for sustenance to soak up the gallons of booze in their stomachs. I was just ready to eat and head home. I claimed an empty table and plopped my bag down and found a place in line. Some young, teenage Native American boys came by, asking everyone to show their room keys, checking to make sure the people in line were actually guests of the hotel and not some drunken freeloaders or some shit like that. The young employees seemed perkier than the typical teenagers that worked at hamburger joints or ice cream shops or wherever teenagers flocked to so they could make minimum wage and buy useless shit at the mall. They must have been making more than minimum wage, probably because they were in on the "stick-it-to-the-man" racket the rest of the Indians were in on. I was sure of it.

The buffet was a cornucopia of southern comfort food with every yummy dish you could imagine. They even had steamed corn on the cob which I thought was strange but ignored that nonetheless and piled everything imaginable on my plate, pancakes and sausage and bacon and eggs and biscuits and French toast and bagels and gravy and whatever I could get my hands on. The other guests were a bunch of goddamn pigs so I had to make it snappy or otherwise I'd miss out. I dressed a perfect cup of coffee for myself and found my table. Finally, I was about to be satisfied and happy. I sipped my coffee and slowly enjoyed my food. I watched the other hotel guests, most of them elderly, some middle-aged, occasionally a young couple in their 20s. They all looked tired and wiped out. I imagined if they were winners then they were probably cashing in their player's cards (if they were smart) or putting their winnings back into the slot machines (if they were idiots). I figured if my luck improved before I left that I might try my luck at a game or two but I doubted it. It was probably best that I just went home. Sometimes, when you're down on your luck, it's best just to go home. It's true.

As I was gobbling my delicious food, I accidentally nudge my plate and tipped over my coffee. Hot, steaming coffee splashed on the table top. I grabbed some napkins from a dispenser on the table and quickly tried to sop up the hot coffee before it dripped off the table and scalded my lap or some shit like that. As I was sopping and cleaning, I noticed a stack of business cards between the napkin dispenser and the salt and pepper shakers. I picked one up and read it. It said:

Do you want to win a FORTUNE? Find out what the future holds for YOU. Let an authentic NATIVE AMERICAN SHAMAN interpret what the future has in store for YOU!

The card went on to say that his store-front was next to the hotel and the casino in a shopping mall and I wondered if this was the shaman that Gina was telling me about, the one that walked around the casino drinking rum and cokes and telling old ladies if they were going to win at the slot machines or at Craps or Black Jack or whatever they were going to play. I was very intrigued by this so I decided right then and there that after I finished my breakfast and checked out from the hotel that I would pay this shaman a quick visit. What would it hurt, right? Maybe I did have some luck in store for me. It's true.

***

Behind the hotel was a strip mall filled with all kinds of Native American-owned businesses like a tax preparer and a check-cashing place and a pawn shop and a cell phone store and whatnot. They all had these signs in their windows stating how they all belonged to the Chickasaw Nation, I guess their equivalent to the Better Business Bureau or some shit like that. It made me feel like I was in a foreign nation or foreign country or something. It's true. At the end of the strip mall was a shop that had a sign that simply said, "Fortune!" In the window, besides the Chickasaw Better Business Bureau sign, was some adhesive letters that spelled out:

Tom Goodheart, Phd., Shaman, No. 137-4-56-325

I thought it very strange that he had this number listed next to his name like it was some kind of license number or serial number or some shit like that. Did shamans get licensed by the Chickasaw Nation? Did he have to pass some kind of certification to be declared a true "shaman?" I was going to have to find out. And a Phd, no less, too? I was very curious. It's true.

Inside the shop was a little reception area with a small couch, a coffee table with a bunch of copies of Sports Illustrated on top, and a fake potted plant in one corner. On the walls were some Native American inspired artworks and a small window with a little plastic sign that read, "Back in 15 minutes." A plain, white door was locked with a combination padlock. The shaman must have been taking a potty break or a smoke break or a breakfast break or some kind of break. I sat on the couch and thumbed through a two-year old copy of Sports Illustrated. It had a profile about how Kobe Bryant wasn't a jackass anymore and how he had become the greatest basketball player of our generation. What a bunch of shit! Our society really loved goddamn celebrities even if they were assholes. I mean, athletes and movie stars and rock stars could get away with absolute murder like sexual assault or drug crazed lunacy or alcoholic benders or whatever and people stilled loved them. Celebrities had a hold on our society's hearts no matter what they did. It's true. On the other hand, poor writers like good ol' James Frey, the genius behind the partially true masterpiece, were vilified. Oprah Winfrey, in front of millions of people, skewered him to *his face* on national TV because he lied a little bit. What a pile of shit! Writers should be the celebrities in our society not jackass athletes like Kobe Bryant, a married man who sexually assaulted a young woman in a Colorado hotel room. Geesh. It was almost too much for me to handle. I could go on for days about it. It's true.

The front door to the shop opened, a little bell on the handle ringing as it swung out, and this giant of a man walked in. He was tall with broad shoulders, his long, black hair pulled back in a frizzy pony tail, wearing blue jeans and a black leather vest, silver rings on every finger, black motorcycle boots on his feet. It must have been Tom Goodheart but his name really should have been Big Chief. He was massive, one of the most imposing men I had ever encountered. He saw me and smiled. He extended his hand to mine for a shake. His hand was like the paw of a grizzly bear. It's true.

"Good morning," he said. "Are you here to discover your fortune?" he asked, releasing my hand from his giant paw and turning the sign that read, "Back in 15 minutes" to the other side which read, "The doctor is in." I thought that was kind of funny. "What is your name?" he asked.

"Simon. Simon Burchwood. You're not really a doctor, are you?" I asked.

"Actually, Mr. Burchwood, yes I am. I have a doctorate in Native American Studies from Oklahoma State."

"Please call me Simon. Shouldn't you be teaching or writing scholarly papers or doing something like that?"

"Yes, I could do that but there's no money in it for me. Besides, this is a lot more fun. Come with me." He unlocked the combination padlock and opened the door, extending his arm for me to walk through. "Let's see what your future holds for you."

I stepped through the door into a small room with a table and two chairs in the middle. The walls had an assortment of framed photos and diplomas, more Native American inspired artwork and some newspaper clippings. The lights were low and he lit a few candles. He motioned for me to sit at the table as he putzed around, lighting candles and straightening up a bit. I looked at the photos on the wall. Some were of Dr. Goodheart standing with what looked like Native American friends. Some of the other photos were of him next to old white ladies just like the ones that were pumping their savings into the slot machines. Were these the ladies he duped into telling their futures? I had to know. It's true.

"Who are these people in these photos?" I asked.

"Oh, some are old college buddies, some are people who have won lots of money after paying for my services. They always come back to see me after they win and ask for a photo. Some of the winners mail copies of the photos to me as their way of saying thank you. So, Simon, what do you do for a living?"

"Well, I work as a support technician during the day but I'm really a writer, a struggling writer but a writer."

"How interesting. And working as a support technician pays your bills?"

"Yes."

"What kind of things do you write?"

"My novel *The Rise and Fall of a Titan* came out last year. They said it was going to be the next great bestseller of the decade but it didn't do as well as I had hoped. But I'm working on a new book. Hopefully I'll be done with it this year."

"Fantastic," he said, sitting down with me at the table. The room had a cozy feeling to it even though it was rather small. The scent and glow from the candles had a hypnotizing effect on me. Maybe that was how he duped his customers. "Are you married?"

"No, I'm divorced unfortunately."

"I see. I'm sorry to hear that. Divorce is difficult, especially for children. And do you have any children?"

"Yes, I have a son and a daughter. Their names are Jessica and Sammie."

"How sweet. And how have they been since the divorce?"

"They seem to have adjusted to it OK," I said. He sure was asking a bunch of personal questions. It was starting to get on my goddamn nerves. I wanted to know my future, not tell him about my miserable present. It's true. "Are you going to tell me my future soon?"

"Patience. I have to get to know you before I can tell you your future. I can't read your mind, you know? I can only see the future with pertinent information to guide me."

"I see." What a bunch of bullshit. This guy was a grade-A swindler, I could tell.

"Would you say that you are happy with your current situation in life?" he asked.

"I guess so, as happy as I can be." Now, that was a big fat lie. I was fucking miserable! But I wasn't going to tell him *that*. He was being a really nosy bastard. It's true. Plus, I didn't even know this guy. I mean, I didn't know him from jack shit. I wasn't going to lay out all of my dirty laundry. "Yes, I'm happy."

"Are you dating anyone?"

"No. Not yet."

"Would you ever consider getting married again?"

"I don't know. I haven't thought about it."

"And your writing? Do you hope that your writing career would be successful in the future?"

"Absolutely! I want that more than anything."

"Fantastic. Before I begin, do you have any questions for me?"

Questions? I had all kinds of questions. It's true. But you know the question I think about most, don't you? Of course you do. I had to ask.

"Yes."

"Then shoot."

"Why does life have to be so hard?"

Now, this must have been a whopper of a question because he sat back in his seat, placing both hands to the side of his face, and he sat there puzzled for a minute. I bet he wasn't expecting that one. That was a pretty big question, the biggest of the biggest. It's true.

"Mr. Burchwood..."

"Simon. Please call me Simon."

"Simon, I do not claim to be some kind of guru. I am not the master of the universe. I do not know everything but I will say this from my experience and the history of my people. One of the biggest burdens of all mankind is the ability to question our existence. It has troubled mankind since the beginning of time and is the common thread through all cultures and societies throughout the world. Just asking 'why' separates us from the animal kingdom. But my people knew from the beginning that we were part of the animal kingdom. We were no different than the other creatures that walked the Earth or flew in the sky or swam in the rivers."

"Mmm hmm."

"Separating ourselves from what we truly are will be our undoing. Birds don't ask why life is hard. Mountain lions don't ask why life is hard. The fish don't ask why life is hard. To them, life is life. They don't ask why. They just live. It's that simple."

"I see."

"And my question to you would be why ask why life is hard? Why aren't you just living? A fox doesn't ask why it's hard to catch his next meal. He just does it. An eagle does not ask why it's hard to raise its eaglets. She just does it. And you shouldn't ask why life is hard. You're a writer and that's what you should be doing. You're a father and that's what you should be doing. Am I right?"

"Yes, you are right."

"The French have a saying. C'est la vie. It's cliché but it's true."

The goddamn French. I was right back to where I started. It's true. I had come full circle in a small candle-lit room in Craplahoma with a giant Indian espousing clichés about 'that's life' and roadrunners searching for worms and snakes looking for fat rats to eat and this and that and whatever. It was a goddamn disaster. Disaster, I tell you! I was ready to end my session without knowing my fortune or my future. I was ready to get up and walk out of that goddamn place. But then he smiled and looked quite pleased with himself. I guess he was trying, at least.

"Thanks," I said.

"Like I said, I'm not a guru. I only know what I know. Are you ready for me to tell you your future?"

"Yes." Thank God. I thought he would never ask.

"OK. Do you have two $20 bills in your wallet?"

"Uh, I think so." I pulled out my wallet and looked inside. There were two $20 bills and a single $2 bill. The $2 bill was a souvenir from Sammie boy. He gave it to me a while back, telling me it was special. It was special to me. So I kept the $2 bill in my wallet and pulled out the two $20 bills. I gave them to Dr. Goodheart.

He pulled out a black marker and drew a sun on the face of one of the bills and a moon on the face of the other bill. Then, quick as a flash, he crumpled the bills into two wads. Placing them in front of me, he shuffled the two bills like a shell game, moving his hands back and forth and side to side, concealing in a blur of movement which bill was which. It was a pile of shit, if you ask me. It's true. Then he sat back, the two paper wads sitting in front of me.

"Pick one. If you pick the $20 with the sun, then you will have great fortune in the near future. If you pick the $20 with the moon, then life goes on unchanged."

I remembered what Gina said about this guy and how he was spot on when it came to telling the future and how he helped old ladies win lots of money, even helping Gina win $1,000. I looked at all of the photos on the wall of the happy old ladies, their arms around Dr. Goodheart, probably with jackpot winnings in their purses, and I thought, 'What can it hurt? Maybe I'll be lucky.' I closed my eyes and picked one of the waded bills. I looked at it in my hand and looked at Dr. Goodheart looking at me, a big fucking smile stretched across his noble goddamn face. I unfolded the bill to find a picture of the sun on it. He nodded an approving nod. I felt a surge of excitement run through my body. Did this mean I was going to be fortunate?

All I could say was, "Wow."

"And so it is." He grabbed the other crumpled $20 bill, folded it, and slipped it in his shirt pocket. "Good luck to you, my friend."

"That's it?" I asked.

"That is it," he said, standing up and opening the door to the reception area. "Don't forget to come back for a photo with me. OK?" He patted me on the back and sent me on my way.

Outside, the morning sun had risen close to high noon. I was feeling lucky, luckier than I did before I saw Dr. Goodheart. I decided to test my newfound good luck. I walked across the parking lot to the casino with my lucky $20 in my back pocket.

24.

Clink clink clink. That was the first sound I heard when I walked into the casino. It was the sound of hopes and dreams and I was hoping it would be the sound for my fortune. At first, good ol' Dr. Goodheart seemed like a real swindler with his leather vest and his Native American mumbo jumbo and his fancy business cards and his strip mall storefront and his fuzzy ponytail and all. But it's really hard giving someone grief when they are trying to send good fortune your way. It's true. Most people in life like to give you all kinds of trouble or grief or pain or whatever other bullshit makes them feel better. People can be real assholes. I mean, it doesn't matter who it is, family, friends, coworkers, strangers, waiters, bartenders, flight attendants, strippers, convenience store clerks, anybody, all they want to do is whatever makes them feel better about themselves, even if it means making you feel like a petrified turd. It's the rare person who will give you more than what they want in return. My good ol' buddy Jason was like that. He's my true friend. And I think Dr. Goodheart was that rare person too. His entire business was about giving people hope for the future. What could be better than that? Even if he did charge me $20, it was worth it. You know why? Most things you buy have a diminishing return but there is no diminishing return when it comes to hope. It's true.

I made my way through the lobby and into the labyrinth of slot machines. I was looking for the ONE, the one that would be my lucky slot machine. I didn't know how to find it but I was hoping that my intuition would lead the way. They had every type of game you could imagine from the classic fruit games to themed slot machines like the TV show Happy Days or American Idol. They had the classic mechanical reel machines and they also had fancy video game-type machines. It was a truly awesome sight and every person sitting at those machines had the same hope I had: to win big. But they didn't have what I had: a blessed $20 bill from the one and only Dr. Goodheart. Well, I take that back. That was a little presumptuous of me, maybe one of these old cronies had a blessed $20 bill from Dr. Goodheart but that didn't matter to me. They didn't have MY blessed $20 bill. It's true.

I could hear the various gamblers tell their companions their methods for winning, whether it was pulling the old mechanical lever instead of pushing the button (like that made a difference?) or memorizing the patterns they thought would be next so they would bet the max or devising a betting pattern like two bets of 25 cents then 1 bet at 50 cents then three bets at 75 cents and repeat ad nauseum or some shit like that. It was all a crock of shit. These silly old bastards felt like they knew how to beat the system but the system was devised for them to lose over the long haul. That's why there is a saying that says,

"Never bet against the house." It's because the house was setup to win otherwise the house would be gone. It's true. But, and this was a BIG but, sometimes, just sometimes, there was always that one lucky bastard, sitting in the right place at the right time, that hits that jackpot. That's the trick that gets everyone else sucked in. They see that one lucky bastard who hits it big, then the sirens go off, the lights flash, the casino staff converges around the winner, and everyone else sees this lucky bastard who won a big, fat pile of cash. The first thing that goes through their mind is, "If that fucker can win, then so can I. Where's the ATM machine? I need to pulse out some more money from my savings!" That's when the casino got everyone else into its sticky tentacles. It's true. And don't get me started on all the booze and cigarettes that the casino handed out for FREE to get everyone lit and throw their sanity out the window. It was all part of their evil plan and it was working except that I had the secret weapon. I had my lucky $20 bill.

After walking past quite a few slot machines I finally found one that caught my eye. It was the classic cherries game, you know, where you get 3 cherries in a row and you win big? That one. I sat on the stool and pulled out my lucky $20 bill, the one with the sun drawn on it. I looked down to find where the machine took the money, the slot that ate your cash. There were some nooks and crannies, places that looked like I could insert my lucky bill but every single one was a dud. I tried cramming my $20 bill in various places but the machine just wouldn't take it. An old lady sitting next to me started laughing all over the goddamn place. She thought what I was doing was the funniest goddamn thing she had ever seen in her entire life. She smelled like moth balls and hand cream and cheap perfume.

She put her hand on my shoulder and said, "Son, are you new at this?"

"I just want to put my money in and play. That's all."

"Well, this machine only takes player's cards. You have to go to that machine over there, swipe your player's card, then insert your money. It'll put the money on your card."

"But I want to put *this* money in THIS machine."

"That machine only uses player's cards."

I reluctantly got up, walked over to the machine she was pointing at, swiped my card, fed my lucky $20 bill into it, and the machine put $20 of credit on my card in addition to the complimentary $10 that was already on there. More chances to win! I went back to my cherry machine and sat down.

"You feeling lucky?" the old stinky lady asked me. She was really engaged with her machine. She was pushing buttons and pulling levers all over the goddamn place. It's true.

"I feel lucky right now," I said.

"Well, if you're feeling lucky, then you should bet the max."

"What's the max?"

"Well, that's a $1 machine. The max is $3. How much money do you have on your card?"

"I think $30."

"Then that's 10 spins at the max."

"How do I do that?"

"Swipe that card and hit the button that says MAX." She pointed her scrawny, wrinkly hand at a big, yellow button in front of me. "There."

What did you know? There were two buttons on the machine, one that said SPIN and one that said MAX. I swiped my card and the machine displayed the amount of money I had allowed it to ingest. It beckoned for me to hit the flashing buttons.

"Just hit this one?"

"Do it, boy."

So I did. I hit the button. A cherry, a 7, and some bars. Nothing to win. I hit it again. A 7, a 7, and some bars. Nothing. I hit it eight more times with a variety of non-winning combinations and on the very last spin, I won $1. What the fuck? Where was my lucky payout? Was Dr. Goodheart messing with me? The old lady looked at me and sighed.

"Just play that last $1. Why not? You have nothing to lose."

I pressed the SPIN button. Nothing. My money was gone and so was my luck. I sat there and stared at the machine. I stared at the machine until my vision became unfocused, turning the flashy slot machine into a rainbowy smear of colored lights and all I could hear was the sound of all the other goddamn winners: clink clink clink.

***

I found a place at the bar, threw my empty player's card in the trash, and debated what I should do next. My luck was a bust. Good ol' Dr. Goodheart had really worked me over. He fed me a tall pile of shit. It's true. He had a goddamn business based on hope and took advantage of me, the bloodsucker. He sat there with his fuzzy ponytail and his leather vest and his Native American mumbo jumbo and his strip mall store front with his adhesive-letter credentials and filled me up to my eyeballs with bullshit. That bastard! And I lost $40 too, $50 if you count my $10 in player's credit. I should have called the Better Business Bureau or the Chickasaw Nation Shaman Licensing Unit or the Oklahoma Workforce Commission or some shit like that. I think I had enough evidence to shut his business down but I didn't do it. That was just too much effort. I sat at the bar and considered ordering an alcoholic drink but I ordered a glass of water and sat there like a sad bastard. I was a really sorry, unlucky, sad, worthless bastard. It's true.

The bartender, a young fellow dressed in a snazzy semi-tuxedo uniform with perfect hair and perfect teeth and a perfect smile, tried to get me to order a drink but I just wasn't up for it. I had a long drive ahead of me back to Austin, back to my home, back to my kids, back to my shitty job, back to a writing career that was dead in the water. It was a really sad situation. It's true. That bartender was a pretty persistent bastard though. He just wouldn't leave.

"Come on, buddy. Just one drink. Why else would you sit at the bar?"

"Because I'm contemplating what I should do next. I have to drive back to Austin soon. It's a long drive. Drinking would make it even longer."

"I understand," he said, drying off some bar glasses with a towel. "Well, if you change your mind, then call me. All you have to do is lift a finger and I'll come serve you." He raised his right index finger in the air as if giving some secret signal. What do you know? That surely must be a universal signal in a bar since the bartender back at the Austin International airport did the same thing when I was waiting to board my flight for my trip to New York via Montgomery, Alabama. Maybe they taught that in bar school or wherever it was he went to become a bartender. It's true. He went to the other side of the bar to clean some more bar glasses.

I pulled out my wallet to see how much cash I had left and all I had was that $2 bill that good ol' Sammie boy gave me. One day, when he and Jessica were staying with me, he brought this $2 bill to me, telling me how he found it on the playground at school and how it was a lucky $2 bill and that I was supposed to keep it forever. He drew little cartoons on it with crayons and markers, pictures of him and me holding hands, our stick-figure arms wrapped around each other, with word balloons that said, "I love you, daddy" and "You're the best dad ever!" and shit like that. It was adorable. I placed the $2 bill on the bar and stared at it. I stared at it so hard, so deeply, that I could hear Sammie boy's voice. He was telling me how proud he was of me and that I was the best daddy in the world. The little stars and suns and moons he had drawn on the bill started to spin and pulsate as we walked toward the pyramid on the back, the one with the ominous eyeball hovering over it. Little did Sammie boy know that I was an absolute failure, a failure at everything really: failed marriage, failed careers, pretty much a failure at everything really. My ex-wife was right. I was a spectacular failure, a spectacular asshole, a spectacular letdown, a spectacularly bad lover, a spectacular idiot, and a spectacular waste of time. What could I say? I was the spectacular Simon Burchwood. It's true.

I must have been talking to myself because I noticed a waitress giving me a queer look like I was crazy or something. I looked at her and she continued to look at me, turning her head like I was an alien. It was the weirdest thing. Then she walked over and sat next to me.

"Are you all right?" she asked. She had a name tag on her shirt. It said, "Stacey."

"Yes," I said, straightening up. My imaginary talk with my son must have been audible. How ridiculous! I'm such an idiot sometimes. It's true.

"Did you not win at the slot machine?"

"What?"

"I saw you over there at the slot machine. That old lady was helping you. But those machines never payout big, at least not since I've been here."

"How long have you worked here?"

"A few weeks."

"I see," I said. She didn't look a day over 21 or 22 at the most. She had a fresh face and she held herself high with the naivety of a young person. Isn't it funny how young people carry themselves like they can conquer the world? Boy, did she have a thing coming in the next few years of her life. It's true. "Well, what machines payout big?"

"Hmmm," she said, placing her hand on her chin, thinking about the layout of the casino. She perched her head high and scanned the maze of slot machines. Her eyes widened when she saw something, a machine in the distance. "Personally, I've had luck on the older machines, the ones that are not video games. I'll slip a few dollars in them on my break and win a couple of hundred bucks every once in a while. It's not a lot but at least I get something instead of just putting more money into the machine and get nothing."

"True. True. Which one pays out?"

"There is a row of older machines against the wall over there. They are not electronic, no buttons. You have to pull the lever. Sometimes it's hard to pull them. They are old, you know?"

"Why are they still here then?"

"Nostalgia, I guess. Some of the players prefer them. There's not a lot who do but they are very vocal about it. You should give it a shot."

"No, that's not a good idea."

"Why not?"

"This $2 bill is the last of the money I have and my son gave it to me for good luck. I can't spend it."

"Well, if he gave it to you for good luck then don't you think it'll give you good luck?"

Stacey had a point there. It's true. I wasn't sure if it was a GOOD point but it was a point nonetheless. Maybe she was right. Maybe good ol' Sammie boy told me it was good luck for a reason. And maybe, just maybe, the $20 bill Dr. Goodheart blessed wasn't where the good luck was; maybe it was just a symbol for good fortune. It was an intriguing thought.

"I don't know. I haven't had any good luck so far."

"I'll go over there with you and give you some lady luck. Do you want to try? What would it hurt?"

Stacey was a real professional. I could tell. As young as she was, she had a way about her that made me feel easy, easy enough to want to spend the lucky $2 bill my son gave me. Isn't it funny how that happens? Sometimes, just sometimes, a little different perspective can make all the difference in the world. It's true.

"OK. Only if you come with me though."

"Deal! Let me tell the bartender I'm on a break." She took off her apron and set her tray on the bar. She told something to the bartender about taking a smoke break or some shit like that and he obliged, taking her apron and tray and stashing it behind the bar. She put her arm around my shoulder. "Let's go! This will be fun."

She lit a cigarette and led me to the other side of the casino, slipping one of her arms into mine and holding the cigarette with her other hand. I have to admit, it sure did feel nice having a beautiful, young woman on my arm, even if she was a waitress at a casino.

"Do you think there is anyone on those machines?"

"Maybe," she said. "But I'm sure we can find an empty one. What's your name?"

"Simon. Simon Burchwood."

"Well, hello there, Mr. Burchwood. What do you do for a living?"

"Please, call me Simon. I'm a writer."

"A writer?!" she said, looking at me with a surprised look. "How fucking cool is that?!"

Pretty cool, if I must admit. People always get all excited and shit when I tell them that I'm a writer. It never fails. It's true. She led me through the maze of slot machines, maneuvering around row after row of old white people spinning away. We got to the end of one aisle and turned left and there they were, a row of slot machines that looked like they were from the 1980s. There wasn't a soul around. All of the stools were empty.

"Pick one," she said, smiling at me. I looked at the six or seven machines and found one that looked good. They were all the same game: Three Card Poker. I pulled out the stool and sat down then pulled out my $2 bill.

"Do I have to put this money on my player's card? I threw my card away."

"No, these machines can take money." She pointed down at the front of the machine. There was a slot for inserting dollars. I held my lucky $2 bill in front of me.

"If I win the jackpot, how much would I win?" I asked. She pointed to the machine.

"If you win the jackpot, you'll get about $15,000. Pretty cool, huh?"

"And this machine will accept $2 bills?"

"It sure will."

"I don't know. My son would be really disappointed if I spent this $2 bill."

"Maybe. But if you WIN, then you can just get another $2 bill and draw silly cartoons on it."

Good ol' Stacey had a point there. If I won $15,000, then I could get a stack of $2 bills a mile high. Sammie would never know the difference.

"Ok then. Here it goes." I slipped the $2 bill into the machine and it consumed it. I grabbed the lever and gave it a tug. When the reels stopped spinning, I saw that I had a Queen of Spades, an eight of Hearts, and a four of Diamonds. Nothing. "I didn't win."

"Keep trying, dummy."

I pulled the lever again and got two Kings and a seven of Hearts. Quarters started falling from the machine into a metal tray at the front. Clink clink clink.

"You won!" she said. "Keep going!"

The machine was a quarter machine which meant I had eight spins. Well, six spins now. I pulled the lever again and got nothing. Then again, nothing. Then again, nothing. Then again, nothing. I was getting discouraged.

"It doesn't look like I'm going to win much."

"Don't stop. Don't stop. Keep going!"

"Are you sure?" I asked. She placed both of her hands on my cheeks and smooshed my face. It was the weirdest feeling but she was so excited that the weirdness faded away pretty quick. It was hard NOT to get wrapped up in her enthusiasm. Ah, young people's enthusiasm. It was too cute. It's true.

"I'm sure!" she said.

I reached for the lever, gripping it tightly, looking at the payout table glued to the slot machine then looking at Stacey. It looked like her head was going to explode she was so goddamn excited. It's true.

"OK. Here I go."

I pulled the lever and the reels spun. The first reel stopped. It was the Jack of Spades. The second wheel then stopped. It was the King of Spades. The last reel stopped. It was the Queen of Spades. Sirens immediately started blaring, lights flashing like the lights on top of a cop car above the slot machine, red beams spinning around and around. It was kind of embarrassing but I won something. It was obvious. Quarters poured out of the machine, filling the metal tray quickly, then pouring onto the floor. Stacey stood back, stunned. Her hands were plastered to her face and she had a look like she had just seen a goddamn ghost. It's true.

"Oh my God. I can't believe it. You won!"

"What do you mean you can't believe I won?" I asked.

"You got a straight flush. You won the jackpot! You better give me a good tip for helping you."

Pretty soon, I was surrounded by some security guards. They were there to make sure I was the real winner and that none of the other losers were coming around trying to get my quarters. I stood there in shock. How much did I win? I guess I was going to find out. One of the guards opened the machine and flipped a switch, turning off the siren and lights. The other scooped up the quarters that had fallen out and put them into a plastic bucket. Both of the security guards were big as shit, real brawny bastards. Stacey congratulated me.

"I still can't believe you won. That's awesome."

"I can't believe it either."

"I'll help you at the cashier. Make sure they treat you right."

"OK," I said, still stunned. I guess good ol' Dr. Goodheart was right. I did have some fortune in my future. I felt bad for doubting him but what was I to do? My lucky $20 was a bust but my lucky $2 bill was a winner. I was going to have to get Sammie boy a nice gift and I was going to have to replace his $2 bill for the one I spent. I was sure he wouldn't mind. I was sure of it.

The security guards asked me to follow them to the cashier and Stacey followed right behind me, patting me on the back every once and a while. They led me to a window with bars on it. A sign that read, "Cashier" hung above the window, a portly lady sat in the room behind it. She didn't look too enthused that I had won. She didn't look enthused about a goddamn thing, actually. One of the security guards handed her a piece of paper from the slot machine. She started filling out some paperwork, doing some calculating on a calculator. It really seemed like she hated her job. I could tell. It's true. The security guards shook my hand then walked off, probably to bully some old drunk man. Stacey hung close by.

"I wonder if you won it all?" she asked.

"The jackpot?"

"Yes dummy. The jackpot."

I was curious as hell so I looked at the unenthused lady behind the bars. She was busy calculating away, filling out papers.

"Ma'am? How much did I win?"

She poked at the calculator some more then looked at me.

"Looks like you won $14,997. Would you like a check or would you like for me to do a wire transfer to your bank account?"

"$14,997?! Did you say $14,997?"

"Yessir, $14,997."

"Oh, I'll take a check then." I looked at Stacey and she smiled at me and I realized that she was waiting for her tip, the tip she deserved because she told me to play that slot. And she DID deserve a tip. I was happy to oblige because without her, I would have only $2. "Ma'am?" I asked.

"Yessir?"

"Can you make the check for... $14,977? And give me the difference in cash?"

"Yessir."

She did her thing and handed me a $20 bill then handed me a check. I looked at the check. Right on the front it said, "$14,977." It was amazing. It's true. I handed Stacey the $20 bill and extended my hand for a shake. She reluctantly took the $20 bill and gave me a limp shake in return.

"Gee, thanks."

"Well, you deserve it. What can I say? I wouldn't have won all that money without you."

"You know, most people tip 10 to 15 percent for winning advice like that."

"I'm not most people, darling."

"I can see that," she said, annoyed. She slipped the $20 bill into her pocket and walked off without saying goodbye. What was bothering her? Did she think I was going to give more than $20 of my hard earned money?! Crazy talk, I tell you. Crazy. It's true. I had the fortune of hitting it big and I wasn't going to waste it on a waitress in a casino. It was time for me to go home. It was time to head back to Austin. I walked out of that casino like I was walking on clouds.

Outside, I walked back toward the hotel. At the front, I gave the valet my validation slip and he ran off, fast as lightning. I found a bench and sat down, waiting for Clint the Caddy to come take me home. I couldn't believe it. I absolutely could not believe it. What was I to do when I got back to Austin? Should I quit my job and start writing my next book? Or should I continue to work and have a nice, fat savings account? Questions, so many new questions. I knew I would make a decision on my way home to Austin. I would have plenty of time to think about it then.

Shortly, Clint the Caddy pulled up and the valet got out and ran around to me. He extended his hand but I didn't have any cash on me for a tip. Poor bastard. He was going to have to bother some other sucker.

"Sorry, buddy, no cash on me. I'll get you next time."

"Yessir. I'll see you next time," he said. He handed me the keys then he ran back to his post by the door.

I thought it was funny that he thought there would be a next time because in my heart of hearts, I knew there would *never* be a next time. There would only be this time and it was time to go home. It's true. I put my seatbelt on and shifted Clint the Caddy into drive. I knew I would not be back in Oklahoma for a long time, if ever, so I waved goodbye to the valet and drove off. I drove off past the other losers walking back to their cars, their hearts sunk low in their chests, their hopes and dreams crushed. I got on the highway and headed home.

25.

All the windows in Clint the Caddy were rolled down and the warm air rushed into the cabin. I drove home at top speed, zipping through all the shithole towns on the way, not stopping to eat or piss or take a break or sight-see or nothing. I was on a mission and, boy, was I ready to get home. I had plans to make. Big plans. There was absolutely no point in stopping in Ardmore or Gainesville or Denton or Waxahachie or Ennis or Waco or anywhere. I felt something big was coming around the corner. I didn't know what it was but I was sure $14,977 was going to come in real handy. It's true. There was quite a bit I could do with $14,977 but what interested me the most was the idea of quitting my job and writing full-time, at least for a while. I was going to have to figure out if that was possible. I was going to have to do some number crunching, you know? I needed to add up all my expenses and see just how far $14,977 would take me. If I could pull it off, then I could write my next book without having to worry about showing up to some goddamn job every day and pretend that I gave a shit about my menial tasks and work and work and work. What was the point in doing that? Nothing I tell you. Nothing.

I tried crunching the numbers in my head but that didn't do me any good. I couldn't concentrate for shit. I was just too excited. Plus, all the goddamn 18-wheelers were pissing me off with their road hogging and swerving and horn honking and lane weaving and everything. It was just too much to handle. It's true. Those truckers could be real assholes, the way they drove. It was enough to conjure up a severe case of road rage in me that would invite murderous thoughts into my otherwise docile mind. If I had a gun in the car, then I would have been mighty dangerous. It's true. Thankfully, the closest thing in the car to a gun was a tire iron. That's about it.

As I zipped through all the shithole towns I thought of the past couple of weeks and felt like someone had been playing a cruel joke on me. My life was completely in the crapper before I bumped into good ol' Stacey, convincing me to put my last $2 bill into that goddamn lucky slot machine. I made a point to remember that I was going to have to replace that lucky $2 bill before Sammie found out it was gone. That would be the ultimate disaster. No amount of money, not even $14,977, would mend Sammie's broken heart knowing his daddy spent that $2 bill. I was going to have to get a new $2 bill the minute I arrived in Austin. But the more I thought about it, the more I convinced myself that ultimately Sammie would understand my situation. Little did my boy know just how hard his daddy had it. I had it pretty bad. Surely he would understand why I risked spending that $2 bill. I was sure of it. It's true.

I decided right then and there not to dwell on it too much and just get home. Like I said, I had big plans to make, the biggest plans ever, and all I wanted to do was get home and start planning.

***

I walked into the government building where I worked. The building smelled just the way it did before I left on my trip, mildewy, stale, and miserable. Nothing had changed while I was gone, not a goddamn thing. Even the walls were still that same government version of gooey tan they were painted before, decades before even. It was an interior decorator's goddamn nightmare. It's true. The same security guard sat at the front desk, bored, unassuming, useless. If a terrorist ran in with a bomb strapped to his chest and threatened to blow all of the capitalist pigs to Kingdom Come, this security guard would have been first to duck under his desk. In the halls, the same trolls limped casually around, pretending to be going somewhere important, avoiding work at all costs. As I walked down the hall, I avoided eye contact with the trolls. Eye contact would have been an excuse for them to start talking to me, another distraction from their miserable work lives, another reason to gossip about their coworkers. Unfortunately, my efforts to keep my anonymity were thwarted. I heard an annoying voice calling my name down the hall, an annoying woman's voice. I looked up and that nosy administrative assistant I helped last week spotted me. She was waving her arms all over the goddamn place like a goddamn idiot, trying to get my attention, scurrying my way. Valerie Johnson. Remember her? I was trying to forget her. I tried to find a door to escape through, quickly. I found one with a sign that said "Stairs" on it but as soon as I grabbed the door knob, she cornered me. She leaned in close, her hand holding the door shut, her cheap perfume ripping into my nose like a poisonous gas. I was trapped. It's true.

"Simon, I'm glad I bumped into you."

"Oh yeah?" I said, nervous.

"Yes. My computer is still acting up. I keep getting that darn blue screen. It won't let me work. I have to restart it over and over."

"I see."

"My boss is really riding me too. Can you come by and help me?"

"I'll see if my boss will let me."

"Please. I beg you."

"I'll see. I have to go clock in now."

"We can catch up too. I want to hear more about your sweet children."

"I really have to go," I said, pushing her arm aside. I opened the door, slipped through, and quickly descended the stairs. She kept calling to me, pleading, her voice echoing in the stair well.

"Simon! Simon! I need your help!"

I entered the basement and found the room where I worked. I opened the door and was met with smiles from some of my coworkers, not all had arrived yet. It was still early for government workers to all arrive. On my desk was a large bouquet of flowers with a little card pinned to it. It said, "Our condolences for your loss." I had to admit, it was a nice gesture on my coworkers' part, even if my trip wasn't exactly what they thought it was. But I wasn't going to say anything about that. There just was no point. I looked around and my boss Rod was sitting at his desk, his phone headset propped on top of his head, his arms crossed. He nodded at me, a sincere nod, and I smiled back. Good ol' Rod really was a good man. I could tell. I was expecting to be accosted by Snaggle but, to my surprise, he was absent. He must have been running late. Or maybe he was hiding in the bathroom, playing with his goddamn nuts. That must have been it.

I sat down at my desk and expected a long queue of support calls for me to have to slog through. To my surprise, there was only one ticket. Valerie Johnson. The blue screen of death. My only work for the morning. I ignored it and started gathering my things together. I made a small pile of my belongings, a framed photo of my kids, Jessica and Sammie, my copy of Breakfast of Champions by Kurt Vonnegut, my copy of Amazing Spider-Man, Vol. 1 by Stan Lee and Steve Ditko, and my copy of Mad Libs, all the things I brought on my first day of work. I tossed some papers in the trash that had piled up during my week at work and a rotten shmapple that I had mistakenly forgotten to eat before I left for my trip. It was a goddamn waste of a good shmapple. It's true.

I immediately got to work drafting an important email to my boss. My resignation letter. It was going to be a glorious manifesto, a declaration of my independence. It went something like this:

> Dear Rod, due to unforeseen circumstances, I'm submitting my letter of resignation to you. I have been offered an opportunity that is too good to pass up and I look forward to reestablishing my writing career in the very near future. I want to thank you for the opportunity to work at this fine government agency and I am sure that your able leadership and fine support staff will lead this agency into a future of productive employees with few, if any, technical issues with their desktop computers. Please accept my sincerest gratitude for the opportunity to work here and I wish you nothing but the best in your career as the help desk manager. Kind regards, Simon Burchwood, soon-to-be famous author.

I quickly read through my resignation letter for typos and misspellings but found none. I am a goddamn professional writer, you know? Professional writers make few mistakes. It's true. I clicked the "Send" button, closed all the programs I had open, and shutdown my computer.

I gathered my things together and placed them in a small, cardboard box. As I walked out of the room, Rod gave me a puzzled look but he was so busy with a goddamn phone call that he didn't have a chance to say anything to me. It was all for the best anyway. I'm sure his call was of an important nature. He was probably helping the Director of Public Relations or the Controller or the Director of Operations or some important asshole like that. Since he was the manager, he got stuck supporting all of the important assholes of the agency. He was good at sucking up to important government assholes. He had a bright future ahead of him. I was sure of it. It's true.

* * *

I have a confession to make. It's very important. Are you ready? I hope so. In reality, $14,977 really isn't that much money. It's true. After I looked at all of my expenses and added up rent and utilities and bills and child support and all of the things that weighed down on me on a monthly basis, I realized that $14,977 wasn't going to get me too far. I could spend a good three months or so writing without having to work some bullshit job but that was about it unless I wanted to rip through all of it and have nothing to show for it. But I decided that it was too good of an opportunity to pass up so I went for it.

I walked down to the office of my apartment complex and wrote a check for three months of rent and handed it to the office lady. Her eyes opened wide as she looked at it, surprised no doubt that one of her lowly tenants could afford to let go of that amount of money at one time. I told her that I was not to be disturbed by any of the handymen or exterminators or deliverymen or whoever would come snooping around. I had important business to attend to for the next three months. She understood and gave me her word, whatever that was good for.

I sent off money for all of my bills and mailed Jessica three months worth of child support and wrote a kind letter saying that I was sorry for all of the animosity that had developed between us and that I hoped she was happy and doing well. But most of all, I told her that I wished she would let me see my children more often because I loved them more than anything. To my surprise, she called me after receiving that letter and said she was sorry too. Can you believe that shit? It's amazing what an apology can to do, even if I didn't really feel like I had to apologize about anything. She let me talk to my kids and little Jessica told me that she was singing in a choir at her little school. How sweet, I thought. And good ol' Sammie boy told me that he had a worm he found outside and placed it in a jar and had made the slimy thing his pet, except he called it a "shworm." How about that? Good ol' Sammie boy was good at inventing new words for things. Maybe he would grow up and become a writer like his good ol' dad. Maybe. It's a tough business being a writer, you know? Not just anyone can be a writer. It's true.

After setting up all of my expenses and taking care of all of my bills, I went to a used office supply warehouse and bought the biggest, most massive solid wood desk I could find. I found this monster of a desk made of solid oak tucked away in a corner of the warehouse, covered with dust and cob webs and dead bugs. I sat at it, pretending I was typing away at my computer, checking the height to make sure it would work for me. It was perfect. I asked them to deliver it to my place, along with a matching chair, and they promptly loaded it onto their delivery truck and asked for directions to my apartment. I paid for that sucker and told them to follow me in my crappy little car.

At my apartment building, the burly deliverymen struggled to carry that oak beast up the stairs to my apartment but they managed, nearly dropping it once or twice. That massive desk would have crushed them if it fell. It was that big. Inside, I told them to place it in the middle of my living room facing a window that overlooked the parking lot outside. I gave the deliverymen a $5 tip for their troubles and they left satisfied that they hadn't killed themselves bringing that desk up those stairs. They were two lucky bastards, for sure, but not as lucky as me. I was, for a small moment in time, the luckiest bastard in the world.

It's true.

***

After a lot of thought and a lot of contemplation, I realized that life wasn't so hard after all. Life wasn't so easy either. It was none of those things. Life was just life. Those French bastards really were a bunch of smarty, fancy schmancy pants. I mean, when they came up with that clichéd phrase "c'est la vie," they really knew what the hell they were talking about. It must have been all the wine they drank and the cheese they ate and the cigarettes they smoked and all of the womanizing and pontificating and whatever. It's a tough thing to admit when you are wrong. But I'll admit it. I was wrong about those French bastards. They really knew what they were talking about. It's true.

Remember when I told you that I had this brilliant idea to write a memoir that was completely fabricated? Good ol' James Frey really had something there when he wrote a partially fabricated memoir but I was going to go all the way with MY memoir. Completely fabricated! Nothing less than complete fabrication was going to do. It was a grand idea. My grand idea also needed a grandiose goddamn title. I racked my head for days and days. It had to be perfect. It had to denote exactly what my fabricated memoir was about to a tee. After much thought, I finally came up with the grandiose title I was looking for. Would you like to hear it? I know you would. So here it is:

THE SPECTACULAR SIMON BURCHWOOD.

THE SPECTACULAR SIMON BURCHWOOD.
THE SPECTACULAR SIMON BURCHWOOD.
THE SPECTACULAR SIMON BURCHWOOD.
THE SPECTACULAR SIMON BURCHWOOD.
THE SPECTACULAR SIMON BURCHWOOD.

It had a really nice ring to it. It was a great title. My new book deserved nothing but the best and I was absolutely sure that my writing career was about to take off. Why wouldn't it? I was determined to be great. With determination and a little effort, greatness was within my grasp. It's within all of our grasps. Don't doubt what I'm saying. I really know what I'm talking about.

Then I wrote the completely fabricated memoir and now you've read it.

It's true.

About the Author

Scott Semegran lives in Austin, Texas with his wife, four kids, two cats, and a dog. He graduated from the University of Texas at Austin with a degree in English. He is a writer and a cartoonist. He can also bend metal with his mind and run really fast, if chased by a pack of wolves. His comic strips have appeared in the following newspapers: The Austin Student, The Funny Times, The Austin American-Statesman, Rocky Mountain Bullhorn, Seven Days, The University of Texas at Dallas Mercury, and The North Austin Bee. Books by Scott Semegran include Sammie & Budgie, Boys, The Meteoric Rise of Simon Burchwood, The Spectacular Simon Burchwood, Modicum, Mr. Grieves and more. He is a Kindle bestselling author.

Books by Scott Semegran

If you enjoyed this book, then check out the novel **The Meteoric Rise of Simon Burchwood** by Scott Semegran. On his way to New York to celebrate his impending literary success, Simon Burchwood is the prototypical American careerist. But a quick detour to Montgomery, Alabama to visit a childhood friend sends Simon on a bizarre journey, challenging his hopes and dreams of becoming a famous writer. **The Meteoric Rise of Simon Burchwood** is a character study that delves into the psyche of a man who desperately tries to redefine himself.

Is Simon pompous? Yes. A jerk? Yes. Will you like him? Absolutely! "The book is told entirely from Simon's viewpoint. Simon is not a very likeable guy; as a matter of fact, he is a self-centered, pompous jerk. But for some reason, it's pretty fun to be inside his head, mainly because he is an inadvertent, oblivious jerk... you will learn Simon's views on smoking, cleanliness and going to the bathroom, just to name a few. There were times that I laughed out loud... A very good novel that was humorous throughout." -- 4 1/2 Stars / *Red Adept Reviews*

The Meteoric Rise of Simon Burchwood was selected as one of the "5 Best Summer Indie Beach Reads" by the editors of *IndieReader*. Their verdict: "An ambitious, enjoyable read with a superb ending that changed my interpretation of the entire text."

"A clever and surprising twist... cutting observations of the writerly demeanor." -- *Kirkus Reviews*

Buy it today!

***

"Illustrated throughout by Semegran, this book is the author's best. In these pages, his steadfastly idiosyncratic style really begins to click. An unconventional, beguiling, and endearing family tale." -- *Kirkus Reviews*

From Kindle bestselling writer and cartoonist Scott Semegran, **Sammie & Budgie** is a quirky, mystical tale of a self-doubting IT nerd and his young son, who possesses the gift of foresight. The boy's special ability propels his family on a road trip to visit his ailing grandfather, a prickly man who left an indelible stamp on the father and son. The three are connected through more than genetics, their lives intertwined through dreams, imagination, and longing.

Simon works as a network administrator for a state government agency, a consolation after a promising career as a novelist flounders. He finds himself a single parent of two small children following the mysterious death of his adulterous wife. From the ashes of his failed marriage emerges a tight-knit family of three: a creative, special needs son, a hyperactive, butt-kicking daughter, and the caring, sensitive father. But when his son's special ability reveals itself, Simon struggles to keep his little family together in the face of adversity and uncertainty.

Sammie is a creative third-grader that draws adventures in his sketchbook with his imaginary friend, Budgie, a parakeet that protects him from the monsters inhabiting his dreams. Sammie is also a special needs child but is special in more ways than one. He can see the future. Sammie seemingly can predict events both mundane and catastrophic in equal measure. But when he envisions the suffering of his grandfather, the family embarks on a road trip to San Antonio with the nanny to visit the ailing patriarch.

Sammie & Budgie is an illustrated novel brought to you from the quirky mind of writer and cartoonist Scott Semegran. The novel explores the bond between a caring father and his children, one affected by his own thorny relationship with his surly father, and the connection he has with his sweet son is thicker than blood, going to the place where dreams are conceived and realized.

Praise for **Sammie & Budgie**:

"A quirky, mystical tale of a self-doubting IT nerd and his young son, who possesses the gift of foresight. Engaging and fun, with wonderfully crafted characters." –Derf Backderf, bestselling creator of the graphic novel *My Friend Dahmer*

"**Sammie & Budgie** is instantly absorbing, its affable narrator hooking you with wit and whimsy, then reeling you into the boat, where larger revelations await. Scott Semegran is a lively, vivid storyteller, and this book will delight readers of all ages, while leaving them with plenty to ponder about their own lives. I loved this book!" -Davy Rothbart, author of *My Heart is an Idiot*, creator of *Found Magazine*, and contributor to public radio's *This American Life*

"Scott Semegran's loose charm and conversational style brings his shaggy narrator to vivid life in this story of a loving, if imperfect father and his maybe-psychic son. A sweet story about an extraordinary everyday family, **Sammie & Budgie** will find its way into your heart, and stay there." -Emily Flake, *New Yorker* cartoonist, author of *Mama*

Tried: Dispatches from the Seamy Underbelly of Modern Parenting, and creator of *Lulu Eightball*

Get it today!

***

If you enjoyed this book then check out **MODICUM**, a collection of short stories, musings, and cartoons by writer / cartoonist Scott Semegran. The book explores such themes as suicide, parenting, religion, masculinity, the apocalypse, and, most importantly, erections. It's guaranteed to make you laugh, cry, and pee your pants (hopefully, not at the same time).

Praise for **MODICUM**:

"Funny, sweet, dark, and sad, Scott Semegran's comics and short stories create a wholly convincing world of love, loss, and fear. His light touch with heavy subjects is a gift, and his forays into silliness are a delight. I can't tell if his kids should read it as soon as possible, or never." - Emily Flake, cartoonist and author of *LuLu Eightball*

"Hilarious, poignant, twisted... and those are just the stories. Scott Semegran's cartoons bring an added one-two visceral punch to a powerful collection of work." - Davy Rothbart, author of *The Lone Surfer of Montana, Kansas* and publisher of *FOUND Magazine*

Buy it today!

***

Mr. Grieves started as a poke at human nature through the use of talking, narcissistic animals. It has evolved into a full-on assault to your funny bone. Where else will you find rats fighting over cubicles, camels worrying about aging, a parrot talking to aliens, and a lonely water snail longing for a friend? Welcome to the world of **Mr. Grieves**!

Praise for **Mr. Grieves**:

"An animal or plant — or maybe even an ovum — talks. Sometimes to itself, but more often to another of its kind. The idea is simple, but the execution is smart and almost always funny in Scott Semegran's collection of 140 four-panel comics drawn between 2004 and 2008, **Mr. Grieves**." -- Reviewed for *Indie Reader* by Andrew Stout

Get it today!

Boys is a collection of stories about three boys living in Texas: one growing up, one dreaming, and one fighting to stay alive in the face of destitution and adversity. There's second-grader William, a shy yet imaginative boy who schemes about how to get back at his school-yard bully, Randy. Then there's Sam, a 15-year-old boy who dreams of getting a 1980 Mazda RX-7 for his sixteenth birthday but has to work at a Greek restaurant to fund his dream. Finally, there's Seff, a 21-year-old on the brink of manhood, trying to survive along with his roommate, working as waiters and barely making ends meet. These three stories are told with heart, humor, and an uncompromising look at what it meant to grow up in Texas during the 1980s and 1990s.

"The writing is sharp and unpretentiously thoughtful, and since each of the main characters finds solace in companionship, this is an affecting literary depiction of the comforting power of friendship. Each of the stories can be read on its own, but taken together, they make a coherent, thematic whole, skillfully produced. An endearing collection that deftly captures the need for youthful fellowship." -- *Kirkus Reviews*

"Verdict: With nary a dull moment, Scott Semegran's **Boys** features short stories filled with unexpected nuances that draws readers right into the heart of his well-developed characters." -- *IndieReader*. 5 Stars. IR Approved.

Buy it today!

Find Scott Semegran Online:
https://www.scottsemegran.com
https://www.goodreads.com/scottsemegran
https://www.twitter.com/scottsemegran
https://www.facebook.com/scottsemegran.writer/
https://www.instagram.com/scott_semegran
https://www.amazon.com/author/scottsemegran
https://www.smashwords.com/profile/view/scottsemegran

Mutt Press:
https://www.muttpress.com